...EEN HOURS

Arvin Larn is terrified. On the battlefields of the far future, only an insane man wouldn't be. Seventeen years old and still new to the Imperial Guard, he is thrust straight into his first war and must face horrors that his sheltered upbringing could never prepare him for.

The trenches of the 41st millennium are filled with worse things than rats and trenchrot. For one, the world they fight for is being contested by the monstrous barbarian orks. The orks live for battle and know no fear, so it's no wonder that the average life-span of an Imperial Guardsman on this forsaken world is only fifteen hours...

More storming action from the
grim darkness of Warhammer 40,000

• GAUNT'S GHOSTS •

The Founding
FIRST AND ONLY by Dan Abnett
GHOSTMAKER by Dan Abnett
NECROPOLIS by Dan Abnett

The Saint
HONOUR GUARD by Dan Abnett
THE GUNS OF TANITH by Dan Abnett
STRAIGHT SILVER by Dan Abnett
SABBAT MARTYR by Dan Abnett

The Lost
TRAITOR GENERAL by Dan Abnett

• SPACE WOLF •

SPACE WOLF by William King
RAGNAR'S CLAW by William King
GREY HUNTER by William King
WOLFBLADE by William King

• CIAPHAS CAIN •

FOR THE EMPEROR by Sandy Mitchell
CAVES OF ICE by Sandy Mitchell
THE TRAITOR'S HAND by Sandy Mitchell

• THE SOUL DRINKERS •

SOUL DRINKER by Ben Counter
THE BLEEDING CHALICE by Ben Counter
CRIMSON TEARS by Ben Counter

A WARHAMMER 40,000 NOVEL

FIFTEEN HOURS

Mitchel Scanlon

To Mum and Dad – Hey, look it, I done wrote my first book without pictures!

A BLACK LIBRARY PUBLICATION

First published in Great Britain in 2005 by
BL Publishing,
Games Workshop Ltd.,
Willow Road, Nottingham,
NG7 2WS, UK.

10 9 8 7 6 5 4 3 2 1

Cover illustration by Klaus Scherwinski.

A CIP record for this book is available from the British Library.

ISBN 13: 978 1 84416 231 4
ISBN 10: 1 84416 231 1

Distributed in the US by Simon & Schuster
1230 Avenue of the Americas, New York, NY 10020, US.

Printed and bound in Great Britain by
Bookmarque, Surrey, UK.

See the Black Library on the Internet at
www.blacklibrary.com

Find out more about Games Workshop
and the world of Warhammer 40,000 at
www.games-workshop.com

It is the 41st millennium. For more than a hundred centuries the Emperor has sat immobile on the Golden Throne of Earth. He is the master of mankind by the will of the gods, and master of a million worlds by the might of his inexhaustible armies. He is a rotting carcass writhing invisibly with power from the Dark Age of Technology. He is the Carrion Lord of the Imperium for whom a thousand souls are sacrificed every day, so that he may never truly die.

Yet even in his deathless state, the Emperor continues his eternal vigilance. Mighty battlefleets cross the daemon-infested miasma of the warp, the only route between distant stars, their way lit by the Astronomican, the psychic manifestation of the Emperor's will. Vast armies give battle in His name on uncounted worlds. Greatest amongst his soldiers are the Adeptus Astartes, the Space Marines, bio-engineered super-warriors. Their comrades in arms are legion: the Imperial Guard and countless planetary defence forces, the ever-vigilant Inquisition and the tech-priests of the Adeptus Mechanicus to name only a few. But for all their multitudes, they are barely enough to hold off the ever-present threat from aliens, heretics, mutants – and worse.

To be a man in such times is to be one amongst untold billions. It is to live in the cruellest and most bloody regime imaginable. These are the tales of those times. Forget the power of technology and science, for so much has been forgotten, never to be re-learned. Forget the promise of progress and understanding, for in the grim dark future there is only war. There is no peace amongst the stars, only an eternity of carnage and slaughter, and the laughter of thirsting gods.

THE SKY WAS dark, and he knew he was dying.

Alone and frightened, unable to stand or even move his legs, he lay on his back in the frozen mud of no-man's land. Lay there helpless, his body shrouded in darkness, eyes gazing up at the nighttime sky overhead as though trying to read some portent of his future in the cold distant stars. Tonight, the stars kept their own counsel. Tonight, the bleak and foreboding heavens held no comfort.

How long has it been now, he thought. *How many hours?*

Finding no answer to his question, he turned his head to look out at the scenery about him – hoping at last to see some sign of rescue but there was nothing: no movement in the darkness, no cause for hope. Around him, the bleak expanses of no-man's land lay still and silent. A landscape rendered featureless by the hand of night, painted black with threatening shadows, holding nothing that spoke to his hopes or could even help him to find his bearings. He was lost and alone, abandoned to a world of darkness, with no prospect of help or salvation. For a moment it seemed to him he might as well be the last man left alive in the entire galaxy. Then, the thought of it gave him cause for fear and he quickly put it from his mind.

How long now, he thought again. *How many hours?*

He had felt nothing when the bullet struck him. No pain, no agony, nor even anguish, just a strange and sudden numbness in his legs as he slid toward the ground. At first, not understanding what had happened, he had thought he had tripped. Until, cursing himself for his clumsiness, he had tried to rise only to find his legs curiously unresponsive. It was then, as he felt the spreading warmth of his own blood seeping across his belly, that he had realised his mistake.

In the hours since, unable to see the extent of his wounds in the darkness, he had used his probing fingers to tell him what his eyes could not. He had been hit at the base of the spine, the bullet leaving a fist-sized hole at the front of his stomach as it exited his body. Treating his wounds to the best of his medical knowledge, he had stuffed them with gauze to stem the bleeding and placed dressings over them. Though there were phials of morphia in his Guard-issue med-pack and he had learned the 'Prayer of Relief from Torment' by heart, he had no need for them. There was no pain from his wounds – even when his probing fingers had slid past the knuckle into the ragged hole in his stomach he had felt no physical discomfort. He did not need to be possessed of any great medical knowledge to know that was not a good sign.

How long now, the question came to his mind again, unbidden. *How many hours?*

There were other discomforts, though. The chill of the cold night air biting at the exposed skin of his face and neck, a terrible mind-wearying fatigue that made his thoughts seem dull and leaden: the fear, the loneliness, the isolation. Worst of all, there was the silence. When first he had fallen wounded, the night had thundered with all the cacophony of battle: the high-pitched whine of lasguns, the *crack* of slugthrowers, the roar of explosions, the screams and cries of the wounded and the dying. Sounds that gradually subsided, growing slowly more distant before finally giving way to silence. He would never have thought a man could draw comfort from such sounds. As terrifying as the clamour of battle had been, the quiet that followed was worse. It compounded his isolation, leaving him alone with all his fears. Here, in the darkness, fear had become his constant companion, plaguing his heart without remorse or respite.

How long now? The question would not leave him. *How many hours?*

At times, the compulsion came over him to cry out. To shout for help, to beg for mercy, to scream, to yell, to pray – anything to break that dreadful silence. Every time it came he fought it with all his strength, biting his lip hard to stop the words from spilling out. He knew that to make even the slightest sound would only be to bring death upon him all the sooner. For though his comrades might hear him, so would the enemy. Somewhere, out there on the other side of no-man's land, the enemy waited in their countless millions. Waited, ever eager to fight, to maim, to kill. No matter how terrifying it was to be trapped alone and wounded in no-man's land, the thought of being found by the enemy was worse. For what seemed like hours now, he had endured the silence. Knowing that, as desperately as he might hope for rescue, he could do nothing to speed it on its way towards him.

How long now, the thought pounded insistently in his head. *How many hours?*

There was so little left to him now. So little of real substance. All the things that had once meant so much – his family, his homeworld, his faith in the Emperor – now seemed dim and distant. Even his memories were insubstantial, as though his past was fading away before his eyes as swiftly as was his future. His inner world, the world of his life which had once seemed so full and bright with promise, had been diminished and reduced by circumstance. He was left with only a few simple choices: to cry out or keep his silence; to bleed to death or take his knife and end it quickly; to stay awake or fall asleep. At the moment, sleep seemed a tempting prospect. He was tired and bone-weary, fatigue pulling at his sluggish mind like an insistent friend, but he would not yield to it. He knew if he fell asleep now he would likely never awaken. Just as he knew that all these so-called choices were simply illusions. In the end, there was only one stark choice left to him now – to live or to die – and he refused to die.

How long now, the question again, relentless. *How many hours?*

But there was no answer. Resigning himself to the thought that his fate was now in the hands of others, he waited in the silence of no-man's land. Waited, hoping that somewhere out in the night his comrades were already searching for him. Waited, refusing to give in or fall asleep. He waited, caught between life and death. His life a last fitful burning spark lost amid a sea of darkness, his mind wondering how it was he had ever come to be there at all…

CHAPTER ONE

20:14 hours Jumal IV Central Planetary Time
(Western Summer Adjustment)

THE LAST OF A THOUSAND SUNSETS – A LETTER EDGED IN
BLACK – A GHOST IN THE CELLAR – THE LOTTERY AND THE
TALE OF HIS FATHERS

THE SUN WAS setting, its slow descent reddening the vast
reaches of the westward sky and bathing the endless
wheat fields below it in shades of gold and amber as they
stirred gently in the evening breeze. In his seventeen years
of life to date, Arvin Larn had seen perhaps a thousand
such sunsets, there was something about the beauty of
this one that gave him pause. Enraptured, his chores for
the moment forgotten, for the first time since his child-
hood he simply stood and watched the setting of the sun.
Stood there, with the world still and peaceful all about
him, gazing toward the gathering fall of night as he felt a
nameless emotion rising deep within his heart.

There will be other sunsets, he thought to himself. *Other
suns, though none of them will mean as much to me as this*

11

one does, here and now. Nothing could mean as much as this
moment does, standing here among these wheat fields,
watching the last sunset I will ever see at home.

Home. The mere thought of the word was enough to
make him turn his head and look over his shoulder
across the swaying rows of ripening grain toward the
small collection of farm buildings on the other side of
the field behind him. He saw the old barn with its sloping, wood-shingled roof. He saw the round tower of the
grain silo; the ginny-hen coops he had helped build
with his father; the small stock pen where they kept the
draft horses and a herd of half-a-dozen alpacas.

Most of all, he saw the farmhouse where he had been
born and raised. Two-storeyed, with a low wooden
porch out front and the shutters on the windows left
open to let in the last of the light. Given the unchang-
ing routines of his family's existence, Larn did not need
to see inside to know what was happening within. His
mother would be in the kitchen cooking the evening
meal, his sisters helping her set the table, his father in
the cellar workshop with his tools. Then, just as they
did every night, once their chores were done the family
would sit down at the table together and eat. Tomorrow
night they would do the same again, the pattern of their
lives repeating endlessly day after day, varying only with
the changing of the seasons.

It was a pattern that had endured here for as long as
anyone could remember. A pattern that would continue
so long as there was anyone left to farm these lands.
Though, come tomorrow night at least, there would be
one small difference.

Come tomorrow, he would no longer be here to see
it.

Sighing, Larn returned to his work, turning once more
to the task of trying to repair the ancient rust-pitted irrigation pump in front of him. Before the sunset had

distracted him he had removed the outer access panel to reveal the inner workings of the pump's motor. Now, in the fading light of twilight, he removed the motor's burnt-out starter and replaced it with a new one, mindful to say a prayer to the machine spirit inside it as he tightened and re-checked the connections.

Taking a spouted canister from beside the foot of the pump he dribbled a few drops of unguent from it into the workings. Then, satisfied everything was in order, he reached out for the large lever at the side and worked it slowly up and down a dozen times to prime the pump before pressing the ignition stud to start the motor. Abruptly, the pump shuddered into noisy life, the motor whining as it strained to pull water up from aquifers lying deep below the ground. For a moment, Larn congratulated himself on a job well done. Until, just as the first few muddy drops of water emerged from the mouth of the pump to stain the dry earth of the irrigation trench before it, the motor coughed and died.

Disappointed, Larn pressed the ignition stud again. This time though, the motor stayed sullenly silent. Leaning forward, he carefully inspected the parts of the mechanism once more – checking the connections for corrosion, making sure the moving parts were well-lubricated and free from grit, searching for broken wires or worn components – all the things the mechanician-acolyte in Ferrusville had warned them about the last time the pump was serviced. Frustratingly, Larn could find nothing wrong. As far as he could see, the pump should be working.

Finally, reluctantly forced to concede defeat, Larn lifted the discarded access panel and began to screw it into place once more. He had so badly wanted to be able to fix the pump; with harvest time still three weeks away, it was important the farm's irrigation system should be in good working order. Granted, it had been a good season so far and the wheat was growing well but the life of a farmer was always enslaved to the weather. Without the irrigation system to fall back upon, a couple of dry weeks now could mean the difference between feast and famine for an entire year.

But in the end he knew that was only part of it. Standing there, looking down at the pump after he had screwed the panel back in place, Larn realised his reasons for wanting to see it repaired went far beyond such practical considerations. Like it or not, tomorrow he would be leaving the farm forever and saying farewell to the only land and life he had ever known, never to return. He understood now that he had felt the need to perform some last act of service to those he would be leaving behind. He had wanted to complete some final labour on their behalf. An act of penance almost, to give closure to his grief.

This morning, when his father had asked him to look at the pump and see if he could fix it, it had seemed the perfect opportunity to achieve that aim. Now though, the recalcitrant machine spirits inside the pump and his own lack of knowledge had conspired against him. No matter how hard he tried, the pump was broken beyond his powers to repair it and his last act of penance would go unfulfilled.

Larn collected his tools together and made ready to turn for home, only to pause again as he noticed a change in the sunset. Ahead, the sun had already half disappeared below the horizon, while the sky around it had turned a deeper and more angry red. What gave him pause was not the sun or the sky, but the fields below them. Where once they had been bathed in spectacular shades of gold and amber, now the colour of the fields had become more uniform, changing to a dark and unsettling shade of brownish red, like the colour of blood. At the same time the evening breeze had risen almost imperceptibly, catching the rows of wheat in the fields and causing them to flow and shift before Larn's eyes as though the fields themselves had become some vast and restless sea. *It could almost be a sea of blood*, he said to himself, the very thought of it causing him to shiver a little.

A sea of blood.

And, try as hard as he might, he could read no good omen in that sign.

BY THE TIME Larn had put his tools away, the sun had all but set. Leaving the barn behind, he walked towards the farmhouse, the yellow glow of lamplight barely visible ahead of him through the slats of the wooden shutters now closed over the farmhouse windows. Stepping onto the porch Larn lifted the latch to the front door and walked inside, carefully removing his boots at the threshold so as not to track mud from the fields into the hallway. Then, leaving the boots just inside the doorway, he walked down the hall towards the kitchen, unconsciously making the sign of the aquila with his fingers as he passed the open door of the sitting room with its devotional picture of the Emperor hung over the fireplace.

Reaching the kitchen he found it deserted, the smell of woodsmoke and the delicious aromas of all his favourite foods rising from the pans simmering on the stove. Roasted xorncob, boiled derna beans, alpaca stew and taysenberry pie; together, the dishes of the last meal he would ever eat at home. Abruptly it occurred to him, in whatever years of his life might yet come, those self-same aromas would forever now be linked with a feeling of desperate sadness.

Ahead, the kitchen table was already laid out with plates and cutlery ready for the meal. As he stepped past the table toward the sink, he remembered returning from the fields two nights earlier to find his parents sitting in the kitchen waiting for him, the black-edged parchment of the induction notice lying mutely on the table between them. From the first it had been obvious they had both been crying, their eyes red and raw from grief. He had not needed to ask them the reason for their tears. Their expressions, and the Imperial eagle embossed on the surface of the parchment, had said it all.

Now, as he moved past the table Larn spotted the same parchment lying folded in half on top of one of the kitchen cupboards. Diverted from his original intentions, he walked towards it. Then, picking up the parchment and unfolding it, he found himself once more reading the words written there below the official masthead.

Citizens of Jumael IV, the parchment read. *Rejoice! In accordance with Imperial Law and the powers of his Office, your Governor has decreed two new regiments of the Imperial Guard are to be raised from among his people. Furthermore, he has ordered those conscripted to these new regiments are to be assembled with all due haste, so that they may begin their training without delay and take their place among the most Holy and Righteous armies of the Blessed Emperor of All Mankind.*

From there the parchment went on to list the names of those who had been conscripted, outlining the details of the mustering process and emphasising the penalties awaiting anyone who failed to report. Larn did not need to read the rest of it – in the last two days he had read the parchment so many times he knew the words by heart. Yet despite all that, as though unable to stop picking at the scab of a half-healed wound, he continued to read the words written on the parchment before him.

'Arvin?' He heard his mother's voice behind him, breaking his chain of thought. 'You startled me, standing there like that. I didn't hear you come in.'

Turning, Larn saw his mother standing beside him, a jar of kuedin seeds in her hand and her eyes red with recently dried tears.

'I just got here, Ma,' he said, feeling vaguely embarrassed as he put the parchment back where he had found it. 'I finished my chores, and thought I should wash my hands before dinner.'

For a moment his mother stood there quietly staring at him. Facing her in uncomfortable silence, Larn realised how hard it was for her to speak at all now she knew she would be losing him tomorrow. It lent their every word a deeper meaning, making even the most simple of conversations difficult while with every instant there was the threat that a single ill-chosen word might release the painful tide of grief welling up inside her.

'You took your boots off?' she said at last, retreating to the commonplace in search of safety.

'Yes, Ma. I left them just inside the hallway.'

'Good,' she said. 'You'd better clean them tonight, so as to be ready for tomorrow…' At that word his mother paused, her voice on the edge of breaking, her teeth biting her lower lip and her eyelids closed as though warding off a distant sensation of pain. Then, half turning away so he could no longer see her eyes, she spoke again.

'But anyway, you can do that later,' she said. 'For now, you'd better go down to the cellar. Your Pa's already down there and he said he wanted to see you when you got back from the fields.'

Turning further away from him now, she moved over to the stove and lifted the lid off one of the pans to drop a handful of kuedin seeds into it. Ever the dutiful son, Larn turned away. Towards the cellar and his father.

THE CELLAR STEPS creaked noisily as Larn made his way down them. Despite the noise, at first his father did not seem to notice his approach. Lost in concentration, he sat bent over his workbench at the far end of the cellar, a whetstone in his hand as he sharpened his wool-shears. For a moment, watching his father unawares as he worked, Larn felt almost like a ghost – as though he had passed from his family's world already and they could no longer see or hear him. Then, finding the thought of it gave him a shiver, he spoke at last and broke the silence.

'You wanted to see me, Pa?'

Starting at the sound of his voice, his father laid the shears and the whetstone down before turning to look towards his son and smile.

'You startled me, Arv,' he said. 'Zell's oath, but you can walk quiet when you've a mind to. So, did you manage to fix the pump?'

'Sorry, Pa,' Larn said. 'I tried replacing the starter and every other thing I could think of, but none of it worked.'

'You tried your best, son,' his father said. 'That's all that matters. Besides, the machine spirits in that pump are so old and ornery the damned thing never worked right half the time anyway. I'll have to see if I can get a mechanician to come out from Ferrusville to give it a good look-over next week. In the meantime, the rain's been pretty good so we shouldn't have a problem. But anyway, there was something else I wanted to see you about. Why don't you grab yourself a stool so the two of us men can talk?'

Pulling an extra stool from beneath the workbench, his father gestured for him to sit down. Then, waiting until he saw his son had made himself comfortable, he began once more.

'I don't suppose I ever told you too much about your great-grandfather before, did I?' he said.

'I know he was an off-worlder, Pa,' Larn said, earnestly. 'And I know his name was Augustus, same as my middle name is.'

'True enough,' his father replied. 'It was a tradition on your great-grandfather's world to pass on a family name to the first-born son in every generation. Course, he was long dead by the time you were born. Mind you, he died even before I was born. But he was a good man, and so we did it to honour him all the same. A good man should always be honoured, they say, no matter how long he's been dead.'

For a moment, his face grave and thoughtful, his father fell silent. Then, as though he had made some decision, he raised his face up to look his son clearly in the eye and spoke again.

'As I say, your great-grandfather was dead long before I could have known him, Arvie. But when I was seventeen and just about to come of age my father called me down into this cellar and told me the tale of him – just like I'm about to tell you now. You see, my father had decided that before I became a man it was important I knew where I came from. And I'm glad he did, 'cause what he told me then has stood me in good stead ever since. Just like I'm hoping that what I'm going to tell you now will stand you in good stead likewise. Course, with what's happened in the last few days – and where you're bound for – I've got extra reasons for telling it to you. Reasons that, Emperor love him, my own father never had to face. But that's the way of things: each generation has its own sorrows, and has to make the best of them they can. That's all as may be, though. Guess I should just stop dancing around it and come out and say what it is I have to say.'

Again, as though wrestling inwardly for the right words, his father paused. As he waited for him to begin, Larn found himself suddenly thinking how old his father looked. Gazing at him as though for the first time he became aware of the lines and creases across his father's face, the slightly rounded slump of his shoulders, the spreading fingers of grey in his once black and lustrous hair. Signs of aging he would have sworn had not been there a week previously. It was almost as though his father had aged a decade in the last few days.

'Your great-grandfather was in the Imperial Guard,' his father said at last. 'Just like you're going to be.' Then, seeing his son about to blurt out a string of questions, he held his hand up to gesture silence. 'You can ask whatever you want later, Arvie. For now, it's better if you just let me tell it to you like my father told me. Believe me, once you've heard it you'll know why it is I said I thought you should hear it.'

Hanging on every word in the quiet stillness of the cellar, Larn heard his father tell his tale.

'Your great-grandfather was a Guardsman,' his father said again. 'Course, he didn't start out to be one. No one does. To begin with he was just another farmer's son like you or me, born on a world called Arcadus V. A world not unlike this one, he would later say. A peaceful place, with lots of good land for farming and plenty of room for a man to raise a family. And if things had followed their natural course, that's just what your great-grandfather would have done. He would have found a wife, raised babies, farmed the land, same as generations of his kin on Arcadus V had done before him. And in time he would have died and been buried there, his flesh returning to the fertile earth while his soul went to join his Emperor in paradise. That's what your great-grandfather thought his future held for him when he came of age at seventeen. Then he heard the news he'd been conscripted into the Guard and everything changed.

'Now, seventeen or not, your great-grandfather was no fool. He knew what being conscripted meant. He knew there was a heavy burden that goes with being a Guardsman – a burden worse than the threat of danger or the fear of dying alone and in pain under some cold and distant sun. A burden of *loss*. The kind of loss that comes when a man knows he is leaving his home forever. It's a burden every Guardsman carries. The burden of knowing that no matter how long he lives he will never see his friends, his family, or even his homeworld again. A Guardsman never returns, Arvie. The best he can hope for, if he survives long enough and serves his Emperor well, is to be allowed to retire and settle a new world somewhere, out among the stars. And knowing this – knowing he was leaving his world and his people for good – your great-grandfather's heart was heavy as he said farewell to his family and made ready to report for muster.

'Though it may have felt like his heart was breaking then, your great-grandfather was a good and pious man. Wise beyond his years, he knew mankind is not alone in the darkness. He knew the Emperor is always with us. Same as he knew that nothing happens in all the wide galaxy without the Emperor willing it to be so. And if the Emperor had willed that he must leave his family and his homeworld and never see them again, then your great-grandfather knew it must serve some greater purpose. He understood what the preachers mean when they tell us it isn't the place of Man to know the ways of the Emperor. He knew it was his duty to follow the course laid out for him, no matter that he didn't understand why that course had been set. And so trusting his life to the Emperor's kindness and grace, your great-grandfather left his homeworld to go find his destiny among the stars.

'Now, the years that followed then were hard ones. Although he would never speak of it much afterwards, in his time as a Guardsman your great-grandfather saw more than his fair share of wonders and horrors. He saw worlds where billions of people lived right on top of each other like insects in giant towers, never able to breathe clean air or see the sun. He saw worlds that lay gripped all year long in perpetual winter, and dry desert worlds that never saw a flake of snow nor felt a drop of rain. He saw the blessed warriors of the holy Astartes – god-like giants in human form, he called them – and great walking machines so big this entire farmhouse would fit inside one of their footprints. He saw terrors by the score, in the shape of all manner of twisted *xenos* and things even ten times worse.

Though he faced a thousand and more dangers, though he was at times wounded and seemed close to death, still his faith in the Emperor never faltered. Five years become ten. Ten became fifteen. Fifteen became twenty. And still your great-grandfather followed his orders without thought of complaint, never once asking when he would be released from service. Until at last, nearly thirty years after he'd first been conscripted, he was posted to Jumael IV.

'Course this world didn't mean much to him then. Not at first. By then he'd seen dozens of different planets, and at first sight Jumael didn't seem to have anything much to recommend it more than most. His regiment had just finished a long campaign, and they had been sent to Jumael to rest up and recuperate for a month before being shipped out to war once more. By then your great-grandfather didn't have too many wars left in him. Oh, he tried to put a brave face on it, never complaining. But he was getting old, and the wounds he'd sustained in thirty years of battles were starting to take their toll. Worst of all was his lungs – they'd never healed right after he breathed a mouthful of poison gas on a world called Torpus III, yet still he didn't waver in his duty. He had given his life over to the service of the

Emperor, and he was content that it was at the Emperor's will whether he lived or died.

'Then one day, as the time grew closer when they would be leaving Jumael, news came among the regiment of something extraordinary. Emperor's Day was coming, and with it the thirtieth anniversary of the founding of their regiment. As an act of celebration it was decreed that lots would be drawn from among all the men, and whichever man won would be released from service and allowed to remain behind when the regiment left Jumael. A lottery that, for one man among thousands, might well mean the difference between life and death. As the day of the lottery came upon them there was a sudden outbreak of piety among the men, as each man in the regiment prayed fervently to the Emperor to be the one to be chosen. All except your great-grandfather. For though he prayed to the Emperor every morning and night, it was never his way to ask for anything for himself.'

'And so great-grandfather won the lottery?' Larn asked, breathless with excitement and no longer able to keep his peace. 'He won it, and that's how he came to live on Jumael?'

'No, Arvie,' his father smiled benignly. 'Another man won. A man from the same squad as your great-grandfather, who'd fought by his side through thirty years of campaigning. Though that man could've just taken his ticket and walked away, he didn't. Instead, he looked at your great-grandfather with his worn-out face and half-healed lungs and handed him the ticket. You see, he'd decided your great-grandfather needed to be released from service more than he did. And that's how your great-grandfather came to settle on Jumael IV, through the kindness and self-sacrifice of a comrade. Though in the years to come, your great-grandfather would always say there was more to it than that. He would say sometimes the hand of the Emperor can be seen in the smallest of things, and that it was the Emperor who had decided to work through this man to save his life. In the end it was a miracle of sorts. A quiet miracle, perhaps, but a miracle all the same.'

With that, his father fell silent again. Looking at him Larn could see the first beginnings of tears shining wetly in his eyes. Then, at length, his father spoke once more, his every word heavy with barely suppressed emotion.

'You see now why I thought you should hear the tale, Arvie?' he said. 'Tomorrow, just like your great-grandfather before you, you're going to have to leave your home and your kin behind, never to return. And, knowing full well you may have some hard years ahead of you, before you left I wanted you to hear the tale of your great-grandfather and how he survived. I wanted you to be able to take that tale with you. So that no matter how dark, even hopeless, things might seem to you at times, you'd know the Emperor was always with you. Trust to the Emperor, Arvie. Sometimes it's all that we can do. Trust to the Emperor, and everything will be all right.'

No longer able to keep the tears from flowing, his father turned away so his son could not see his eyes. While his father cried into the shadows Larn sat there with him as long uncomfortable moments passed, struggling to find the right words to soothe his grief. Until finally, deciding it was better to say something than nothing at all, he spoke and broke the silence.

'I'll remember that, Pa' he said, the words coming with faltering slowness from him as he tried to choose the best way of saying it. 'I'll remember every word of it. Like you said, I'll take it with me and I'll think of it whenever things get bad. And I promise you: I'll do what you said. I'll trust to the Emperor, just like you said. I promise it, Pa. And something else. I promise, you don't have to worry about me doing my best when

I go to war. No matter what happens, I'll always do my duty.'

'I know you will, Arvie,' his father said at last as he wiped the tears from his eyes. 'You're the best son a man could have. And when you're a Guardsman, I know you'll make your Ma and me proud.'

CHAPTER TWO

12:07 hours Jumal IV Central Planetary Time
(Western Summer Adjustment)

MARCHING PRACTICE – CONVERSATIONS WITH SERGEANT
FERRES – A MEAL AMONG COMRADES

'HUP TWO THREE four. Hup two three four,' Sergeant Ferres yelled, keeping pace with the men of 3rd Platoon as they marched the dusty length of the parade ground. 'You call that marching? I've seen more order and discipline in a pack of shithouse rats.'

Marching in time with the others, painfully aware of his own visibility, Larn found himself silently praying his feet kept in step. His place midway along the platoon's left outer file put him out in plain view right under the sergeant's eyes. The two months' worth of basic training he had endured so far had left him with few illusions as to what happened to those who failed to live up to the sergeant's exacting standards.

'Keep your feet up,' the sergeant screamed. 'You're not courting in the wheat fields with your cousins now, you inbreeds! You are soldiers of the Imperial Guard, Emperor help us. Put some vim into it.' Then, seeing the platoon was nearly at the far edge of the parade ground, Ferres yelled again, his voice strident and shrill with command. 'Platoon. About face. And march.'

Turning smartly on his heel with the others, as they resumed marching Larn found himself feeling dog-tired and exhausted. So far today, like each of the sixty days before it, Ferres had had them running training exercises since dawn. Marching, weapons drill, kit inspection, hand-to-hand training, basic survival skills: every day was a never-ending series of challenges and tests. Larn felt he had learnt more in the last two months than he had in his entire life. Yet, no matter how much he and the rest of the platoon learned or how well they did, none of it seemed to satisfy their vengeful sergeant.

'Hup two three four. Keep in step, damn you.' the sergeant bellowed. 'I'll keep the whole damned lot of you drilling here for another two hours if that's what it takes to make you keep to time!'

Larn did not doubt Ferres meant his threat. Over the last two months the sergeant had repeatedly shown an inclination to hand out draconian punishments for even the most minor infractions. Having been on the receiving end of such punishments more than once already, Larn had learned to dread the sergeant and his idea of discipline.

'Company halt,' Sergeant Ferres yelled at last, hawkish eyes watching to see if any of the Guardsmen overran their mark. Then, apparently satisfied that every man had stopped the instant they heard his order, he yelled again, loudly elongating every syllable of the command. 'Turn to the left!'

With a sudden clatter of clicking heels the company turned to face their sergeant. Seeing Ferres advance purposefully towards them, Larn did his best to keep his shoulders back and his spine ramrod straight, his eyes staring fixedly ahead as though gazing blindly into the middle distance. He knew enough of Sergeant Ferres's ways by now to know that an inspection would follow immediately they had finished marching. Just as he knew Ferres would not be any kinder to the soldier who failed to pass muster now than he would to anyone whose marching did not meet his standards.

From the corner of his eye Larn saw Sergeant Ferres move to the end of the outer file of Guardsmen to begin his inspection. Moving slowly along the line to inspect each man in turn, the sergeant's dark eyes darted swiftly up and down, scanning for any flaw in equipment, dress or manner. At times like these, no matter where in line he stood, it always felt to Larn as though it took the sergeant forever to reach him. A slow torturous eternity, spent waiting like the head of a nail to be struck by the hammer – all the time knowing that, no matter how well he had worked or what pre-cautions he had taken, the hammer would fall regardless.

Abruptly, still three men away from Larn, the sergeant stopped to turn and face the fair-haired trooper standing in front of him. It was Trooper Leden – his favourite target. Tall and broad-shouldered, with a thick neck and big hands, Leden looked even more the farmboy than the rest of the men in the company. Even now, standing to attention under Ferres's wither-ing glare, Leden's face was open and guileless, his mouth looking as though it could break into a warm and friendly smile at any moment.

'Your lasgun, trooper,' the sergeant said. 'Give it to me.' Then, taking the gun from Leden's outstretched hands, he checked the safety, before inspecting the rest of the gun in turn.

'What is the best way for a Guardsmen to prevent his lasgun from failing him in battle?' Ferres asked, eyes boring into Leden's face as he spoke.

'I… uh… first he should check the power pack is not empty. Then, reciting the Litany of Unjamming, he should…'

'I asked what is the best way to *prevent* a Guardsman's lasgun from failing him, Leden,' the sergeant said, cutting him off. 'Not how he should clear a jam after it malfunctions!'

'Umm…' for a moment Leden seemed stymied, until his eyes lit up with sudden inspiration. 'The Guardsman should clean his lasgun every day, taking care to recite the Litany of Cleanliness as he…'

'And if, because he has *failed* in his duty to keep his lasgun clean, the Guardsman finds his weapon jams in the heat of battle and he cannot fix it?' the sergeant cut him off again. 'What then, Leden? How should the Guardsman proceed?'

'He should fix his bayonet to the mounting lugs on his lasgun's flash suppressor, sergeant, and use it to defend himself,' Leden replied, an edge of pride to his voice now as though he was sure he had finally answered one of his sergeant's questions correctly.

'In the heat of combat? With the enemy right on top of him? What if he doesn't have time to fix his bayonet, Leden?'

'Then, he should use his lasgun as a club, sergeant.'

'A club you say?' the sergeant asked, suddenly placing both his hands at the end of the lasgun's barrel and lifting the butt of the weapon above his head. 'What, he should hold his lasgun above his head as though it were a bat-stick and he was playing shreev-ball?'

'Oh no, sergeant,' Leden replied mildly, apparently unaware that with every word he was digging a deeper hole for himself. 'He should hold his lasgun horizontally with his hands widely spaced as though it were a short-staff and strike the enemy with the butt.'

'Ah, I see,' the sergeant said, bringing the lasgun down and holding it in front of him with his hands in the positions Leden had indicated. 'And to best disable the enemy, what target should the Guardsman aim at – the face, the chest, or the gut?'

'The face,' Leden said, an idiot smile on his face, while every other Guardsman in the company winced inwardly at what they knew was coming.

'I see,' Sergeant Ferres said, bringing the butt of the lasgun up quickly to smash Leden in the bridge of the nose. Screaming, a gout of blood geysering from his nose, Leden collapsed to his knees.

'Get up, Leden,' the sergeant said, tossing the lasgun back to him as Leden shakily rose to his feet once more. 'You aren't seriously injured. Much less disabled. Look on it as a lesson. Perhaps next time you'll remember to clean your lasgun more carefully. The power node on this one is so filthy, chances are it'd burn out after a few shots.'

Turning away from Leden, the sergeant resumed his inspection. Standing three men down the line, Larn felt weighed down by the expectation of impending disaster. *Ferres is really on the warpath today*, he thought. *There's no way he'll let me pass muster. He'll find something I've done wrong. Some little thing. He always does.* Then, his heart rising in his mouth, Larn saw the sergeant pause in his slow procession down the line and turn to face him.

'Your lasgun, trooper!' the sergeant said. Then, as he had done with Leden before him, he checked the safety before inspecting the rest of the gun in turn. Sights, barrel, stock, holding lugs – for long seconds Ferres pored minutely over the lasgun as Larn felt sweat gathering at the back of his collar. Next, pressing the release catch

Ferres pulled the power pack free to check the contacts and the cell well were clean. Then, glowering as he snapped the power pack back into place, Ferres raised his eyes to look at Larn once more.

'Name and number!' he barked.

'Trooper First Class Larn, Arvin A, sergeant. Number: eight one five seven six dash three eight nine dash four seven two dash one!'

'I see. Then, tell me, Trooper First Class Larn, Arvin A, why did you join the Guard?'

'To defend the Imperium, sergeant. To serve the Emperor's will. To protect humanity from the alien and the unclean.'

'And how will you do those things, trooper?'

'I will obey orders, sergeant. I will follow the chain of command. I will fight the Emperor's enemies. And I will die for my Emperor, if He so wills it.'

'What are your rights as a member of the Imperial Guard?'

'I have no rights, sergeant. The Guardsman willingly forfeits his rights in return for the glory of fighting for the just cause of our Immortal Emperor.'

'And why does the Guardsman willingly forfeit his rights?'

'He forfeits them to better serve the Emperor, sergeant. The Guardsman has no need of rights – not when he is guided by the infinite wisdom of the Emperor and, through Him, by the divinely ordained command structure of the Imperial Guard.'

'And if you should meet a man who tells you these things are wrong, Larn? If you should meet a man who claims the Guard's command structure sometimes makes mistakes and needlessly wastes the lives of the men under its command?'

'Then I will kill him, sergeant. That is the only way to treat with traitors and dissenters.'

'Hnn. And if you should hear a man spout heresy, Larn, how will you persuade him of the error of his ways?'

'I will kill him, sergeant. That is the only way to treat with the heretic.'

'And if you should meet the *xenos*?'

'I will kill it, sergeant. That is the only way to treat with the *xenos*.'

'Very good, Larn,' the sergeant said to him, tossing Larn's lasgun back to him before turning to inspect the next man in line. 'You're learning. Perhaps we'll make a Guardsman of you yet.'

'No bruises, no extra laps, not even a demerit,' Jenks said. It was an hour later, and Larn sat with the other men of his fireteam at one of the long tables inside the mess hall as their company waited for the midday meal to be served. 'You passed muster with flying colours this time, Larnie. Looks like Old Ferres is starting to like you.'

'Like me? I don't think he likes *anyone*,' Larn replied. 'Still, I can hardly believe it myself. The way he glowers at you, you always think he's going to put you on report no matter what you do.'

'Ah, the sergeant isn't so bad,' said Hallan, the squad medic, from nearby as he busied himself putting a dressing on Leden's damaged nose. 'I mean, granted he can be tough, but he's pretty fair with it.'

'Dair?' Leden said, outraged. 'Da dastard doke by dose!'

'It could have been worse, Leden,' Hallan said. 'Usually when Ferres thinks a trooper's gun isn't clean enough he kicks him in the balls. At least this way I haven't got to get you to drop your pants to tend your injuries. And besides, next time the sergeant gives you a choice between face, chest, or gut maybe you'll be smart enough to say "toe".'

'Ha, say that and you'll definitely catch one in the balls,' Jenks laughed. 'No, once Ferres has a burr riding him he's going to hurt you one way or another. You ask me, only thing you can do is take your lumps and tough it out. Unless you're like Larnie here, of course. The perfect Guardsman.'

At that, they all smiled. Even though the jibe – such as it was – was directed at him, Larn smiled with them. Even without the light tone in his companion's voice, he would have known Jenks was only joking. *The perfect Guardsman*. Larn might well have just passed muster, but he did not have any pretensions in that regard. Even after two months of basic training, he felt no more a Guardsman now than he had on the day when he had first been drafted.

For a moment, while the others continued their conversation around him, Larn considered how much his life had changed in the space of a few short months. The day after his conversation with his father in the cellar he had taken the landrailer to the town of Willans Ferry, and from there on to the regional capital Durnanville to report for induction. From Durnanville he had been sent two hundred kilometres east, to a remote staging post where for the last two months they had trained him to become a Guardsman.

He found himself looking at his comrades. Hallan was small and dark, Jenks tall and fair, but despite the differences between them he realised they did not look any more like Guardsmen than either him or Leden. Himself included, they all still looked like what they were – farmboys. Like him, they were all the sons of farmers. So for that matter were most of the men in the regiment. They were all of them farmboys, fresh from the fields and accustomed to lives of peaceful obscurity. The arrival of the induction notices had changed that forever. Now, for better or worse, they found themselves conscripted as Guardsmen. Two thousand green and unproven recruits, sent for basic training at this staging post before they left Jumael IV for good. Two thousand would-be Guardsmen, given over to the tender mercies of men like Sergeant Ferres in the hope they could be made into soldiers by the time they got their first taste of action.

'Anyway, if you ask me, Hallan is right,' Jenks said, his voice breaking into Larn's thoughts. 'I mean, hard as Ferres is, at least you know where you stand with him. Besides, I suppose he's earned the right to be hard. Unlike the rest of us, I hear he was regular PDF back before he got drafted. He's probably the only man in this entire regiment who knows anything about soldiering. And, believe you me, when we make our first drop and the lasfire starts flying we'll be glad they gave us a man like that to lead us.'

'Do you ever think about it, Jenks?' Larn asked. 'Do you ever think about what it will be like the first time we see action?'

In response the others fell silent then, their faces troubled and uneasy. For as long as the silence lasted, Larn worried he had said too much. He worried that something in his voice, some tremor perhaps or even the very fact he had thought to ask the question at all had been enough to cause the others to start to doubt him. Then, finally, Hallan smiled at him; the smile telling him that all of them felt the same nervousness he did at the thought of seeing combat.

'Don't worry, Larnie,' he said, 'Even if you do get hit I'll be on hand to patch you up.'

'Lot of comfort that is,' Jenks said. 'I thought you said the only reason they made you a medic was because you were a veterinary back home.'

'Actually, it was my *father* who was the veterinary – I just used to help him out,' Hallan said. 'So not only do

I know how to mend wounds, Jenks, but if we come across a pregnant grox I'll be able to assist with the birthing as well.'

'Just so long as you don't get the two mixed up, Hals,' Jenks said. 'Bad enough if I should get wounded, without having to worry about you trying to put your hand up my backside because you think I'm about to calf.'

They all laughed, the sombre mood of a few moments before gratefully forgotten. Then, seeing something at the other end of the mess hall, Jenks nodded towards it.

'Hey oh,' he said. 'Looks like dinner's here at last.'

Following the direction of Jenks's nod, Larn looked over to see Vorrans – the fifth member of their fireteam – hurrying over towards them with a stack of mess trays balanced in his hands in front of him.

'It's about time,' Hallan said. 'I swear my stomach's so empty I was starting to think my throat'd been cut.' Then, as Vorrans arrived at the table and began to hand out the mess trays: 'Zell's tears, what took you so long, Vors? This food is barely warm!'

'It's not my fault the mess line is so crowded this time of day, Hals Vorrans said. 'Besides, yesterday when it was *your* turn at mess duty I don't remember you getting the food here any faster. And anyway, remember what you said then? Your exact words were "It's not like this slop tastes any better hot". That's what you said.'

'Excuses, excuses,' Hallan replied, before turning his attention fully to the contents of his mess tray. 'Though I was right enough about this slop. Back home we wouldn't have fed this to the grox. Still it fills a hole, I suppose.'

'Fills a hole is right,' Jenks said, pulling a spoon from his mess kit and using it to prod suspiciously at the sticky grey stew in his own mess tray. 'You should keep back some of this and take it into battle with you, Hals.

Anybody gets wounded you can use this stuff to glue them back together.'

'I try to pretend to myself it's alpaca stew,' Larn said. 'You know, like they make back home.'

'And does that work, Larnie?' Jenks said. 'Does it make it taste any better?'

'Not so far,' Larn admitted with a shrug.

'What amazes me,' said Vorrans, 'is here we are, surrounded by wheat fields on every side in one of the most productive farming regions on the entire planet. Yet, every day, instead of giving us real food they give us this reconstituted swill. If you ask me, it makes no sense.'

'Well, that's your mistake right there, Vors,' Jenks said. 'Asking questions. Don't you remember the big speech Colonel Stronhim gave us on the first day of induction?'

'Men of the Jumael 14th,' Hallan said, his voice taking on a false gravity as he mocked the stern patrician tones of their regimental commander. 'In the months and years to come you will find yourselves assailed by a thousand questions every time you are dispatched to a new theatre of operations. You will ask yourselves where you are going, how long will it take to get there, what will the conditions be like when you arrive. You must put such things from your mind. The Guard's divinely ordained command structure will tell you what you need to know, when you need to know it. Always remember, there is no place in a Guardsman's mind for questions. Only obedience!'

'That was really good, Hals,' Larn said. 'You captured the old man's voice perfectly.'

'Well, I've been practising,' Hallan said, delighted. 'Though I tell you there are only two questions I want answered: *where* are they sending us for our first posting, and *when* is it going to happen.'

'I wouldn't hold your breath on that count, Hals,'
Jenks said. 'I wouldn't expect them to tell us anything of
the sort until they're good and ready. And anyway, even
if they have decided where and when we're going, you
can be sure we'll be the last to know about it.'

CHAPTER THREE

15:17 hours Imperial Standard Time
(Empyreal Variance Revised Approximation)

ANSWERS IN THE BRIEFING ROOM – WARP SICKNESS AND
THE RHYTHMS OF SLEEP – ON THE CARE AND HANDLING
OF IMAGINARY ORDNANCE

'WE SHOULD BE there in three weeks, maybe four,' the naval officer said, standing illuminated in the glow of the star chart on the pict-display behind him. 'Though given the vagaries of warp travel and the relativity of time in the Empyrean, you should understand that giving anything even resembling a definite answer in this regard is entirely out of the question. Furthermore, there is always the possibility that what may seem like three weeks to us may prove to have been a somewhat longer period once we emerge from the warp. As I say, time is relative in the Empyrean.'

The officer droned on, his sentences strewn with terms like "trans-temporal fluidity", "real-space eddies", and a dozen other similarly indecipherable phrases.

Sitting in the confines of a briefing room already made cramped and stifling by the presence of an entire company of Guardsmen crammed inside it, Larn found himself forced to suppress a sudden yawn. Two months had gone by since the day he had first passed muster on the parade ground, and for the last four weeks of that period Larn's regiment had been billeted on an Imperial troopship en route to what promised to be their first campaign. Four weeks, and today at last their superiors had finally decided to tell them where in hell it was they would be going.

'Seltura VII, gentlemen,' Lieutenant Vinters the company commander said, stepping forward to address his men as the naval part of the briefing ended. 'That's where we are going. And that is where you will get your first chance to serve your immortal Emperor.'

Behind the lieutenant the image on the pict-display abruptly changed, the naval star chart giving way to a static image of a round blue world set against the blackness of space. With it there was a stirring in the room as, almost as one, two hundred Guardsmen leaned forward from their lines of metal chairs for a better view. Then, satisfied he had their attention, Lieutenant Vinters used the remote device in his hand to change the pict-display once more, revealing an aerial view of a forest landscape.

'Seltura VII is heavily forested,' Vinters continued. 'Over eighty per cent of the planet's landmass is covered in temperate rain forest. The climate is mild – not unlike that back on Jumael IV, I'm told – though with something like twice the mean average rainfall per annum. It should be about early summer by the time we arrive to make planetfall, so you can expect the weather to be hot and wet.'

Finding himself yawning once more, Larn hurriedly raised his hand to cover his mouth. Even travelling through the depths of the void, Sergeant Ferres had not let up on them. If anything, Ferres's daily training regime since they had left their homeworld was harder than it had been back on Jumael IV, the only difference being they did their training now in one of the troopship's loading bays while sardonic naval crewmen paused in their own duties to watch them with sneering smiles. Every day, Ferres had had them running training exercises from breakfast to lights out. It was not just the effect of today's exertions that had left Larn feeling so exhausted.

They had been on the troopship nearly a month now, jumping in and out of the Immaterium for a few days' warp travel here, a few days there. Each time, during every night they spent in the warp, Larn had been troubled by terrible nightmares. In his dreams he saw alien landscapes populated with strange and horrific creatures – dreams that had him waking in a cold sweat in his bunk every night, his heart heavy with a sickening and nameless dread. *Warp sickness*, the ship apothecary had called it when half of the regiment had reported for sick duty after their first night in the warp. *You will get used to it in time*. For Larn, the pills the apothecary had given him to help him sleep had proven of little use. He had not had a decent night's sleep in weeks. While, no matter how many pills he took, every night he spent in the warp seemed just as bad as the first.

'Obviously, for reasons of secrecy, there is a limit to the details I can give you at this stage as to the specific operational aspects of our mission on Seltura VII,' Lieutenant Vinters said. 'What I can tell you is that we have been sent to help suppress a mutiny among elements of the local PDF and restore the legitimate government to power. If Intelligence is to be believed we can expect heavy resistance on the part of rebels. We are the Imperial Guard, gentlemen. We will prevail. Of course, we may take it for granted we are likely to experience some hardships at first – not least in matters of acclimatisation to local conditions.'

Acclimatisation, thought Larn, *that's half my problem. The warp sickness is bad enough but it feels to me like it should have been lights out hours ago.* Larn knew that in order to acclimatise their body clocks to the thirty-hour day/night cycle of their destination world, the light-cycle in the parts of the ship inhabited by his regiment had been altered accordingly. Even after weeks now of living by the new cycle, Larn was still finding it difficult to adjust. He felt time-lagged, in the grip of constant fatigue, as though his body was wondering why it was still awake. As hard as the warp sickness was to endure, Larn found the strange sleep rhythms he was now forced to live by made his sleeplessness infinitely worse.

'But as I say, gentlemen,' Vinters said, 'we are Guardsmen and we will prevail. I know this is to be your first campaign. Be assured, your commanders have faith in you all the same. Now, I think that covers everything. If you have any questions you may refer them to your sergeants.'

With that, the lieutenant pressed the remote device once more, causing the image on the pict-display to fade away to darkness as the assembled Guardsmen rose and filed silently from the room. Though as Larn walked away with the others, he found himself wondering how well Lieutenant Vinters really knew the character of the men under his command.

For, from among all the men in the company, who in their right mind would ever dare refer a question to Sergeant Ferres?

'YOU CALL YOURSELVES soldiers?' Sergeant Ferres yelled, his voice echoing stridently off the bulkhead walls of the loading bay. 'I've seen higher lifeforms sticking to my father's arse after his ablutions. Now, attack that blockhouse like you mean it or I'll make the whole lot of you sorry you ever crawled from your inbred mothers' idiot wombs!'

Five hours had passed since the briefing. Five hours which Larn had spent in one of the troopship's loading bays with the rest of his platoon, experiencing the latest training regime to issue from the febrile mind of Sergeant Ferres. All around them rectangular shapes had been painted on the metal floor. Shapes representing the imaginary outlines of bunkers, fixed emplacements, and blockhouses, on which the Guardsmen were expected to hone their skills in close tactical assault. Despite the hours spent already in conflict with invisible enemies, Sergeant Ferres seemed far from happy.

'Keep crouched as you run,' the sergeant yelled, running alongside Larn and his fireteam as they assaulted another non-existent objective. 'There's lasfire and shrapnel whistling all around you. Keep crouched and stay in cover if you don't want to get hit.'

To Larn, the whole thing seemed like madness. Even accounting for his normal fear of the sergeant, as they raced from one imaginary target to another it was all he could do to stop from bursting into laughter. The only thing that stopped him was the expression on Ferres's face. Whatever Larn and the others might think of the folly of spending five hours attacking the outlines of imaginary buildings full of invisible enemies, it was clear that to Sergeant Ferres it was no laughing matter.

'Faster,' Ferres shouted, his voice so shrill it seemed on the verge of breaking. 'I want you to clear that blockhouse room by room. No quarter to the enemy. No survivors. For the Emperor!'

Reaching the outer wall of the 'blockhouse' Jenks took point while the others covered him, kicking in an imaginary door in time for Leden to throw an imaginary grenade into the room to kill the imaginary enemies inside.

'Halt!' the sergeant screamed, spittle spraying from his mouth with the force of the command.

In an instant, Larn and the others froze where they stood. Then, unsure what to do next, they watched as Sergeant Ferres marched past them towards the blockhouse. Stepping carefully into the blockhouse as though he picking his way through a splintered doorway only he could see, Ferres advanced into the centre of the imaginary room before bending forward to wrap his fist around some imaginary object. Straightening his back, he turned and walked towards Leden, his fist held knuckles down in front of him at waist height as though he was still carrying something there.

'What is this, Leden?' the sergeant asked, indicating the invisible object gripped in his fist.

'I... I don't know, sergeant,' Leden replied, jaw sagging open in confusion.

'This is the grenade you just threw into the blockhouse, Leden,' Ferres said. 'Now, can you tell me, what is *wrong* with this grenade?'

'Umm... I don't know, sergeant,' Leden said, shrinking down into himself as he answered as though melting beneath the hot glare of Sergeant Ferres's eyes.

'What is wrong with this grenade is that its pin is still in place, Leden,' the sergeant said. 'And the reason I know the pin is still in place is because when you threw it, you didn't remove it. Now, tell me, Leden: what use is a thrown grenade that still has its pin in place?'

'I... I... didn't think I had to remove the grenade pin, sergeant,' Leden said, his voice trailing away to nothing as he realised what he was saying. 'It is only an imaginary grenade...'

'Imaginary? Not at all, Leden. I assure you, this grenade is quite solid. Here, let me show you,' the sergeant said, suddenly balling his hand into a fist and punching Leden in the stomach. The air exploding from his mouth, Leden fell to his knees. Then, Ferres turned to face the others.

'There,' he said, holding the imaginary grenade up in the air for them all to see it, 'you see I was right – this grenade is just as solid as my fist. As solid as the door of this blockhouse, the walls of the emplacement, even the plasteel of that bunker. The next man who dares even to suggests to me that these things are not real and solid will get the same as Leden just got, but worse. Now, I want to see you attack that blockhouse again. And, this time, I want to see you doing it like Guardsmen!'

At that, the sergeant screamed the order to attack. Chastened by the example of Leden, Larn and the others hurried to assault the blockhouse once more while Leden painfully pulled himself to his feet and came to join them. So it continued, with assault after assault on imaginary buildings and invisible enemies, as Sergeant Ferres moved from fireteam to fireteam to inspect their labours. Larn felt himself growing more and more tired as his sleeplessness took its toll until at last, after hours more of manoeuvres, the sergeant finally called a halt to training and dismissed them. So tired by then, Larn was sure he knew what it meant to be a dead man walking.

INTERLUDE

A Day in the Life of Erasmos Ng

'COORDINATE: TWO THREE three point eight six three nine,' the voice blared into Erasmos Ng's ear as he dutifully typed the number 233.8639 into the cogitator before him. 'Coordinate: two four two point seven four six eight. Coordinate: two three eight point five nine six one. Correction: two three eight point five *eight* six one. Further coordinates pending. Wait.'

With that, the voice in his earpiece fell abruptly silent. Granted brief respite from the endless stream of numbers that assailed him every minute of his working life, Erasmos Ng turned his tired eyes to gaze at the cavernous interior of the room around him. As ever, Data Processing Room 312 was a hive of mindless activity as a thousand other bored and dispirited souls just like him went about their labours. Here, numbers were crunched, data entries updated, reports filed, then collated, then cross-indexed – all amid a constant din of clattering type-keys and whirring logic-wheels that put him in mind of nothing so much as the sound of an insect army on the march. Still, he realised it was a spurious analogy. The labours of insects at least served some useful purpose. While he had long ago begun to doubt that what went on in Room 312 served any purpose at all.

'Coordinate: two three five point one five three zero,' the voice in his earpiece crackled into life again. 'Coordinate: two two two point six one seven four. Coordinate: two three six point one zero one five.' And so on, *ad infinitum*.

Resuming his task with a weary sigh, as he typed the new set of coordinates into the cogitator, Ng found himself reflecting sadly on how often the shape of a man's life came to be dictated by the happenstance of birth. If he had been born on another planet he might have been a miner, a farmer, or even a huntsman. As it was he had been born on *this* world – on Libris-VI. A world whose only industry of note resided in a single enormous Administratum complex the size of a city – one of many thousands of such complexes the Administratum maintained across the galaxy. Lacking other prospects, like his parents before him Erasmos Ng had entered Imperial service, becoming just another small cog in the vast bureaucratic machine responsible for the functioning – smooth or otherwise – of the entire Imperium. A selfless and noble calling, or so they told him. Though, as with so much else he had been told in his life, he no longer believed it.

'Coordinate: two one eight point four one zero zero,' the voice – his unseen tormentor – said, his tone smug and mocking even through the static. 'Coordinate: two two one point one seven two nine.'

Now, at the age of forty-five and with thirty years of mind-numbing tedium behind him Ng knew he had risen as far in the Administratum hierarchy as he was likely to go. Specifically, to the heady heights of Assistant Scribe, Grade Secundus Minoris. A records clerk by any other name, condemned to spend every day of his life hunched over the cogitator at his workstation in Room 312. His appointed task: to type into the cogitator the never-ending series of numbers spoken to him by the disembodied voice over his earpiece. A task he performed seven days a week, twelve hours a day, barring two permitted fifteen-minute rest-breaks, a full half-hour for his midday meal, and a single day's unpaid holiday every year on Emperor's Day.

Beaten down by the bleak dreariness of his existence, Erasmos Ng found he had long ago stopped caring what purpose his labours served. Instead, for thirty years now, he had simply performed his allotted task, repetitively typing coordinates into the cogitator again and again and again, no longer caring what – if anything – they meant. A lost soul, adrift in a dark and endless sea of numbers.

'Coordinate: two three three point three three two one,' the voice said, grinding his soul down a little more with every word. 'Coordinate: two two three point seven seven one two.'

Then, just as he finished typing a new set of coordinates into the machine, Erasmos Ng abruptly realised he might have made a mistake. That last coordinate – was it 223.7712 or 223.7721? But long past giving a damn one way or another he simply shrugged, put it from his mind, and went on to the next one. After all, he consoled himself, it hardly really mattered whether or not he had made a mistake. He had long ago realised his labours, like his life, were of no importance.

And, in the end, they were only numbers…

CHAPTER FOUR

22:57 hours Imperial Standard Time
(Revised Real-Space Close Planetary Approximation)

CURIOUS ORDERS AND UNWELCOME DESTINATIONS –
EXHORTATIONS TO DUTY AND UNANSWERED QUESTIONS –
THE LANDER AND INTIMATIONS OF FALLING

MAGNIFIED BY THE enhancement devices cunningly hidden in the transparent surface of the forward viewing portal the planet looked huge and foreboding, its red-brown bulk reminiscent of nothing so much as an enormous globule of half-dried blood. As he stood watching it from his usual vantage on the bridge of the troopship he commanded, Captain Vidius Strell found himself briefly pitying the men who would be forced to make planetfall there. *Poor devils*, he thought. *I have seen a lot of planets, absolute hellholes some of them, but there is something about the look of that damn place that makes you think landing there wouldn't be pleasant.*

'Captain?' he heard the voice of his first officer, Gudarsen, behind him. 'Navigation Liaison reports we are currently fifteen point three five minutes from reaching orbit. Gravitational conditions normal. All systems running clean and smooth. We are green for go, Captain. Request permission to relay the order to launch control to prepare a lander for planetary descent.'

'Permission denied,' Strell said. 'I want you to check the confirmation codes on that last astropathic message again, Number One. Then, report back to me.'

'Aye, sir. Understood,' Gudarsen replied, before bustling energetically away with what seemed to his captain a commendable eagerness to follow his instructions.

Left to his thoughts once more, while around him the crew of the command bridge went about their duties, Strell again turned his attention to the planet looming ever larger through the viewing portal. As he did, he wondered if the disquiet he felt gazing at the world before him had less to do with anything sinister in the appearance of the planet itself and more to do with his puzzlement at the orders that had brought them to it. His ship, *Inevitable Victory*, had been en route with escorts and another thirty troopships to the Seltura system when they had received orders to break convoy and proceed here alone. It had been only a small detour requiring no more than a four hour jump through the warp, but the precise nature of the mission they had come here to perform was enough to have the *Victory's* captain grinding his teeth in frustration.

A single company, thought Strell. *Why in the name of the Divine would Naval Operations Command divert an entire starship just to drop a single company of Imperial Guardsmen on some backwater, Emperor-forsaken world?*

Aggravated by the thought, Strell cast an ill-humoured eye over the printout of the ship's transport manifest held in his hand until he came to the listing for the offending company. *6th Company, the 14th Jumael*

Volunteers, Company Commander: Lieutenant Vinters.
There was nothing out of the ordinary in the company's
listing on the manifest. Nothing to explain why he and
his crew had been diverted from their duties and the
protection of the convoy to ferry two hundred men to a
planet that, in galactic terms, might as well be in the
middle of nowhere.

Perhaps there is more to this than meets the eye, thought
Strell again. *Perhaps the manifest listing is only a cover, and
they are special troops on a secret mission. Why else would
we have been sent here? The only other reason could be if
some mistake had been made but the Imperium does not
make mistakes. Yes, a secret mission. It is the only explanation that makes any sense...*

Satisfied at last that he had found the answer, Strell
turned to see Gudarsen hurrying towards him once
more, holding the text of the astropathic message
gripped tightly before him.

'All confirmation codes read correct, captain,'
Gudarsen said. 'The specifics of our mission are confirmed.'

'Very good. You have my permission to relay instructions to Launch Control to prepare a lander for launch.
Oh, and Number One? This is strictly a "drop-and-depart"
mission. Tell Liaison to have the navigator plot a new
course for Seltura-III. Once the lander has dropped its
passengers planetside and returned to the ship, I want
us to underway within the hour.'

'Orders received and understood, captain,' said
Gudarsen, ending with a standard phrase of acknowl-
edgement as he hurried away to carry out his duties.
'The Emperor protects.'

'The Emperor protects, Number One,' Strell echoed,
already turning to redirect his gaze towards the planet
once more as he waited for the lander to be launched so
he could watch its descent.

Yes, he thought. *A secret mission. That's the only thing it could be. If Operations Command has decided we are to be denied information as to the nature of that mission, so be it. It is like they used to teach us in the scholarium.* Then, he allowed himself a small smile of nostalgia as his mind turned to the half-remembered wisdoms of long ago days. *How did it go now,* he thought. *Ah yes, it was something like: 'Ours is not to reason why.'*

'Ours is but to do and die.'

'IT IS BETTER to die for the Emperor than live for yourself!' the vox-caster screamed, drowning out the sound of trampling feet and shouted orders as the men of 6th Company ran through the troopship's cramped corridors towards the launch bay. 'The blood of martyrs is the seed of the Imperium! If you want peace, prepare for war!'

The vox-caster blared on through the bowels of the troopship, on and on in a pre-recorded loop of exhortations to duty, as Larn ran stumbling with the others under the weight of the heavy pack on his back. Barely three hours had passed since Sergeant Ferres had at last relented and dismissed them from training to return to their quarters. Three hours since, exhausted, Larn had finally been allowed to go to sleep. Only to be roused blearily from his slumbers two and a quarter hours later by the wail of sirens as Sergeant Ferres had ordered the men of the platoon from their bunks and told them to make ready for a planetary drop.

'Be vigilant and be strong!' the vox-caster shrieked ever louder, harsh echoes rebounding from loudspeakers set in the metal walls and ceiling all around them. 'The Emperor is your shield and protector!'

Now, three quarters of an hour's worth of hurried preparations later, Larn found himself running in full kit as he and the rest of his company were herded like sheep through the troopship's maze of corridors. Here and there they passed naval crewmen who paused from their duties long enough to cheer them on, offering half-heard words of encouragement in place of the sardonic laughter that had greeted their earlier training exercises. With the prospect that their erstwhile passengers might soon be seeing combat, it seemed the normal antipathy between the Navy and the Guard had abruptly given way to mutual respect. With a sudden tremor in the pit of his stomach, Larn realised he was about to go to war.

'You shall know no reward other than the Emperor's satisfaction!' the vox-caster continued. 'You shall know no truth other than that which the servants of your Emperor tell you!'

This is it, Larn thought. *After all the training and briefings, all the preparations, the moment for which it was all in aid of is here at last. I am finally going to war.* As much as that thought filled his mind, he found himself distracted as a second thought pushed itself insistently to the fore. *Three weeks,* he thought. *Three weeks, maybe four. That is what the naval officer said in the briefing only yesterday. He said it would be at least three weeks before we saw any action.* Confused, Larn wondered what could have changed in the meantime. If yesterday they were still three weeks from combat, how was it today they were about to make their first drop?

'The mind of the Guardsman has no place for questions,' the vox-caster screamed unnervingly. 'Doubt is a vile cancer whose symptoms are cowardice and fear, steel yourself against it. There is room for but three things in the mind of the Guardsman: obedience, duty, and love of the Emperor.'

Abruptly, as though the blaring of the vox-caster was somehow the sound of his own conscience, Larn felt a sudden shame. He thought of his family far away on

Jumael, and how every night they would be offering a
prayer for his safety as they knelt before the votive picture of the Emperor above the fire mantle. He thought
about the tale his father had told him, about his great-
grandfather and the lottery. He thought about all the
promises he had made his Pa about doing his duty. He
realised, for all his talk and promises then, how close he
had coming to failing them at the very first hurdle. It did
not matter that the facts given him in yesterday's briefing now seemed at odds with today's reality. He was a
Guardsman, and all that mattered was that he did his
duty. Putting his questions aside he found himself comforted by the memory of his father's words in the cellar,
his recollection of his father's voice serving as a kinder
and more gentle counterpoint to the vox-caster's wail
and bombast.

'Trust to the Emperor,' his father had told him with
tears in his eyes. 'Trust to the Emperor, and everything
will be all right.'

EMERGING FROM THE cramp and narrowness of the corri-
dor, the launch bay seemed huge as Larn followed the
men in front of him inside it. Ahead he saw the imposing bulk of a lander, steam rising from the hydraulics of
the platform it rested on as tech-adepts scurried around
it like mindful ants giving succour to a fallen giant. He
saw adepts manning the massive fuel lines that ran
from a recessed spout in the far wall of the launch bay
to the lander's engines, while others anointed the sur-
faces of the lander with unguents, burned incense,
performed blessings, or made final adjustments to the
lander's systems with the diverse instruments of holy
calibration. All the while the lander hummed with
power, the thrumming of its restive engines vibrating
through the metal floor of the launch bay towards
where Larn and the others stood gazing at it uncertainly,

like wary travellers unsure whether to risk waking a sleeping tiger.

'Get moving, you inbreeds!' Sergeant Ferres yelled, the volume of the continuing vox-caster broadcasts around them having been diminished enough by the open spaces of the launch bay for them to at last hear their sergeant's commands. 'A man might almost think you bumpkins hadn't seen a lander before.'

In truth, none of them had: their journey from Jumael to the orbiting troopship having been undertaken inside local planetary shuttles of much less startling dimensions. As Larn rushed towards the lander with the others he found himself in awe to be approaching so enormous a vehicle. *It looks like it could hold a couple of thousand men at least,* he thought. *Not to mention tanks and artillery besides.* For the first time he truly appreciated the extraordinary scale of the troopship he had been travelling within for the last twenty-nine days. *Sweet Emperor,* he thought in amazement, *to think they say this ship carries twenty such landers!*

At the front the mouth of the lander lay open, the primary assault ramp stretching towards them like the tongue of some improbable metal beast. Running up the ramp into the cavernous and dimly lit interior of the lander itself, Larn and the others found a grim-faced member of the lander's crew waiting to point them in the direction of a nearby stairwell. Then, following the stairwell to its summit, they came to the vast rows and aisles of seats of the lander's upper troop-deck.

'Find a seat and fasten your restraints,' Ferres barked. 'I want you seated together in fireteam, section, and platoon order. Any man who isn't in his seat and ready for drop in two minutes' time is going to find himself on a charge.'

Hurrying to his seat Larn quickly sat down, carefully fastening the buckles of the seat's impact restraints across his waist, shoulders and chest, before tightening them to fit him. Making sure the safety on his lasgun was set to 'safe', he pushed the gun upright and butt-first into the shallow recess of the weapon holder set at the front of his seat and clipped the barrel lock closed to hold the gun in place. Then, looking about him at the other Guardsmen as they did likewise, Larn found himself briefly confused as he realised just how few men there were inside the lander. Despite the fact that the lander was built to house a minimum of two thousand men, there was at most a single company of men inside it. *It looks like they are only dropping my company,* he thought. *6th Company. But that would make no sense. Why would they only put only two hundred men on board, when this lander can hold ten times that? No. They must be going to load more men on board. No doubt we are just the first aboard and rest of the regiment will be following us soon enough.*

'Ready for launch in "T" minus two point zero zero minutes,' a harsh metallic voice announced over a hidden vox-caster speaker as, in the distance, Larn heard the slow grinding of the lander's assault ramp closing.

'Sounds like we got into our seats just in time, Larnie,' Jenks said, as Larn realised he had taken the seat next to him. 'Good thing, too. Never mind old Ferres and his threats, I wouldn't want to be wandering around out of my seat when this monster finally gets going.'

With that Jenks turned away to fasten his own seat-restraints. For a moment, still confused, Larn found himself fighting the urge to ask Jenks where he thought the rest of the regiment was. Then, abruptly, he realised it made no difference. It was too late to turn back now. Like it or not, it looked like 6th Company would be making their first planetary drop on their own.

'Ready for launch in "T" minus one point zero zero minutes,' the voice said again, as Larn felt the vibrations of the lander's engines grow stronger.

'Don't worry, Larnie,' said Jenks by his side as, trying as much to allay his own anxieties as comfort a friend, he turned to give Larn a kindly smile. 'They say it's not the *fall* you need to worry about. It's hitting the *ground* that kills you.'

'Ready for launch in "T" minus zero point three zero minutes,' the metallic voice continued its countdown as Larn realised, too late, he had forgotten to pray to the Emperor for a safe descent.

'Ready for launch in "T" minus zero,' the voice said as the lander's engines fired and Larn found himself feeling suddenly weightless. 'All systems ready. Launch!'

And then, quicker than Larn would have thought possible, they were falling.

CHAPTER FIVE

23:12 hours Imperial Standard Time
(Revised Real-Space Close Planetary Approximation)

EVASIVE MANOEUVRES – FALLING AND THE TASTE OF VOMIT
– LANDFALL, DEATH AND GRIM REALISATIONS – THE
CALAMITY OF SERGEANT FERRES – NO-MAN'S LAND AND
THE EAGLE IN THE DISTANCE – WELCOME TO BROUCHEROC

'BEARING ONE EIGHT degrees one five minutes,' the navigation servitor's voice croaked, the parchment-thin tones of its voice barely audible in the lander's crew compartment over the roar of engines. 'Recommend course correction of minus zero three degrees zero eight minutes for optimal atmospheric entry. All other systems reading normal.'

'Check,' said the pilot, automatically pushing his control stick forward to make the adjustment. 'New bearing: one five degrees zero seven minutes. Confirm course correction.'

'Course correction confirmed,' the servitor said, its yellowing sightless eyes rolling back in their sockets as it rechecked its calculations. 'Atmospheric entry in 'T' minus five seconds. Two. One. Atmospheric entry achieved. All systems reading normal.'

'Look at that glow, Dren,' Zil the co-pilot said, his eyes lifting from his instruments for a fraction of a second to look out the view-portal at the nose of the lander as it was surrounded by a nimbus of bright red fire. 'No matter how many planetary drops we do, I never get used to it. It's like riding in a ball of flame. It makes you thank the Emperor for whoever first made heat shields.'

'Heat shields reading normal,' said the servitor, gears whirring inside it as it mistook the comment for a question. 'Exterior temperature within permitted operational thresholds. All systems reading normal.'

'That's because you've only got a dozen drops behind you,' the pilot said. 'Trust me, by the time you've done another dozen you won't even notice it. How's the signal from the landing beacon? I don't want to miss the drop point.'

'Beacon signal reading strong and clear,' Zil replied. 'No air traffic, friendly or hostile. Looks like we've got the sky to ourselves. Wait! Auspex is reading some–'

'Warning! Warning!' the servitor interrupted, the whirring of its mechanisms reaching an abrupt crescendo as it burst into life. 'Registering hostile missile launch from ground-based battery. Recommend evasive manoeuvres. Missile trajectory eight seven degrees zero three minutes, airspeed six hundred knots. Warning! Registering second missile launch. Missile trajectory–'

'Evasive manoeuvres confirmed!' the pilot said, pressing his control stick forward as he pushed the lander into a dive. 'Servitor: belay hostile trajectories and airspeeds until further orders. Zil, deploy chaff!'

'Chaff activated. Instruments reading chaff successfully deployed,' Zil said, his voice growing suddenly hoarse as he looked at one of the screens before him.

'Wait. The chaff, it's not done any good. It's as though…
Holy Emperor! None of the hostile missiles have guid-
ance systems!'

'What do you mean?' the pilot asked as he saw Zil's
face go pale. 'If that's the case we have nothing to worry
about. If they're firing blind there's not one chance in a
thousand of them being able to hit us.'

'But that's exactly it,' said Zil, his voice frantic. 'I'm
reading a *thousand* hostile missiles as airborne already.
And hundreds more are being launched every second.
Holy Throne! We're flying into the biggest shitstorm I've
ever seen!'

'Emergency evasion procedures!' the pilot said, bark-
ing out orders as he pushed the lander forward into an
even steeper dive while from outside they could hear
the first of the missiles exploding. 'Servitor: override
standard flaps and navigation safety protocols – I want
full control! Make sure your strapped in tight, Zil –
we're going to have to go in hard and heavy! Looks like
this is going to be a *close* one…'

> *Falling.*
> *They were falling.*
> *With nothing to slow or stop them.*
> *Like a comet.*
> *Falling headlong from the stars.*

In the lander's troop compartment, slammed back in
his seat by the force of acceleration, it felt to Larn as
though his stomach was trying to push its way up from
his throat. Around him he could hear men screaming,
the sound all but drowned out by the dull thud of
explosions from outside the lander. He heard cries for
pity and muttered oaths, all the while the skin being
pulled so tight across his face he was sure it was about
to rip free from his bones. Then, sounding much louder

than any noise he had ever known before, there came the boom of another explosion and with it the gut-wrenching sound of tearing metal. With those sounds he found himself forced back against his seat with even greater force as the fall began in earnest.

We've been hit, he thought, overcome with sudden panic while the world began to spin crazily around him as the lander turned over and over on its axis out of control. *We've been hit*, the thought crowded his mind and held him at its mercy. *We've been hit! Holy Emperor, we're in freefall!*

He felt himself struck in the face by a warm and semi-solid liquid, the acrid smell and the taste of the droplets dribbling past his lips telling him it was vomit. Half mad with desperation, he found himself wondering incongruously whether it was from his own stomach or someone else's. Then another thought forced its way fearfully into his mind and he no longer cared who the vomit belonged to. A thought more terrible than any he had ever considered in his seventeen years of life to date.

We are falling from the sky, he thought. *We are falling from the sky and we're going to die!*

He felt his gorge rise in a tide of sickly acids, the half-digested remnants of his last meal spewing uncontrollably from his mouth to soak some other unfortunate elsewhere in the lander. Certain he was on the brink of oblivion he tried to replay the events of his life in his mind. He tried to remember his family, the farm, his homeworld. He tried to think of fields of flowing wheat, magnificent sunsets, the sound of his father's voice. Anything to blot out the terrifying reality around him. It was hopeless though and he realised the last moments of his life would be spent with the following sensations: the taste of vomit; the sound of men going screaming to their deaths; the feeling of his own heart beating wildly in his chest. These were the things he would take with him to death: the last sensations he would ever know. Just as he began to wonder at the unfairness of it all the world stopped spinning as, with a bone-jarring impact and a terrible screech like the death-knell of some mortally wounded beast, the lander finally hit the ground.

For a moment there was silence while the interior of the lander was plunged into total darkness. Next, Larn heard the sound of coughing and quiet prayers as the men in the lander drew a collective breath to find, despite some initial misgivings, they were very much alive. Abruptly, darkness gave way to dim shadowy light at the activation of the lander's emergency illumination system. Then, he heard a familiar strident voice begin to bark out orders as Sergeant Ferres sought to re-establish control of his troops.

'Fall in!' the sergeant shouted. 'Fall in and prepare to disembark. Get off your arses, damn you, and start acting like soldiers. You've got a war to fight, you lazy bastards.'

Releasing his seat-restraints Larn staggered unsteadily to his feet, his hands warily prodding his body as he checked to see whether any of his bones were broken. To his relief, it seemed he had survived the landing little the worse for wear. His shoulders were sore, and he had the painful beginnings of a bruise where the clasp of one of the seat-straps had bitten into his flesh. Other than that, he had escaped from what had seemed like certain death remarkably unscathed. Then, just as he began to congratulate himself on surviving his first drop, Larn turned to retrieve his lasgun and saw that the man sitting in the seat next to him had not been so lucky.

It was Jenks. Head lolling sideways at a sickening angle, eyes staring blankly from a lifeless and slack-jawed face,

Jenks sat in his seat dead and unmoving. Staring at his friend's body in numb disbelief, Larn noticed a thin stream of blood trickling from Jenks's mouth to stain his chin. Then, spotting a small bloody-ended piece of pink flesh lying on the floor of the lander beside his feet, Larn realised that with the force of the landing Jenks must have inadvertently bitten off the end of his tongue. As horrified as he was by that discovery, Larn could not at first understand how Jenks had died. Until, looking once more at arrangement of seat-restraints around his friend's body and the way his head lolled sideways like a broken puppet, Larn realised the restraints had been improperly fastened, causing Jenks's neck to snap at the moment of their landing. The realisation brought him no comfort. Jenks was dead. Understanding how his friend had died did nothing to lessen Larn's grief.

'Fall in.' the sergeant shouted again. 'Fall in and get ready to move out.'

Still numb with shock, Larn grabbed his lasgun and stumbled past Jenks's body to join the rest of the company as they lined up in one of the aisles between the upper deck's endless rows of seating. As he did, he became aware for the first time of the sound of distant ricochets clanging off the exterior of the hull. *We are being fired at,* he thought dully, his mind still reeling at the sight of Jenks's corpse. Until, noticing an almost palpable sense of unrest among the other Guardsmen as he took his place in the line and waited for the order to move out, Larn realised he could smell smoke and with it, there came an unwelcome realisation that cut through the fog of his grief and seemed to grip at his heart with clutching icy fingers.

The lander was on fire.

Spurred on by horror at the prospect of being trapped in a burning lander, the Guardsmen began to hurry for the stairwell while behind them Sergeant Ferres shouted profanities in the vain hope of maintaining some form of order. No one was listening. Frenzied, they rushed down the stairs towards the lower deck, treading on the corpses of those already killed in the landing.

Running with the others, Larn caught a brief glimpse of their company commander, Lieutenant Vinters, sitting dead in his seat with his neck broken just like Jenks. He had no time to dwell on the lieutenant's death; caught in the crush of fleeing Guardsmen he could only run with the crowd as they made for the lower deck, to the assault ramp and freedom. As they came within sight of it they found that the assault ramp was still sealed shut, while from all around them the smell of smoke grew ever stronger.

'Open that ramp!' screamed Sergeant Ferres, pushing his way through the crowd of milling Guardsmen to where a small group stood studying the control panel governing the ramp's mechanism. Seeing the group raise their eyes to look at him in confusion, he pushed them aside and stretched out a hand towards a metal lever set in a recess by the edge of the ramp. 'Useless bastards!' he spat in contempt, his hand closing around the lever. 'The master control panel must have been damaged in the landing. You need to pull the emergency release lever – like this.'

Pulling the lever, Sergeant Ferres shrieked in sudden agony as one of the ramp's explosive release bolts misfired, a bright tongue of yellow fire bursting from the side of ramp to engulf his face. Screaming, a halo of flame dancing around his head, he stumbled blindly against the assault ramp as the other bolts fired and the ramp fell open behind him. Falling into the suddenly vacated space, his body rolled down the ramp and came to a stop partway down it as one of his legs caught on a protrusion at its side. For a moment, seeing the

strugglings of their sergeant's body grow still as the life
left him, his troops stood gazing at him in shocked
silence, hypnotised by the brutal calamity of their
leader's death.

'We have to move,' Larn heard someone say behind
him as he realised how warm it had grown in the lander. 'The smoke is getting closer. If we don't get out of
here now we'll either burn to death or choke.'

As one, the Guardsmen burst forward to rush down
the ramp. The light outside seemed blinding in its
intensity after the shadowed dimness of the interior of
the lander. Barely able to keep his feet as the men
behind him pushed to get out, Larn stumbled down the
ramp with the rest, his first experiences of the new
world before him registering as a disconnected jumble
of sights and sensations. He caught snatches of an
empty landscape through the press of bodies around
him, saw a grey and brooding sky above them, felt a savage chill that bit gnawingly into his flesh. Worst of all
was the sight of Sergeant Ferres's burnt and disfigured
face. The fire-blackened sockets that had once held his
eyes glimpsed briefly at the edge of Larn's vision as he
followed the others down the ramp. Then, as the first
ranks of Guardsmen reached the foot of the ramp and
apparent safety, the frenzied herd instinct of a few
moments before abruptly abated.

Released from the crushing pressure of the crowd as
the Guardsmen in front moved to take advantage of the
open space before them, Larn was relieved to find himself able to breathe properly once more. Then, standing
uncertainly with the others as they milled leaderless in
the shadow of the lander, he turned to take his first clear
view of the planet around him.

This is it, he thought, his breath turning to white
vapour in the cold. *This is Seltura-III? It doesn't look much
like how they described it in the briefing.*

Around him, as endless as the wheat fields of his homeworld, was a bleak and barren landscape – a flat treeless vista of frozen grey-black mud, punctuated here and there by shell craters and the rusting silhouettes of burned-out vehicles. To the east of him, he saw a distant cityscape of ruined buildings, as grey, foreboding and abandoned as every other aspect of the landscape around it. *It looks like a ghost town*, he thought with a shiver. *A ghost town, hungry for more ghosts.*

'I don't understand it,' he heard a questioning voice say as he realised Leden, Hallan and Vorrans had come to stand beside him. 'Where are the trees?' Leden asked. 'They said Seltura-III was covered in forests. And it's cold. They said it would be summer.'

'Never mind that,' said Hallan, terse at his side. 'We need into get to cover. I heard shots hitting the hull when we landed. There must be hostiles around here some–' He paused, stopping to look up with anxious eyes at the sky as, overhead, they heard the whistle of a shell coming closer.

'Incoming!' someone screamed as the entire company raced frantically to seek shelter at the side of the lander. Seconds later, an explosion lifted up dancing clods of frozen mud thirty metres away from where they were standing.

'I think it was a mortar.' Vorrans said, an edge of panic to his voice as he huddled with the others beside the lander. 'It sounded like a mortar,' he said, jabbering uncontrollably in a breathless rush of fear. 'A mortar, don't you think? A mortar. I think it was a mortar. A mortar…'

'I wish to the Emperor that was *all* it was,' Hallan said. Around them, more shots and explosions rang out. A fusillade that seemed to ominously increase in volume with every instant, as the noise of bullets and shells striking the hull on the other side of the lander grew so loud they had to shout to be heard over the roar. 'Lucky for us whoever's shooting is on the other side of this lander but we can't stay here forever. We need to find better cover, or it's only a matter of time before their artillery finds the range and starts to loop shells over the lander to land right on top of us.'

'Maybe this is all a mistake?' Vorrans said, his face alive with the glimmer of desperate hope. 'That's it, mistaken identity. Maybe it's our own side doing the shooting and they don't know who we are. We could make a white flag and try to signal them.'

'Shut up, Vors. You're talking like an idiot.' Hallan snapped. Then, seeing Vorrans look at him in shock, he softened his tone. 'Believe me, Vors, there's nothing *mistaken* about it. There's a ten-metre tall Imperial eagle painted on each side of the hull of the lander. The people shooting at us know *exactly* who we are. That's why they're trying to *kill* us. Our only way out of this is to try and make for our own lines. Though we'll need to find out where they are first.'

'There!' Leden said, his finger pointing eastward. 'You see it – the eagle in the distance. Sweet Emperor, we're saved.'

Turning to follow the direction of Leden's jabbing finger, Larn saw a flagpole rising from the rubble-strewn outskirts of the city. At its top a worn and ragged flag: an Imperial eagle, fluttering in the breeze.

'You're right, Leden,' Hallan said, the excitement in his voice drawing the attention of the rest of the company as dozens of eyes turned to look toward the flag. 'It's our own lines, all right. If you look closely you can see the outlines of camouflaged bunkers and firing emplacements. That's where we should be headed.'

'But it's got to be seven or eight hundred metres away at least, Hals,' Vorrans protested. 'With nothing between us and that flag but open ground. We'll never make it.'

'We don't have any choice, Vors,' Hallan said. Then, seeing the eyes of every other Guardsman in the company were on him, he turned to them, his voice raised loud enough to be heard among the din of gunfire. 'Listen to me, all of you. I know you're scared. Zell knows, I am too. But if we stay here we are as good as dead. Our only chance is to make for that flag!'

For a moment there was no response as the Guardsmen cast frightened eyes from the now burning lander to the wide expanse of open ground before them. Each man weighing an unwelcome decision: to stay and risk an undetermined death sometime in the future, or to run and risk an immediate death in the present. Then, suddenly, a shell landed on their side of the lander no more than five metres from where they were standing and the decision was made for them.

They ran.

Breathless, terror dogging his every step, Larn ran with them. He ran, as from behind them there came a remorseless tide of gunfire as the unseen enemy tried to shoot them down. He saw men die screaming all around him, red gore spraying from chests and arms and heads as the bullets struck them. He saw men killed by falling shells, bodies torn apart by blast and shrapnel, heads and limbs dismembered in an instant. All the time he kept his eyes glued on the flag – his would-be refuge – in the distance before him. His every breath a silent prayer in the hope of salvation. His every step one closer to making that salvation a reality.

As he ran, he saw friends and comrades die. He saw Hallan fall first, his right eye exploding from its socket to make way for the bullet passing though it, his mouth open in a cry of encouragement to his fellow Guardsmen that would never be finished. Then Vorrans, his torso ruptured and mutilated as a dozen pieces of shrapnel exploded through his chest. Other men fell:

some he had known by name, others he had known
only by sight. All of them killed as, just as breathless
and desperate as he was, they ran for the flag. Until at
last, with most of his comrades dead already and the
flag still a hundred metres away, Larn realised he would
never make it.

'Here! Over here! Quickly, this way! Over here!'

Suddenly, hearing shouting voices nearby Larn turned
to see a group of Guardsmen in grey-black camouflage
appear as if from nowhere to beckon him towards
them. Changing direction to head for them, he saw they
had emerged from a firing trench and raced towards it
with enemy bullets chewing up the ground around him.
Until at last, reaching the trench, he leapt inside to
safety.

Trying to catch his breath as he lay at the bottom of
the trench, looking about him Larn saw five Guardsmen
standing around him in the confines of the trench: all
clad in the same uniform of grey-black patterned great-
coats, mufflers and fur-shrouded helmets. At first they
ignored him, their eyes turned to scan the killing fields
he had just escaped from. Then, one of the Guardsmen
turned to look down towards him with a grimace and
finally spoke.

'This is Vidmir in trench three, sergeant,' the Guardsmen said, pressing a stud at his collar as Larn realised he
was speaking down a comm-link. 'We have one sur-
vivor. I think a few more made it to the other trenches.
But most of those poor dumb bastards are dead out
there in no-man's land. Over.'

'I can see movement on the ork side,' one of the other
Guardsmen said, standing looking over the trench parapet. 'All this killing must have got their blood up.
They're getting ready for an attack.' Then, while Larn
was still wondering if he had really heard the word 'ork',
he saw the man turn away from the parapet to look

towards him. 'Assuming that uniform you're wearing is not just for show, new fish, you might want to stand up and get your lasgun ready. There's going to be shooting.'

Pulling himself to his feet, Larn unslung his lasgun, stepping forward as the other Guardsmen moved sideways to make space for him on the trench's firing step. Then, as he checked his lasgun and made ready to put it to his shoulder, he saw something that caused him to wonder if his first combat drop might have gone even more badly wrong than he could have thought. As, from the corner of his eye, he spotted a bullet-riddled wooden sign erected behind and slightly to one side of the trench. A sign whose ironic greeting gave him pause to wonder if he really was where he thought he was at all.

A sign that said:

Welcome to Broucheroc.

CHAPTER SIX

12:09 hours Central Broucheroc Time

QUESTIONS OF INTERSTELLAR GEOGRAPHY AND OTHER
REVELATIONS – A BAD DAY IN HELL – THE WAAAGH! –
A BAPTISM OF FIRE – HAND-TO-HAND AGAINST THE
ENEMY – AN OPINION AS TO THE BEST METHOD OF
KILLING A GRETCHIN

'THEY'RE GETTING READY to move all right,' the Guardsman said next to him, spitting a wad of greasy phlegm
over the trench parapet. 'They'll hit us hard this time,
and in numbers. It's the blood that does it, you see. Our
blood, I mean. *Human* blood. The sight and smell of it
always makes 'em more willing and eager for a fight.
Though, Emperor knows, your average ork is usually
pretty *eager* to begin with.'

His name was Repzik: Larn could see the faded letters
of the name stencilled on the tunic of the man's uniform under his greatcoat. Standing beside him on the
firing step, Larn followed the direction of his eyes to
look into the landscape he now knew as no-man's land.

No matter how intently he stared across the bleak fields of frozen mud before them he could see no movement, nor for that matter any other sign of the enemy. Ahead, no-man's land seemed as flat, featureless and devoid of life as it had when he had emerged from the lander to his first view of it barely ten minutes ago. The only difference now was the addition of the burning shell of the lander itself, and with it the bodies of his company strewn haphazard and bloody across the frozen landscape. Abruptly, as he looked out at the remains of men he had known as friends and comrades, Larn felt the beginnings of tears stinging wetly at the corners of his eyes.

Jenks is dead, he thought. *And Hallan, Vorrans, Lieutenant Vinters, even Sergeant Ferres. I don't see Leden. Perhaps he is still alive somewhere. But nearly every man I came here with from Jumael is lying dead out there in no-man's land. All of them slaughtered within minutes of landing, without even having fired a shot.*

'It's a pity about your comrades,' Repzik said, his voice almost kindly as Larn clenched his eyes to try and stop the other men in the trench from seeing his tears. 'But they're dead and you ain't. What you need to start thinking about now is how you're going to stop yourself from *joining* them. The orks are coming, new fish. If you want to live you're going to have to keep yourself hard and tight.'

'Orks?' Larn said, trying to concentrate his mind on the practical in an effort to lay his grief aside. 'You said "orks"? I didn't know there were any orks on Seltura VII?'

'Could be that's true,' Repzik said, as beside him one of the other Guardsmen looked to the sky in silent exasperation. 'Fact is, you'd have to ask somebody who's actually *been* there. Here in Broucheroc though we generally have more orks than we know what to do with.'

'Wait,' asked Larn, confused, 'are you telling me this planet isn't Seltura VII?'

'Well, I wasn't specifically commenting on it, new fish,' Repzik said. 'But since you ask, you'd be right enough. This place isn't Seltura VII – wherever in *hell* that is.'

Stunned, for a moment Larn wondered if he had somehow misunderstood the man's meaning. Then, he looked out again at the treeless landscape and was struck by all the troubling inconsistencies between what he had been told to expect on Seltura VII and the stark brutal realities of the world he saw before him. They had made the drop three weeks early. There were no forests. It was winter rather than summer. The war here was against orks, not PDF rebels. A catalogue of facts that, with a dawning horror born of slow realisation, pushed him inexorably toward a sudden and shocking conclusion.

Holy Throne, he thought. *They sent us to the wrong planet!*

'I shouldn't be here,' he said aloud.

'It's funny how everyone tends to think that when they're waiting for an attack to begin,' said Repzik. 'I wouldn't worry about it, new fish. Once the orks get here you'll soon find yourself feeling right at home.'

'No, you don't understand.' Larn said. 'There has been a terrible mistake. My company was supposed to be going to the Seltura system. To a world called Seltura VII, to put down a mutiny among the local PDF. Something must have gone wrong because I'm on the wrong planet.'

'So? What is that to me?' Repzik said, his eyes as he looked at Larn seemed little warmer than the landscape around them. 'You are on the wrong planet. You are in the wrong system. Not to mention probably the wrong war. Get used to it, new fish. If that is the *worst* thing that happens to you today, you will have been lucky.'

'But you don't understand–'

'No. It is *you* who does not understand, new fish. This is Broucheroc. We are surrounded by ten million orks. And right now some of those orks – maybe only a few thousand or so, if we are lucky – are getting ready to attack us. They don't care what planet you think you should be on. They don't care that you think you're in the wrong place, that you're wet behind the ears, or that you're probably not even old enough to shave. All they care about is *killing* you. So if you know what is good for you, new fish, you will put all this crap aside and start worrying about killing them instead.'

Shocked at the man's outburst Larn said nothing, his reply dying on his tongue as he saw Repzik turn away from him to gaze darkly into no-man's land once more. As though by some sixth sense the other Guardsmen in the trench had already done the same, all of them staring hard into no-man's land as though watching something happening out there of which Larn was entirely unaware. No matter how hard Larn tried, he could see nothing. Nothing except grey-black mud and desolation.

Frustrated, wary of asking the others what they were looking at for fear of drawing another angry outburst, Larn turned to glance around him. Behind him, hidden from his sight when he had first landed by a gentle sloping of the ground, was a series of firing trenches and foxholes. All of them led down towards sandbag emplacements that covered the entrances to a number of underground dugouts set among the shattered husks of buildings at the outskirts of the city. Now his eyes had become accustomed to the relentless grey of the landscape, Larn could see other firing trenches around and to the side of their trench – their parapets cunningly camouflaged to look no different from the countless chunks of crumbling half-buried plascrete and other detritus that lay scattered across this waste-land. From time to time a Guardsman would suddenly emerge from one of the trenches to run half-crouched, zigzagging from one piece of cover to the next until he reached the safety of either another trench or the entrance to one of the dugouts. Behind them, in the dis-tance, the main body of the city stood brooding across the horizon as though watching their lives and labours with disdain. A city of ruined and battle-scarred build-ings set against a grey and uncaring sky.

This is Broucheroc, Larn reminded himself. *That is what they said the city was called.*

'There,' one of the Guardsmen said beside him. 'I see green. The bastards are moving.'

Turning to gaze once more into no-man's land with the others, for a moment Larn found himself vainly struggling to see anything among the wearying grey of the world about them. Then, suddenly, at ground level, perhaps a kilometre away, he saw a brief glimpse of green flesh as its owner stood upright for a split second before abruptly disappearing once more.

'I see it,' Larn said, the words jumping breathless from him, unbidden. 'Holy Emperor! Is that an ork?'

'Hhh. I only wish orks were as small as that, new fish,' Repzik said, spitting over the parapet into no-man's land again. 'That's a gretch. A gretchin. Keep looking and you should be able to see some more.'

He was right. Ahead, Larn saw the creature stand upright once more. This time it stood where it was unmoving, its green flesh plainly visible against the contrast of the grey backdrop of the landscape behind it. Then, after a moment, Larn saw another dozen crea-tures appear beside it, all of them standing still and motionless as though trying to smell something on the wind. Each of them perhaps a metre tall at most, their stunted green bodies appearing curiously hunched and misshapen inside their rough grey garments. Watching them, Larn felt himself recoil in instinctive horror at his first sight of an alien species. Until, before he even knew what he was doing, his finger was on the trigger of las-gun at his shoulder as he sighted in on the *Xenos*.

'Don't bother, new fish,' Repzik said, laying a hand across his barrel. 'Even if you did manage to hit one of the gretch at this range, you would be wasting your ammo. Save it 'til later. Save it for the orks.'

'I don't like it,' one of the other Guardsmen said. 'If the orks are sending their gretch out like that it means they're planning on hitting us with a frontal assault. Another one. What is that now? Something like the *third* one today?'

'Third time is right, Kell,' the Guardsman called Vid-mir said, his face grim as he pressed a finger to his ear to listen to something on his comm bead. 'You'll have to remember to remonstrate with the orks about their lack of originality when they get here. From the reports I'm hearing over the tactical net, you should soon be getting the opportunity to do so.'

'What is it?' the other Guardsman – Kell – asked, while the rest of the men in the trench turned to look at Vidmir. 'What have you heard?'

'Sector Command says auspex is reading a lot of movement in the ork lines,' Vidmir replied. 'Sounds like Repzik was right. They're going to be hitting us hard, and in numbers. Though, from the sound of it, I think there's more to this than just a matter of the orks getting excited over killing the new fish's friends. Could be they were already getting ready to launch an offensive. Which would be bad enough, except it sounds like our own side is trying to get us killed as well. Battery Com-mand are refusing to give us artillery support until they are sure this is really a full-blown assault and not just a feint.'

'A feint, my arse,' Kell grunted. 'When have you ever known an ork to do anything by halves?'

'Agreed,' Vidmir said. 'But, irrespective, it looks like we're going to have to repel the orks on our own. Emperor help us.' Then, turning towards Larn, Vidmir gave him the cold flash of a graveyard smile.

'Congratulations, new fish,' he said. 'Looks like not only did you manage to get yourself dropped right into the middle of hell but you picked a bad day in hell besides.'

REPZIK, VIDMIR, DONN, Ralvs and Kell. These were the names of the five men who shared the trench with him. Larn had learned that much about them at least in the quiet time as they waited for the battle to begin. They were from a planet called Vardan, they told him. They and their regiment, a group of hardened veterans known as the 902nd Vardan Rifles, had come to the city of Broucheroc more than ten years ago and had been here even since. *Ten years!* He could hardly believe it. Nor where those the only things that Larn had learned from the Vardans.

'I don't understand it,' he said, looking out at the group of gretchin on the other side of no-man's land. 'What are they waiting for?'

Ten minutes had passed since the first alien appeared. Though the numbers of those waiting with it had now increased to perhaps a couple of hundred, still the ranks of gretchin stood exposed and out in the open on the other side of no-man's land. Occasionally a squabble would break out, two or three of the aliens suddenly breaking away from the main group to fight a bloody battle with tooth and claw while their fellows watched with lazy interest. For the most part the aliens simply stood there unmoving, their feral faces turned to stare unblinkingly towards the human lines. It was an unnerving spectacle. Not for the first time, Larn found himself fighting the urge to take his lasgun and fire at them. To shoot over and over again until every one of the ugly inhuman faces he could see before him had been obliterated.

'It's an old trick, new fish,' Repzik said. 'They're waiting for us to shoot at them and give away our positions.'

'But that's suicide,' Larn said. 'Why would they be willing to sacrifice themselves like that?'

'Hhh. They're gretch, new fish,' Repzik replied. 'Willing doesn't come into it. If their Warboss tells 'em to go stand out in no-man's land and wait to get killed, it's not like they get much say over it. Of course, even the fact that their boss is smart enough to think of using his gretch that way tells us something. It means the greenskin leading the assault is likely to be one crafty son of a bitch, relatively speaking. And that's likely to be bad news for us, believe me. There's not much worse than a crafty ork. Now quiet down, new fish. There will be plenty of time for questions later, after the attack. Assuming, of course, we survive it.'

At that Repzik fell silent once more, his eyes staring into no-man's land with the rest of the Vardans. Denied the distraction of further conversation, Larn began to realise just how tense the atmosphere was in the trench. *An attack is coming*, he thought. *Although these men have faced dozens, perhaps even hundreds of such attacks in the past, still the tension is plain on every line of their faces for anyone to see.* Briefly, he tried to find comfort in that thought. He tried to tell himself that if hardened veterans like these felt queasy in the face of the impending assault, there was no shame in the churning of his own stomach but he remained unconvinced. *Am I a coward*, he thought. *I am afraid, but will my nerve hold so I can do my duty? Or will it fail? Will I fight when the attack comes or will I break and run?* But as forcefully as those questions rebounded around inside his head, he could find no answer.

The waiting was the worst of it. Abruptly, as he stood there on the firing step, Larn realised that until now he had been inoculated against fear by the sheer breathless pace of events since the lander had been hit. Now, in the silence of the lull before battle, there was no hiding place from his fears. He felt alone. Far from home. Terrified that he was about to die on a strange world under a cold and distant sun.

'Ready your weapons,' Vidmir said, as more gretchin began to appear on the other side of no-man's land. 'This is it. Looks like they got tired of waiting.'

'We hold our fire until they're three hundred metres away,' Repzik said to Larn. 'See that flat grey-black rock over there? That's your mark. We wait 'til the first rank of gretch reach that before we fire.' Then, seeing Larn looking in confusion into no-man's land as he tried to distinguish which of the thousands of grey-black rocks was the mark, Repzik sighed in exasperation. 'Never mind, new fish. You shoot when we do. You follow orders. You do what we tell you to do, when we tell you to do it, and you don't ask any questions. Trust me, that's the only way you going to survive your first fifteen hours.'

Ahead, the group of gretchin out in no-man's land had swelled to become a horde several thousands strong. They seemed agitated now, jabbering to each other in incomprehensible alien gibberish while the more brave or foolhardy among them pushed their way to the front of the group as though restless for their wait to be at an end. Then, finally, the waiting was over as for the first time Larn heard the sound of massed alien voices screaming a terrifying war cry.

Waaaaaaaghhhh!

As one, firing their guns into the air, the horde of gretchin came charging towards them. As unnerving as the sight of the aliens had seemed to Larn earlier, they were nothing compared to the horrors he now saw emerging into view in their wake. Just behind the onrushing gretchin he saw countless numbers of much larger greenskins rise up to join the charge. Each one of them a grotesquely muscled broad-shouldered monster more than two metres tall, screaming with ferocious savagery as they took up the battle cry of their smaller brethren.

Waaaaaaaaghhh!

Sweet Emperor, Larn thought, half-beside himself with terror. *Those must be the orks. There's so many of them and every one of them is huge!*

'Eight hundred metres,' Vidmir said, sighting in on the enemy with the targeter clipped to the side of his lasgun, his calm voice barely audible above the sound of approaching thunder as the greenskins charged ever closer. 'Keep yourselves cold and sharp. No firing until they reach the kill zone.'

'Don't fire until you see the reds of their eyes,' Kell snickered, as if he had found some grim humour in the situation that eluded Larn.

'Six hundred metres,' Vidmir said, ignoring him.

'Remember to aim high, new fish,' Repzik said. 'Don't worry about the gretchin – they're no threat. It's the orks you want to hit. We open up with single shots at first – continuous volley fire. Oh, and new fish? You might want to release the safety catch on your lasgun. You'll find killing orks is easier that way.'

Fumbling at his lasgun in embarrassment as he realised the Vardan was right, Larn switched the firing control from safe to 'single shot'. Then, remembering his training and the words of *The Imperial Infantryman's Uplifting Primer*, he silently recited the Litany of the Lasgun in his mind.

Bringer of death, speak your name,
For you are my life, and the foe's death.

'Four hundred metres,' Vidmir said. 'Prepare to fire.'

The greenskins were closing. Looking past the scut-tling ranks of gretchin, Larn could see the orks more clearly now. Close enough to see sloping brows and baleful eyes, while thousands of jutting jaws and mouths filled with murderous tusks seemed to smile towards him with eager and savage intent. With every passing second the orks were coming closer. As he watched them charging towards the trench, Larn felt himself gripped by an almost overpowering urge to turn and flee. He wanted to hide. To run away as far and fast as he could and never look back. Something deep inside of him – some mysterious reservoir of inner strength he had never known before – stopped him. Despite all his fears, the dryness of his mouth, the trembling of his hands that he hoped the others could not see, despite all that he stood his ground.

'Three hundred and fifty metres!' Vidmir shouted, while Larn could hear the distant popping sound of mortars being fired behind them. 'Three hundred metres! On my mark! Fire!'

In the same instant every Guardsman on the line opened fire, sending a bright fusillade of lasfire burning through the air towards the orks. With it came a sudden flurry of airbursts as dozens of falling mortar and grenade launcher rounds exploded in mid-air in a deadly hail of shrapnel. Then came the blinding flash of lascannon beams; the rat-a-tat crack of autocannons; the flare of frag missiles streaking towards their targets. A withering torrent of fire that tore into the charging orks, decimating them. Through it all, as the Vardans in the trench beside him ceaselessly worked the triggers of their lasguns to send more greenskins screaming to *xenos* hell, Larn fired with them.

He fired without pause, as merciless as the others. Over and over again, his fears abating with every shot, the terrors that had once assailed him replaced by a growing sense of exultation as he saw the green-skins die. For the first time in his life, Larn knew the savage joy of killing. For the first time, seeing orks fall wounded and dying to be trampled under the heedless boot heels of their fellows, he knew the value of hate. Seeing the enemy die, he felt no sorrow for them, no sadness, no remorse for their deaths. They were *xenos*. They were the alien. The unclean. They were monsters, every one of them.

Monsters.

With a sudden insight, he finally understood the wisdoms of the Imperium. He understood the teachings he had received in the scholarium, in the sermons of the preachers, in basic training. He understood why Man made war upon the *xenos*. In the midst of that war, he felt no pity for them.

A good soldier feels nothing but hate.

Then, through the heat and noise of battle, Larn saw something that brought all his fears rushing back to him. Incredibly, despite all the casualties inflicted by the Guardsmen's fire, the greenskins' charge had not wavered. Though the torrent of fire continued from the Vardans' positions, the orks kept on coming. They seemed unstoppable. Abruptly, Larn found himself uncomfortably aware just how much he wanted to avoid having to face an ork in hand-to-hand combat.

'One hundred and twenty metres!' he heard Vidmir yell through the din. 'Change cells and switch to rapid fire!'

'They're getting closer!' Larn said, his hands clumsy with desperation as he struggled to change the cell in his lasgun. 'Shouldn't we fix bayonets – just in case?'

'Hardly, new fish,' Repzik said, his cell already changed and firing with the rest. 'If this battle gets to bayonet range we've as good as lost it. Now, shut up and start shooting!'

Out in no-man's land the charging orks came ever closer. By now most of the gretchin were dead, winnowed away by blast and shrapnel. Though the ranks of the orks had also been thinned, from where Larn stood there looked to be thousands of them left. All bearing down across the battered landscape of no-man's land in a relentless and barbaric tide hell bent on slaughter.

There's no stopping them, Larn thought. *We're going to be overrun!*

He saw orks armed with short bulbous-headed sticks running at the head of the mob, the sticks covered in a lethal profusion of spikes, blades and flanges. At first he took the weapons in their hands to be some form of primitive mace or club. Until he saw the front rank of orks suddenly throw the same 'clubs' to land in the frozen mud before the trenches, each one exploding in a shower of shrapnel. Instinctively, seeing one of the stick-grenades land a few metres from his trench, Larn ducked his head to avoid the deadly fragments whistling through the air above it. An action that drew a terse reprimand for Repzik.

'Damnation, new fish. Keep your fool head up and keep on shooting!' Repzik yelled. 'They're trying to make us keep our heads down so they can get in close.'

Doing as he was told, Larn resumed firing. Only to look on in horror with the rest of the men as, flying through the air so slowly it might almost have been moving in slow motion, another of the stick grenades hit the parapet and bounced inside their trench.

'Stikk bomb!' Vidmir screamed. 'Bail out!'

Rushing to evacuate the trench with the others, Larn scrambled over the trench wall behind him, stumbling

over his own two feet as he made it to ground level and
turned to run for cover. He tripped, his body already
falling towards the ground as the blast of the stikk
bomb ripped through the air behind him. He felt a pain
in his shoulder and a sudden pressure in his ears.

Then, he hit the ground and everything went black.

HE BECAME AWARE of a ringing in his ears, his face cold
against the hard frozen mud beneath him. Through
the haze of returning consciousness, he heard men
screaming and shouting, the sound of lasguns being
fired, the bestial roars and bellows of what could have
only been orks. The noises of a battle going on all
around him.

Starting abruptly awake, with a surge of fear Larn
lifted his head from the mud and looked about him to
try and gain his bearings. He was lying face down on
the ground, the pain in his shoulder having diminished to nothing more than a distant ache, while on
every side around him Guardsmen and orks fought in
brutal combat. He saw an ork shot point-blank in the
face, its feral inhuman features burned away in the
blink of an eye by a lasgun on full burst. He saw a
Guardsman in the uniform of the Jumael 14th die
screaming as another ork disembowelled him with the
blade of a great gore-stained axe. He saw men and orks
fighting, their feet slipping and stumbling over the
bodies of their fallen comrades beneath them, the
details of which side was winning or losing unclear in
the fog and haze of combat. He saw blood and he saw
slaughter. He saw savagery from human and alien
alike. His eyes opened, he saw the reality of war once
all the noble pretensions were stripped away.

Then, as the appalling spectacle continued to unfold
around him, Larn's heart began to beat wildly in his
chest as a dreadful thought suddenly occurred to him.

Where is my lasgun, he thought, looking about him in panic. *Sweet Emperor, I must have lost it when I fell.*

Feeling suddenly naked, Larn began scrabbling frantically among the fallen bodies lying nearby in search of a weapon. No sooner had he started than he all but fell over a gretchin searching among the bodies for reasons of its own. For a second they stood face-to-face, the creature was as astonished to see Larn as he was to see it. Then, noticing a sly smile come over the gretchin's face as it made to lift its gun and point it at him, Larn leapt screaming towards it.

Knocking the gun from the gretchin's hands before it could shoot, Larn made to grab for it himself, only for the gun to skip away from both of them as the force of their impact sent them falling to the ground. Pushing himself on top of the creature, desperately trying to hold it off with one hand as it clawed and bit at him, Larn felt the fingers of his free hand brush a hard object lying on the ground beside him and he grabbed it. As he raised the object and brought it crashing down into the gretchin's face, Larn became dimly aware he was holding his own helmet but he was past caring. In a frenzy born of self-preservation, he raised the helmet and smashed it down into the gretchin's face again and again. Repeatedly smashing the creature in the face until the helmet in his hand was slick with black ichor. Then, finally realising the gretchin had stopped moving long ago, Larn paused to catch his breath. By then, there was no trace left of the smile he had seen from the gretchin when it had tried to kill him. Below him, the gretchin's face had been reduced to a battered shapeless pulp. The creature was dead. It could no longer hurt him.

Hearing the chilling sound of an alien battlecry, Larn looked up from the dead body beneath him to see a group of a dozen orks charging towards him. For a

moment he almost turned, whether to run away or
scramble after the gretchin's fallen gun to defend himself he did not know. Only to realise that no matter
what he did now it would make no difference. The orks
were too close. He was as good as dead already.

This is it, he thought, his panic abruptly displaced by
an unnerving sense of calm. *I am going to die here. I am
a dead man and there is nothing anyone can do to save me*.

'Forward!' he heard a voice yell as a shotgun boomed
behind him and the face of the foremost ork disappeared in an explosion of gore. 'Vardans, by my mark!
Advance and rapid fire!'

Amazed, Larn saw a battle-scarred sergeant in a grey-
black greatcoat stride past him leading a ragtag band of
Vardans in a counter-charge against the orks. Moving at
a slow walk, firing from the hip with shotguns, lasguns
and flamers blazing, they advanced towards the oncoming orks, taking a gruesome toll of the enemy with every
step towards them. While before them orks screamed
and died, the sergeant led his men forward with bullets
and lasbeams flying all around him, his pace never faltering, his voice a clear beacon of authority among the
confusion of battle. Watching the sergeant lead his men
from the front, his every gesture calm and unafraid,
Larn found himself wondering if one of the long-dead
saints of the Imperium had somehow regained human
form and now walked among them. The sergeant
seemed immortal. Unkillable. Like a hero from the tales
they told in the scholarium.

A legend, leading his men to victory.

'Forward!' the sergeant yelled, the counterattack gain-
ing momentum as every man still alive in the trenches
gathered to advance beside him. 'Keep on firing. Forward and advance!'

Following the sergeant's lead the advance continued,
the constant fire of the Vardan guns and the slow

measured pace of their progress seemed every bit as
relentless and unstoppable as had the orks' charge
earlier. Until, wilting before the remorseless ferocity of
the Vardans' attack, the orks did something which Larn
had never thought he would live to see.

They turned and ran.

Watching the surviving orks run back towards their
lines, Larn slowly became aware of a brief hush falling
across the battlefield as the Vardans' advance halted and
they stopped firing. Soon, as it became plain the orks'
attack was ended, new sounds broke the silence: the
cries of wounded men; the shouts of their comrades
calling for a medic; the noise of nervous laughter and
disbelieving oaths as other men found they were still
very much alive. Hearing those sounds, Larn felt the
tension abruptly leave him as the realisation hit him
that he had survived. Still kneeling over the body of the
dead gretchin, he looked down at the thing's ruined face
in with sudden queasiness; afraid he was going to
vomit. Then, he saw a shadow fall across him as a
nearby Guardsman came to stand beside him.

'You must be a new fish?' a cynical voice asked him.
'One of the new groxlings to the slaughter they sent us
in the lander? I think this belongs to you.'

Looking up, Larn found himself staring at an ugly
dwarfish Vardan with a shaven head and a mouthful of
stained and crooked teeth. The Vardan was holding a
lasgun in each hand, one of which Larn recognised
sheepishly as his own gun – the same weapon he had
lost earlier.

'Here, new fish,' the runt said, giving him a sardonic
broken-toothed smile as he tossed the lasgun towards
him. 'Next time you need to kill a gretch, you might try
using this.'

CHAPTER SEVEN

13:39 hours Central Broucheroc Time

THE FIELD STATION – LESSONS IN FUTILITY, PARTS ONE &
TWO – FRIENDS & HEROES AWAITING DISPOSAL –
WELCOME TO THE 902ND VARDAN – CORPORAL VLADEK
AND THE DISTRIBUTION OF RESOURCES – MEETING
SERGEANT CHELKAR AND AN ADDITION TO DAVIR'S WOES

PAUSING FOR A moment to catch his breath while he
waited for the stretcher bearers to bring another patient,
Surgeon-Major Martus Volpenz was surprised to realise
how inured he had become to the sound of men
screaming. Around him, the walls of the apothecarium
field station reverberated with it constantly. He could
hear men shouting, begging, moaning, shrieking, muttering profane oaths and whispering half-remembered
prayers. Not for the first time, ever mindful that it was
his calling to alleviate the pain of others, the surgeon-
major looked about him at the place where he practised
his craft and felt despair.

To a man less accustomed to it, the dimly lit interior of the field station's main operating theatre might have been mistaken for a scene from hell. Along one wall of the station, hundreds of severely wounded men lay in litters stacked four men high on a series of metal racks. Against the other wall a dozen exhausted surgeons worked feverishly to clear the most urgent cases from tables that stank with the blood that stained every surface of the floors and walls. For each man they healed, a dozen more men waited amid the suffocating stink of blood and pus and death, desperately wailing and pleading for help in a cacophony of suffering that never reached its end.

'Stomach wound,' his surgical assistant Jaleal said, breaking into his thoughts. 'He's been given morphia,' he added, checking the treatment notification tag on the patient's ankle as the stretcher-bearers lifted the unconscious form of a wounded Guardsman onto the operating table before them. 'Two doses.'

Taking a pair of scissors, Jaleal removed the tag, before cutting away the Guardsman's tunic in blood-encrusted strips to reveal the wound hidden beneath it. Then, taking a wet cloth from a bucket at the foot of the table, he washed the worst of the blood away from the edges of the wound.

'Looks like a through and through,' he said. 'From the size of the wound I'd say an ork gun was the culprit. The blood's dark. Looks like his liver's been punctured.'

'Give him some ether somnolentus,' Volpenz said, taking a scalpel from a tray of instruments nearby as he stepped to the side of table. 'Standard dosage.'

'We have none,' Curlen, his other assistant, said. 'We used what was left on the last patient.'

'What about the other anaesthetics?' Volpenz said. 'The nitrous oxide?'

'Gone as well,' Jaleal said. 'If he wakes up we'll just have to hold him down.'

'At least tell me we have some blood plasma left?' Volpenz said. 'If I have to go digging around this man's insides in search of a wound in his liver he's going to bleed like a stuck pig.'

'Not a drop,' Jaleal said, shrugging in helplessness. 'Remember the sucking chest wound twenty minutes ago? He got the last of it.'

'How much blood is there in the overspill bag, Jaleal?' Volpenz asked.

Ducking his head under the table, Jaleal checked the contents of the transparent bag underneath it designed to catch the blood bleeding out of the patient as it oozed along the disposal gutters set in the table's sides.

'About half a litre,' he said, pulling the bag up from beneath the table. 'Maybe three-quarters.'

'All right,' Volpenz said. 'Replace that bag with a new one and use the contents of the one you've got to autosanginuate him.'

'You want to transfuse him with his own blood?' Jaleal said. 'There's barely enough in here to keep a dog alive, never mind a man.'

'There's no other choice,' Volpenz said, leaning forward with a practiced hand to make the first incision. 'He'll die anyway if this wound isn't seen to. Now, look sharp, gentlemen. We're going to have to do this fast, before he bleeds to death.'

Cutting an incision to open the wound, Volpenz quickly peeled back the skin around it and fixed a clamp in place to keep it open. Then, while beside him Jaleal used his cloth to mop at the blood welling in the wound cavity, Volpenz searched desperately for the source of the bleeding. It was hopeless. There was so much blood in the wound he could hardly see a thing.

'Vital signs are weak,' Curlen said, his fingers at the man's neck to feel his pulse. 'We're losing him.'

'Lift his legs up, Jaleal. It'll send more blood to his heart,' Volpenz said. 'I only need a few more seconds. There! I think I've found it. He's got a tear in the main artery leading to the liver.'

Pushing his hands deep into the wound cavity, Volpenz clamped the bleeding artery shut. Only to find his hopes frustrated as, abruptly, the cavity began to fill with blood once more.

'Damnation! There must be another bleeder! Curlen, how's he doing?'

'I can't find a pulse any more, sir. We could try to manually resuscitate him?'

'No,' Volpenz said, throwing his bloody scalpel down on the instrument tray in frustration. 'It wouldn't do any good. He's bled out. The round probably hit a rib and caused bone fragments to perforate his liver in a dozen places. Clear the table. We can't save this one.'

Grabbing a piece of discarded cloth to clean his hands, Volpenz stepped away from the table, pausing only to glance at the dead Guardsman as Curlen signalled for the stretcher bearers to take him away. *How old was he*, he thought. *He looks to be in his forties, but that means nothing here. Broucheroc has a way of aging a man. He might only be in his early thirties, even late twenties.* Then, as they lifted the dead man's body from the table, Volpenz noticed an old scar in the patient's side. *He's been wounded before*, he thought. *And patched up. I wonder, was it my work or someone else's? Doesn't matter now, I suppose. Whoever saved the poor bastard's life before, there was no saving him this time.*

Sighing, he turned away to gaze once more at the confines of the operating room around him. As he did, he realised how little good could be done there for the dying and suffering men who came to the field station day after day. *It's not the war or even the orks that kills most of them*, he thought. *It's the shortages. We're short of anaesthetics, antibiotics, plasma; even the most basic of medical equipment. Short it seems of everything except pain, death and futility. Here in Broucheroc, these things at least are never in short supply.*

Then, as he made to throw away the cloth he had used to clean his hands, Volpenz noticed something was written on it. Looking at it more closely, he saw there was a name stencilled in the cloth. Repzik. Abruptly, he realised the cloth must have come from the dead Guardsman's tunic – one of the pieces Jaleal had cut away earlier to reveal the man's wound. *Repzik*, Volpenz thought sadly. *So that was what his name was.* Then, just as abruptly, he realised that it made no difference.

Whatever name the man had come here with, he did not need it now.

IN THE SHADOW of the dugout emplacements, a little way behind the trenches, the corpses of the men killed in the last hour-and-a-half had been piled in a line three cadavers deep. Their feet bootless, their bodies stripped of their equipment, some with faces wrapped in concealing cloth, others with dead features left naked to the biting cold: all of them laid haphazardly atop each other like so many logs ready for the burning. *Like firewood*, Larn thought as he stood gazing down on the dead bodies of the men who had made the journey with him from Jumael IV. Men he had known and liked. Men who had crossed the unimaginable distances of the void only to waste their lives on the wrong planet and in the wrong campaign. His comrades, now reduced to nothing more than a temporary landmark in the unforgiving and war-torn landscape he saw all about him. For what? To Larn, it seemed the most pointless of the many horrors he had witnessed already in this desolate place. A lesson in utter futility.

Hearing the protesting squeal of a rusted axle, Larn turned to see four bent-backed old women bundled in ragged layers of civilian dress pushing an empty hand-cart across the frozen ground towards him. Noticing the faded insignia of the Departmento Munitorium on the khaki-green armbands they wore on their sleeves, Larn realised they must be militia auxiliaries levied from among the local population. Wheeling the cart past him, they halted beside the line of corpse and wearily began to lift them into the cart. Until at last, as their labours revealed the face of a corpse hidden deeper in the pile, Larn saw something that made him cry out and race towards them.

'Wait!' he yelled.

Startled, cringing away as though afraid he might hurt them, the women stopped their work. Then, seeing Larn standing by the pile to peer down at the face of a corpse, one of the women spoke to him in a voice made dull and lifeless with fatigue.

'You knew him?' she said. 'One of the dead men?'

'Yes,' Larn said. 'I knew him. He was a friend. A comrade.'

It was Leden. His face slack and pale, his body covered in gruesome and horrendous wounds, he lay at the centre of the pile with dead eyes staring up at the foreboding sky overhead. Having not seen Leden die during their mad flight across no-man's land, Larn had harboured the hope the simple-minded farmboy might have made it to the Vardan lines and survived just as he had. Now that hope was dashed. Looking down at Leden's face, Larn realised his last living link with his homeworld had been severed. He was truly alone now. More alone than he could have ever thought possible. Alone, on a strange new world that seemed entirely given over to randomness, brutality and madness.

'He was a hero,' the old woman said.

'A hero?'

Unsure of her meaning, Larn looked at her in confusion. For a moment, her eyes dim and uncomprehending with exhaustion, she returned his gaze in silence. Then, barely more animated than the dead bodies before her, she tiredly shrugged and spoke once more.

'They are heroes,' she said in a listless voice, as though reciting a speech she had heard a thousand times herself. 'They all are: all the Guardsmen who die here. They are martyrs. By giving their blood to defend this place they have made the soil of this city into sacred ground. Broucheroc is a holy and impregnable fortress. The orks will never take it. We will break their assault here. Then, we will push them back and reclaim this entire planet.'

'So the commissars tell us,' she added, without conviction.

Returning to their work the women made to lift Leden from the pile. Finding him held fast and stuck to the other bodies by frozen and congealed blood, one of the women took a pry bar from the side of the cart. Sickened to his stomach, Larn watched her slide the bar under Leden's body and put her weight on it, the corpse rising with a crack of splintered ice as her sisters pulled it free and tossed it on the cart. Then, two of them pushing down the handles of the cart while the others stood by the side to stop its contents from falling out, the old women began to wheel away the bodies they had collected.

'What will you do with them?' Larn called out after them, not altogether sure he wanted to know the answer.

'They will be buried,' the women he had spoken to earlier said. 'Like heroes should be. Buried, up on the hill past the old plasteel works on the Grennady Plass. Heroes' Hill, it is called. Or at least that is what they tell us,' she shrugged again. 'We just transport the bodies. Others deal with their disposal.'

With that she turned back to the burden of the cart, pushing it away with the other women in the direction of the outskirts of the city. As he watched them go, Larn belatedly tried to remember one of the prayers he had been taught as a child. A prayer to ease the passage of the departed souls of his comrades into the afterlife as they went to join their Emperor in paradise. His mind was a blank, his heart so sick with grief it felt dull and empty. All his prayers had left him.

'Take off your jacket and pull back your tunic,' he heard a voice say behind him.

Turning, Larn found himself face-to-face with a gaunt Vardan medic wearing a blood-splattered greatcoat and carrying a satchel slung across his shoulder.

'If you want me to treat that shoulder wound I will have to be able to see it,' the medic said, opening his satchel.

Looking at his own left shoulder, much to his surprise Larn noticed a small bloodstained hole in the epaulette of his jacket. Dimly remembering the sudden pain he had felt there when the ork bomb had exploded in the trench behind him, he did as the medic had asked, removing his jacket and pulling down his tunic shirt to allow him access to the wound.

'Hmm. The good news is you'll live,' the medic said, prodding at the wound while Larn shivered in the cold. 'Looks like you were winged by a piece of shrapnel. Took a little bit of flesh with it, but it doesn't look as though the bone is broken.'

Taking a sachet of white powder from inside his bag the medic poured it liberally on the wound and pressed a gauze pad over the hole, applying half-a-dozen pieces of adhesive tape to hold the dressing in place.

'You didn't realise you had a hole in you, I take it?' he said. Then, seeing Larn nod, he continued. 'Probably shock. Get yourself some recaf. Food too, if you can find it. It'll help you get yourself together. Though I warn you, you probably won't thank me for that advice in an hour's time. Once you get your feeling back, chances are you'll find that wound aches like a bitch. You have morphia?'

'Four phials,' said Larn. 'In my med-pack.'

'Good. Let me see it,' the medic said. Then, when he saw Larn hesitate, he held out his hand in command. 'Kit inspection. As company medical officer, it is my job to make sure you are properly equipped.'

Pulling the slim oblong wooden case of the med-pack he had been issued with on Jumael from his belt, Larn handed it over. Breaking the seals on the box lid the medic slid it open and checked the contents.

'Morphia. Vein clamps. Sterilising fluid. Synth-skin canister. Wherever you're from they obviously don't believe in sending their sons under equipped to war. Still, my need is greater than yours. I'm going to have to requisition some of your supplies.'

'But you can't just help yourself to my med-pack,' Larn said in outrage. 'The regulations say–'

'The regulations say a lot of things, new fish,' the medic replied, taking a handful of items from inside the med-pack and dropping them into his satchel. 'Though you can be sure whichever genius wrote them never troubled himself actually finding out if they worked in practice. Anyway, I'm leaving you with half of the gauze, morphia, and clamps. Plus, you get to keep the insect repellent. Given the climate, there's not much call for it hereabouts.'

'But if I should get seriously wounded–'

'Then you'll need a medic. Just scream loudly and I'll come running.'

Tossing the depleted med-pack back to him, the medic closed his satchel before looking at Larn once more.

'Now,' he said, 'seeing as you're standing about here on your own, I take it you've not been assigned to duties yet?'

'No... I... my company was destroyed and...'

'Go see Corporal Vladek,' the medic said. 'He'll sort you out. Tell him Medical Officer Svenk sent you.'

'Corporal Vladek?'

'Over there,' the medic said, pointing to one of the dugout entrances as he turned to walk away. 'Barracks Dugout One. Vladek is our quartermaster – the biggest scavenger, thief, pack rat, and all round scrounger in the sector. You'll know him when you see him. Oh, and a word to the wise, new fish. Don't drink any more than two cups of Vladek's recaf. Or else, next thing you know you could be charging the ork lines on your own in a one-man assault.'

WALKING DOWN THE rough earthen steps underground into the dugout, Larn was greeted with a warm blast of air thick with the smell of smoke and the odour of stale sweat. Eyes watering at the stench of it, he stepped past a couple of Guardsmen playing dice just inside the doorway and made his way into the barracks. Inside, he saw two lines of rusting metal bunks arranged either side of an iron stove at the centre of the room where a group of Vardans sat talking, eating, or cleaning their weapons. For a moment, Larn considered asking them if any of them had seen Corporal Vladek. Then, seeing a flabby unshaven Vardan in a stained undershirt sitting alone at a table in a corner of the room, Larn remembered the medic's description and knew he had found his man.

Crammed on ramshackle shelves and in alcoves cut directly into the earth of the wall behind the corporal was a treasure trove of scavenged equipment. Larn could see lasgun power packs, frag grenades, boxes of dry rations, shotgun shells, bayonets and knives of all shapes and sizes, spades, picks, hand axes, lanterns, uniforms, helmets, flak jackets, even a large metal claw that could only have come from the arm of a dead ork. Meanwhile, on the table and the floor around him were a number of standard issue Guardsmen's field rucksacks, the contents of which the corporal was currently busy digging through with the grim enthusiasm of a bandit chieftain surveying his latest spoils.

'Corporal Vladek?' Larn asked, approaching the table. 'Medical Officer Svenk said I should come see you.'

'Ah, more cannon fodder,' the corporal said, pushing the rucksacks aside to clear a space as he looked up at Larn with the glint of a smile in his red-rimmed eyes. 'Always good to see some new grist for the mill. Welcome to the 902nd Vardan, new fish. Find yourself a chair. You would like some recaf? I have some brewing.'

Turning to the battered pot of recaf perched precariously on a small hotplate beside him, the corporal produced a pair of enamel cups and filled them to the brim with black steaming liquid. He noticed Larn staring darkly down at one of the rucksacks still left on the table.

'Here we go. Two cups of Vladek's special recaf, nice and hot,' the corporal said. 'Sadly, we have to make do with a ground-up concoction of local roots and tubers rather than the real thing. Even the Emperor himself would be hard pressed to find any real recaf in this hellhole, and we all know he can work miracles. To give it a bit more kick I mix in a tenth of a dose of powdered stimms which, incidentally, works wonders for the flavour. But I see you seem to be interested in one of my latest acquisitions, new fish. Though, from the expression on your face, I have a feeling you're not about to make me an offer.'

'This rucksack,' Larn said, feeling dead inside as he looked at the words *Jumael 14th* stamped on the side. 'It could have belonged to one of my friends.'

'I wouldn't be surprised,' Vladek said, then gestured at the pile of rucksacks lying on the floor beside him. 'If not this one, then perhaps one of these other packs did. So? What of it? It is not as though this equipment is likely to be of help to its previous owners any more. While it *could* mean the difference between life and death for someone still living on the line. It is a simple matter of the fair and logical distribution of resources, new fish. Which, in this case, means that the living get to keep the things the dead no longer have any use for. Besides, if I hadn't had the foresight to liberate these packs from the bodies of the dead, someone else would have. You would have preferred I had let the militia auxiliaries get them so they could make us trade for the contents? This is Broucheroc, new fish. Forget all that nine-tenths rubbish. Here, possession is the *whole* of the law.'

'And if I was killed?' said Larn, angrily. 'Would you loot my body as well?'

'In a heartbeat, new fish. Your lasgun, your bayonet, your pack, your boots, not to mention whatever medical supplies the esteemed Svenk was kind enough to leave you with. Anything that might be of use to us. But you needn't feel so put upon. It is the same for everyone here, myself included. If I am killed tomorrow, I should expect to have my equipment stripped and re-allocated before my body even goes cold.'

'Not much likelihood of that happening,' Larn spat. 'Not with you sitting warm and safe in here in this dugout while outside good men are dying!'

'Good men?' Vladek said, his voice low with menace as the warm facade of moments earlier abruptly faded. 'Don't talk to me about good men dying, new fish. In ten years in this stinking cesspit I've seen men – good and bad – die by their thousands. Some of them were friends of mine. Others weren't. But any one of them was worth more than you and all your idiot recruit friends put together. You think just because I'm sitting here I don't know what it is to fight? I was killing the Emperor's enemies when you were still sucking greedily at your mother's teat. How else do you think I ended up with a leg like this?'

Taking an enormous combat knife from the table before him Vladek smacked it down against his left leg for emphasis, the flat of the blade making a dull metallic noise through his trouser leg as it struck his knee.

'You have an augmetic leg?' Larn said, shocked.

'Augmetic? Phah. The chance would be a fine thing! Along with everything else bionics are in short supply hereabouts. This is a Mark 3 Non-Motive Prosthetic, Left Leg Model. I had to barter the salvaged parts from a knocked-out sentinel for it, never mind what it cost me to get the damned apothecary to fit it. Now, I think it's time you sat down and stopped your mewling, new fish. Before I become so offended at your big mouth and flagrant disregard for my hospitality that I waste this good recaf by throwing it in your stupid snot-nosed face.'

Hearing someone laugh in another part of the dugout, Larn suddenly realised the other Vardans must have heard every word Vladek had said to him. His face burning with shame and embarrassment Larn took a chair and sat opposite the corporal with eyes lowered, unwilling to meet the other man's gaze for fear his cheeks were still flaring scarlet.

'Drink your recaf, new fish,' the corporal said, the storm of his anger passing as abruptly as it had started. 'We will begin again, you and I. Wipe the slate clean. I know it has been a hard day for you after all, and so I am willing to make allowances. It is not every day that a Guardsman finds he has been dropped on the wrong planet.'

'You know about that?' Larn said, stunned. 'Did one of the men I was in the trench with tell you? Repzik said–'

'Repzik is dead, new fish,' Vladek said. 'He died in the last attack. We talked about good men? Well, Repzik was one of the best. I knew him nearly twenty years, all told. From back on Vardan, even before we were drafted into the Guard together. The parts from the sentinel I used to buy this leg? It was Repzik who went into no-man's land to get them for me. Like I said, a good man. But no, to answer your question, it wasn't Repzik who told me about your misfortune. It was Kell. Though by then I had heard about it from other sources anyway.'

'Other sources? Who?'

'The Navy. About half an hour ago Sector Command forwarded us a message from an orbiting troopship, requesting that we inform the Guard company they'd just dropped that this planet wasn't in fact Seltura VII. Apparently they forgot to tell you this, what with all the excitement of the drop and so forth. *A regrettable oversight caused by a temporary failure in the lines of communication.* Those were their exact words I believe. A snafu, as we call such things in these parts.'

'A snafu?'

'Situation Normal All Fouled Up. An apt and well-used acronym here in Broucheroc. Though you can substitute other words for fouled if you so desire.'

'But if they have realised their mistake, does that mean I am being reassigned?' Larn asked, his heart grown suddenly hopeful.

'No, new fish. Frankly, the fact the troopship chose to relay the news of your company's predicament at all was more by the way of an afterthought. The main purpose of their message was to demand to know what the hell we had done with their lander. I am told their response when they heard the lander had been shot down and would not be returning was unrepeatable. By now, they are likely already underway again and far from this planet.'

'So, I am stuck here,' Larn said glumly.

'You and the rest of us, new fish.' Vladek said, bending forward to delve through a boxful of grey-black coats sitting under the table. 'Now, drink your recaf and we will see about getting you sorted. A new greatcoat in urban camouflage pattern would seem as good a place to start as any. It will help you blend in and make you less of a target, not to mention keeping you warm. This time of year it's cold enough to have a man passing ice cubes every time he voids his bladder. I have one here that should fit you perfectly, give or take. No need to worry too much about the blood on the lapels. I am sure you will find it brushes off easily enough once it has had time to dry.'

TEN MINUTES LATER, courtesy of Corporal Vladek's scavenged stores, Larn found himself the new owner of a greatcoat, a pair of woollen gloves, two frag grenades, a fur-covered helmet, a small lump of whetstone, and a comm-bead tuned to the local comm-link frequencies used by the Vardans. Then, as Larn finished the last bitter mouthful of ersatz recaf from his cup, Vladek asked to see his dog-tags and wrote his name and number on a clipboard beside him.

'That is it for now, new fish,' Vladek said. 'You will need to come back here and see me again in fifteen hours' time. Then I can issue you with some of the more valuable and sought-after pieces of equipment: hotshot power packs for your lasgun, extra frag grenades, a laspistol, smoke grenades, and so on.'

'Why fifteen hours?' Larn asked.

'Phah. You will learn soon enough in this place there are some questions it is better not to ask, new fish. That is one of them. Just come see me again in fifteen hours, and try not to think about it in the meantime. Oh, and new fish? I almost forgot. You will need one of these.'

Removing a slim black copy of *The Imperial Infantryman's Uplifting Primer* from a shelf behind him, Vladek offered it to Larn across the table.

'But I already have one, corporal,' Larn said. 'I was issued with my copy of the Primer on my first day of basic training back on Jumael.'

'Congratulations, new fish,' Vladek said. 'Now, you have two copies. You will need them, and it is better not to get caught short. You will find this little book to be a vital tool when it comes to the nitty-gritty of day-to-day living here in Broucheroc. The paper it is printed on is most absorbent.'

Handing him the book along with his dog-tags, Vladek turned to the hotplate to pour another steaming cup of recaf.

'Anyway, that's enough equipment for you to be getting on with, new fish,' Vladek said, turning back towards Larn and nodding at something behind him. 'Next, we should see about getting you fixed up with a fireteam. Fortunately here comes our company commander, right on cue.'

Seeing a figure in a greatcoat approaching through the corner of his eye, Larn stood bolt upright from his chair and saluted smartly. Only to find himself facing the same Vardan sergeant he had seen lead the counterattack against the orks earlier.

'Why is there a new fish saluting me, Vladek?' the sergeant said, stepping past Larn to take a cup of recaf from the corporal's hand. 'He has mistaken me for a general perhaps?'

'An entirely understandable mistake given your commanding presence and natural air of authority, sergeant,' Vladek said, smiling. 'Then again, I had just told him you are our company commander. Perhaps he thinks that makes you a lieutenant.'

'A lieutenant? I am disappointed, Vladek. If I am going to be mistaken for an officer, I thought I would have rated colonel at least.' Then, the merest suggestion of a smile ghosting at his lips, the sergeant turned back to Larn. 'You can put your hand down by the way, trooper. Even if I was a lieutenant, we don't hold much with saluting here. It only gives the orks something extra to aim at. I assume you have a name? Other than new fish I mean?'

'Trooper First Class Larn, Arvin A, reporting for duty, sergeant!' Larn said, his hand falling but his back still ramrod straight as he stood to attention. 'Number: eight one five seven six dash—

'At ease, Larn,' the sergeant told him. 'Save it for the parade ground. As I say, we don't stand much on ceremony here. All right then. I take it you have already given your name and number to Corporal Vladek so he can forward them to General HQ?'

'Yes, sergeant.'

'Good. It may be that HQ will order you reassigned to duties elsewhere in the city. In the meantime standing orders on the disposition of new troops are clear. You were dropped into our sector: that means you belong to us. You are hereby seconded to the 902nd Vardan until further notice, Larn. Welcome to Company Alpha. My name is Chelkar. Until you are assigned elsewhere or HQ gets around to sending us a new lieutenant you will be taking your orders from me. We are clear?'

'Clear, sergeant.'

'How long since you took the eagle?'

'The eagle, sergeant?'

'I mean: how long is it since you were inducted into the Guard?'

'Four months, sergeant.'

'Four months? You are green then? You haven't seen much action?'

'No. Today was my first engagement, sergeant.'

'Hmm. Well, you survived it at least. I suppose that shows us something.' For a moment, his eyes grown suddenly sad and distant, Chelkar fell silent. Certain he was being judged somehow by that silence, Larn felt a rising urge to defend his worth.

'You do not need to worry, sergeant,' he said. 'I will not let anyone down. I am a Guardsman. I will do my duty.'

'I am sure you will, Larn.' Chelkar's expression was grave. 'But remember, part of that duty is for you to keep yourself alive so you can fight again tomorrow. To that end, you will do the following things. You will follow orders. You will keep your eyes and ears open. You will watch your comrades' backs, just as they will watch yours. But most of all, there will be no heroics. No fool-hardiness. No unnecessary risks. This is Broucheroc, Larn. There are no heroes here; the orks keep killing them. Do we understand each other?'

'Yes, sergeant.'

'All right then,' Chelkar said, before turning to call out to one of the Guardsmen standing beside the stove. 'Davir. Come over here and meet our new recruit.'

In response to Chelkar's call, Larn saw a stocky diminutive Vardan move away from the stove and come walking towards them. With a sinking heart, he recognised him at once as the same ugly dwarfish Guardsman who had given him his lasgun back after the battle.

'Davir, this is Larn.'

'We have met already, sergeant. Hello, new fish.'

'Good,' said the sergeant. 'Larn, I am assigning you to Fireteam Three under Davir's command.'

'With all due respect, sergeant,' Davir said, 'given the new fish's lack of experience, wouldn't it be better to assign him somewhere else until he finds his feet. Fireteam Three is a frontline unit, after all.'

'This whole company is a frontline unit, Davir,' Chelkar said. 'If you can think of anywhere I could send him in this entire sector where the orks wouldn't be shooting at him, I'd be glad to hear of it. Besides, your fireteam is under strength. You need him and I am sure I can rely upon you to look after him and show him the ropes.'

'You are right of course, sergeant,' Davir said, grudgingly. 'Come on then, new fish. Get your kit and follow me. We have orks to kill, you and I.'

Turning, Davir strode away at a surprisingly brisk stride, forcing Larn to hurry his own pace to catch up. Then, as Davir walked through the door at the end of the barracks and headed up the steps out of the dugout, from behind him Larn heard the Vardan muttering venomously to himself under his breath.

'Need him,' he heard Davir whisper to himself. 'Need him, my Vardan arse! Like I need to be nursemaiding a damn new fish. As though having had to spend ten years in the company of that fat halfwit Bulaven wasn't bad enough, now they've gone and saddled me with a war virgin just to add to my woes. Damnation!'

Reaching the head of the steps to emerge into the cold air outside, Davir turned to give Larn a withering glare as he waited for him to catch up.

'Come on, new fish. I haven't got all day. Though I suppose I should thank the heavens for small mercies that you've managed to negotiate the stairs without losing your lasgun again. Not that I mean that as an invitation, mind. You lose that damned thing again, don't expect me to go finding it for you. You want to go around confronting orks with no other weapons than what nature gave you, next time you're on your own. I'll leave you to it. Now, come on. Let's get moving and when we're heading for the trench, keep your damned fool head down. Not that I've got any qualms about see-ing the orks blow your head off, you understand. I just don't want to run the risk of the damned greenskins missing and hitting me instead.'

So it went on, with Davir unleashing a constant tirade of insults and complaints as, trailing in his wake, Larn followed him up the low rise towards the firing trenches and the frontline. As they ran half-crouched towards their destination and the tirade continued, Larn abruptly found himself briefly entertaining a notion that until a few minutes before would have never occurred to him.

Suddenly, he found himself feeling strangely nostal-gic for the good old days of Sergeant Ferres.

CHAPTER EIGHT

14:59 hours Central Broucheroc Time

CASUALTIES OF WAR – THOUGHTS ON THE KILLING OF
GENERALS – SCHOLARLY ANSWERS AND INSIGHTS – ON
VITAL SUPPLIES & THE MANY AND VARIED USES OF
PROPHYLACTICS – THE MATHEMATICS OF SLAUGHTER &
QUESTIONS OF LIFE EXPECTANCY AT THE FRONT – THE
FACTS OF LIFE AS ACCORDING TO DAVIR

FOR ONCE, THE printing press was silent. Though Lieutenant Dellas had always considered the constant
clattering of the machine to be a source of much-cursed
irritation, now it was idle he found the sound of its
silence filled him with dread. Sitting at his desk in the
claustrophobic confines of his cluttered office, he
looked across the fractured glass of the top half of the
partition wall separating him from the print room and
felt his stomach churn in anxiety as he watched the
militia auxiliaries who made up his staff go about their
labours. The aged caretakers Cern and Votank were busy

maintaining the ancient parts of the press itself: Cern oiling the machine's rollers, while Votank topped up the ink reservoir ready for the next edition. Nearby, head bobbing and his face moving in involuntary tics, the feeble-minded cripple Shulen stumbled past them with a broom flailing spasmodically in his hands as he attempted to sweep the floor. Only the compositor Pheran was without a task. His features pinched in an expression somewhere between expectancy and annoyance, he stood beside the empty expanse of the typesetting board and gazed back towards Dellas through the glass. Then, seeing he had met the lieutenant's eyes, Pheran raised a hand to point at the chronometer hanging above the printing press in a gesture of mute accusation.

1500 hours, Dellas thought, his heart sinking as his eyes followed the direction of Pheran's bony finger to glance at the chronometer. *We only have an hour now before I have to deliver the late edition to Commissar Valk for approval. A single hour! I must find something to write. Anything!*

Despairing, Dellas returned his attention to the dozens of official papers piled in confusion across his desk. Among the jumbled mass of documents before him were copies of situation reports, battlefield dispatches, casualty statistics, terse communiqués, comms transcripts: between them comprising a record of every event of consequence that had happened in the city of Broucheroc in the past twelve hours. Despite what seemed like hours now spent surveying the assembled weight of information before him, Dellas had found nothing there to suit his purpose.

There is no good news to report, he thought bleakly. *Today, the same as every other day, there is only bad news and I cannot print that. The commissar would have me shot on the spot.*

His thoughts drifted back to the day two years previously when he had first heard the news that he was being posted to the imposing edifice of the General Headquarters building in the centre of Broucheroc. At first, sure he was going to be rewarded with a staff assignment, he had rejoiced. Then, when they brought him to the dingy basement print room to tell him it would be his task to produce a twice-daily newsletter and propaganda sheet for the edification of the city's defenders, his heart had thrilled even more. It had seemed the answer to all his prayers: a staff and an office of his own, and more importantly a prestigious assignment that would keep him far from the fighting. He had soon learned however that the lot in life of an official propagandist was rarely a happy one. Even less so when it was his duty to put a brave face to a conflict as prone to sudden reverses and unmitigated disasters as was the war in Broucheroc.

We are losing this war, he thought, so lost in the depths of his own misery now he was barely aware of any wider implication. *We are losing this war. That is the reality and yet I have barely an hour to find some small piece of good news that will allow the newsletter to pretend otherwise. An hour. It just can't be done. I need more time.*

Hearing the sound of his office door opening, Dellas looked up to see Shulen shuffling through the doorway. Mouth working soundlessly, his body twitching with uncontrollable palsies, Shulen tottered towards him with a wastebasket in his hands, the ugly scar left by the ork bullet that had addled his brain clearly visible at his temple.

'What is it, Shulen?' Dellas sighed.

'Cuh cuh cuh… cleaning!' Shulen said, stammering out a spray of spittle as he stooped to start shovelling the papers littering Dellas's desk into the wastebasket.

Aggravated, for a moment Dellas idly wondered if there was a way of making Shulen bear the blame for his problems. *I could tell Commissar Valk it is all Shulen's fault,* he thought. *That we were just putting the finishing touches to the latest edition when Shulen blundered into the typesetting board, knocking it to the floor and destroying all our work. If the commissar decides to shoot the useless oaf in retribution, I for one would not miss him.* Just as quickly he realised for the plan to work the other members of his staff would have to support his story. Pheran and the others would not wear it. They had always protected Shulen, coddling him like some idiot child, and would be sure to oppose any attempt to make him the sacrificial goat. Then, abruptly, Dellas caught a glimpse of the words written on one of the crumpled pieces of paper in Shulen's hand and knew he finally had the answer.

'Stop that!' he snapped at Shulen, reaching out with a metal ruler to rap his knuckles. 'Leave the wastebasket here and go tell Pheran I will have the copy for tonight's edition ready for him in fifteen minutes.'

'Fuh fuh fuh…'

'Fifteen minutes,' Dellas said, retrieving the paper he had seen in Shulen's hand and smoothing out the creases so he could read it. 'Now, get out of my sight.'

It was a contact report, reporting an ork assault in Sector 1-13 two and a half hours earlier. What interested Dellas more was the attached account of the event that had presaged the assault. A single lander bearing a company's worth of battlefield replacements had crashed in no-man's land. Reading it, Dellas realised it was exactly what he had been looking for. Granted, the course of events would need a little rewriting. To keep Commissar Valk happy what had been an entirely futile waste of human life would need to become a resounding victory. All the basic substance of what he needed was there already: he would only have to change the details and the events in Sector 1-13 should suit his purposes admirably. *Yes, this is exactly what I need,* Dellas thought, quickly running through a series of potential headlines in his mind. *Enemy Assault Defeated By Landing From Space. A Sector-Wide Breakthrough. Orks Retreating in Disarray.* Then, the hairs rising at the back of his neck, he thought of a new headline and knew he had cracked it.

Orks Defeated in Sector 1-13: Jumael 14th Victorious!

Smiling, Dellas picked up a stylus and began to write a glowing report of the battle, carefully embroidering the account with a variety of the stock words and phrases he had developed over the years in the course of his duties. *Heroic resistance! Brave and resolute defence! A triumph of faith and righteous fury over Xenos savagery!* Occasionally, as he paused to construct some new sentence full of rhetorical zeal and fire, he felt the vague stirrings of his conscience troubling him but he ignored it. It was not his fault he was forced to lie and twist the facts, he told himself. The truth was always the first casualty in warfare. As an information officer, sometimes it was his task to be creative: to do otherwise would be to risk offering aid and comfort to the enemy. Yes, it was a matter of duty.

And, after all, it was important to do everything humanly possible to keep up the morale of the troops.

'A FIRE,' DAVIR said as they sat in the firing trench. 'That's what I would like to see. A fire to burn down General Headquarters and torch all the stupid bastards inside it. If another blaze could somehow be ignited at Sector Command as well then, all the better. It wouldn't be that difficult. Give me a grenade launcher and a couple of phosphorus rounds, and I would have both damn places on fire in no time.'

Appalled, Larn listened in disbelieving silence. In the last half an hour since they had reached the trench,

Davir's constant stream of complaints had slowly given way to extended musings in which he openly discussed methods of killing the General Staff responsible for the progress of the Broucheroc campaign. Though even more extraordinary to Larn's mind was the fact that the other men in the trench had simply sat there and listened to it, as though it was the most normal thing in the world to talk lightly of mutiny and sedition. As Davir's monologue wore on, Larn found himself with fewer and fewer doubts as to the reasons why the war in this city seemed to be going so badly if these men represented a representative cross-section of the city's defenders.

'Of course, I accept it will be difficult getting close enough to use a grenade launcher,' Davir continued. 'What with the security perimeters around both buildings being so heavily patrolled and defended. But I have already foreseen a solution. It is only a matter of stealing the right credentials, and I can be inside the perimeter and killing the members of the General Staff before you can say poetic justice.'

These men can't be Guardsmen, Larn thought as he looked at the faces of the four men sitting around him in the trench. *Granted, they fought off the ork attack well enough two hours ago. But where is their discipline? Their devotion to the Emperor? It is as though all the traditions and regulations of the Guard mean nothing to them. How can they just sit here and listen to this man spew treason without taking action?*

'You would never get away with it, Davir,' the Vardan sitting opposite Davir said. A tall thin man in his mid-thirties, his name was Scholar. Or at least that was what the others called him. Whether it was his profession or a simple nickname, given his stoop-shouldered build and the owlish cast of his face, the name seemed to fit him.

'I am afraid it is a question of there being major flaws in your *modus operandi*,' Scholar said, fingers playing unconsciously at his chin as though stroking a non-existent beard. 'Even granting that you manage to obtain the necessary credentials, I doubt the perimeter guards would be willing to stand idly by while you shoot grenades at their generals willy-nilly. There are rules in the Guard against the wasting of ammunition, after all. Besides, even if you could somehow elude the guards, you can be sure that the buildings housing General HQ and Sector Command have both been extensively fireproofed. Not to mention equipped with damage controls systems, blast shields, extinguishing devices, and so forth. No, Davir, I think you will have to find some other method of getting your tally.'

Could they be joking somehow, Larn thought. *Is that it? Is this all some kind of joke, intended to do no more than help them pass the time? But they are talking about murdering officers! How could anyone mistake that for a laughing matter?*

'Then I will simply have to seize control of an artillery battery,' Davir said. 'A few high explosive rounds aimed at the GHQ building and I should kill a few generals at least.'

'But you wouldn't want to do that either,' the third one, Bulaven, said earnestly. A hulking figure with a thick neck, brawny arms and a broad bearish build, Bulaven was the fireteam's heavy weapons specialist. He also seemed the only man among the group to harbour anything in the way of concern for the lives of his superiors. 'If you start killing generals, Davir, who would we have left to give us orders?'

'You talk as though that is a bad thing, pigbrain,' Davir spat. 'It is thanks to those arseholes in General HQ and their orders that we are in this mess to begin with! Not that I expect us to suddenly starting magically

winning this war when they are all dead, you understand. Killing them couldn't make it any worse. At least
doing it would give me some small moments of satisfaction. Orders? *Phah!* As though they ever achieved
anything with all their damned orders other than making things ten times worse. You want to know about
orders? Ask Repzik. If it hadn't been for some fool
ordering Battery Command to withhold artillery support during the last attack, he'd probably still be alive.
For that matter, what about our new friend here? You all
saw what happened to that lander earlier. Ask the new
fish what he thinks of the orders that sent him halfway
across the galaxy just to make landfall on the wrong
planet.'

Abruptly, the other men in the trench turned to look
towards him. Fully aware he must have looked like a
rabbit caught in the searchlights of an oncoming vehicle, Larn could only gawp back at them, unsure of what
to say.

'Perhaps he is still in shock?' Bulaven said, his tone
solicitous. 'Is that it, new fish? Are you in shock?'

'Wetting his pants in fear more like,' Zeebers, the
fourth man in the trench, said. Thin and wiry, of average build, Zeebers looked younger than the others:
perhaps in his mid-twenties where Davir and the rest
were in their early to mid-thirties. Red-haired, with a
pitted and pockmarked face, Zeebers looked nastily
towards Larn and sneered at him. 'Look at him. If his
skin was any greyer you wouldn't be able to see him
against the mud. You ask me, he's afraid if he says what
he really thinks some commissar will hear him and
have him shot.'

'Hhh. Not much to be worried about on that score,'
Davir said. 'You hear me, new fish? You can speak freely.
Granted, time was we'd always be getting commissars
coming to the line to lead attacks and so forth.

Thankfully, our friends the orks soon put paid to that. Any commissar who was crazy enough to want to join a frontline combat unit got himself killed off long ago. The commissars left now tend to be those with a sharper instinct for their own survival. Sharp enough to stay away from the front at any rate. So, come on, new fish. You must have an opinion? Let us hear it.'

'Yes, indeed,' said Scholar. 'I for one would be fascinated to know what you think.'

'Come on, new fish,' Zeebers said, his tone harsh and goading. 'What are you waiting for? Gretch got your tongue?'

'Don't rush him,' Bulaven said, more kindly. 'Like I say, I think he's still in shock. I'm sure he'll tell us in time.'

Faces expectant, the Guardsmen fell quiet as they waited for Larn to answer. Uncomfortable, painfully aware of the four pairs of eyes staring at him in silence, for a moment Larn could only sit there with his mouth open, the words dying on his tongue before he could even say them. Then, thinking about all he had seen and heard in the last few hours, in a voice thick with misery he gave them the only answer he had.

'I... I don't understand any of this,' he said at last. 'None of it. Nothing that has happened to me so far today seems to make any sense.'

'WHAT IS THERE to understand, new fish?' Davir had said. 'We are stuck in this damned city. We are surrounded by millions of orks. Every day they try to kill us. We try not to let them succeed. End of story.'

'A concise summary granted, Davir,' Scholar had said next. 'Though you omitted to mention the promethium. And the stalemate. Not to mention some of the wider parameters.'

'Fine, Scholar,' Davir had shrugged. 'I think you're wasting your time, but you tell him all about it then.

While you're at it, you might as well tell him how to go about brushing his teeth and wiping his backside. After all, I wouldn't like to see the consequences if the new fish here somehow got those two vital functions mixed up. Whatever you do, do it from the firing step. It is still your turn to stand watch. And remember: just because we have to nursemaid a war virgin doesn't mean the orks have forgotten they want to kill us.'

'You SEE THEM?' Scholar said a few minutes later, standing pointing into no-man's land from the firing step next to Larn while Davir and the others sat playing a card game on the trench floor below them. 'That dark grey ragged line about eight hundred metres away? That's the ork lines.'

Looking through the field glasses Scholar had lent him, Larn followed the direction of the tall man's pointing finger to stare into the wasteland before them. There. He saw it. A sinuous line of ditches that ran the entire length of the sector on the other side of no-man's land. Watching it, from time to time he saw a gretchin or ork head suddenly come into view. Only for the head to then swiftly disappear as its owner dropped out of sight below the parapets on the ork side once more.

'I don't understand how I didn't see it before,' Larn said. 'Having the field glasses helps. But it seems so clear now. How could I have missed it?'

'It is a question of perception,' Scholar said. 'You have noticed how grey the landscape is? The mud, the rocks, the sky, even the buildings? When a person first arrives here the details of the world about them can easily be lost in the same monotonous tone of grey. But there are subtle differences. Differences you become slowly aware of the longer you spend in this city. You have heard how some jungle-worlders have forty different words for green? In reality of course those forty words correspond to different shades of green. Shades which would all look the same to us. But to them, their perceptions heightened by living their entire lives in a green environment, the difference between each shade is as obvious as the difference between black and white. It is the same here in Broucheroc. Believe me, you'll be amazed how acute you become to the palette of greys once you've been in this city a few months.'

'Of course,' he continued, delighted to finally have an audience willing to hear a lecture, 'normally you wouldn't be able to miss the ork lines if you tried. There'd be an array of makeshift walls, dirt ramparts and bosspoles stretching from one side of the sector to the other. Or piles of burned-out vehicles and corpses used in place of sandbags. The details differ from sector to sector. Up to a month ago we were stationed in Sector 1-11. There, the orks used these large jury-rigged barricades that they would just smash their way through whenever they attacked us. Then they would rebuild them, smashing their way through them again whenever there was a major assault, and so on.

You see, the orks don't follow a centralised command structure as we do. Granted, when their Warbosses are not busy fighting it out amongst each other, they are usually united behind a single Warlord. But when it comes to the disposition of any particular ork sector, the local Warboss is free to do as he wants. And, as it happens, this particular boss seems to have taken a leaf out of our book – ordering his followers to dig camouflaged underground dugouts, foxholes and trenches rather than the usual ostentatious fortress. It could be he is brighter than the usual ork leader. Then again, perhaps he's just aping our tactics without any kind of clear plan in mind. Really, it can be hard to tell with orks. Even after ten years here, I still find it difficult to tell the difference between a stupid ork and a clever one.'

'You have been here ten years as well?' Larn said. 'I could barely believe it when Repzik said he had been here that long.'

'We all have,' Scholar said. 'Me, Davir, Bulaven, Vladek, Chelkar, Svenk, Kell. All the men in the company have. The ones from Vardan, anyhow. Of course, there are plenty of replacements like you and Zeebers who have been here considerably less time.'

'Zeebers isn't from Vardan?'

'Him? No, as I say, he is a replacement. Joined us about two months ago, give or take.'

'What about the rest of the regiment? Are there many replacements among them as well?'

'The rest? You misunderstand me, new fish,' Scholar said sadly. 'Company Alpha *is* the Vardan 902nd. We're all that's left among the Vardans here. The others are dead.'

'You mean your regiment was wiped out?' Larn said horrified. 'Out of an entire regiment, only two hundred men are still alive?'

'Worse than that, new fish. There were three Vardan regiments when we first set down in Broucheroc. But over time we suffered heavy losses. We lost the Vardan 722nd in our first week here, wiped out when General HQ ordered one of their now famous all-out assaults on the ork lines. The survivors were amalgamated into the Vardan 831st, who in turn eventually became part of the 902nd. Then, over the years, there were more casualties and the number of companies in the 902nd were reduced and amalgamated. Until, now, only Company Alpha is left. At last count I believe our current fighting strength is something in the order of two hundred and forty-four men, perhaps three-quarters of whom are from Vardan. Something like one hundred and eighty or so Vardans then, left from the more than six thousand men who first made planetfall in this city ten years ago. Really it is not so different from your situation with your own former company. It is a matter of attrition, you see. It's the same for ever other Guard regiment in this city. Of course, having been on the frontlines so long, we've had it worse than most. I doubt there's a regiment left in this city that is at any more than thirty per cent of its original strength. This is Broucheroc; here, everything is a matter of attrition. But then, given the name of the place, it is hardly surprising.'

'The name?' Larn asked, still stunned by the thought that the men he saw about him were all that was left from six thousand Guardsmen.

'Yes. A while back we spent a month dug in at an old bombed-out building that turned out to be a storage facility for some of the city's oldest archives. I managed to read some of them before Davir and the rest used them for toilet paper. In the days before it became a city the name of this place was Butcher's Rock, or *Bouchers Roc* in the local planetary dialect. Over time, as the city grew, its name was corrupted to the pronunciation we know now. *Broo-sher-rok*. As for the origin of the name, apparently the first settlement to be founded here served as the centre for the planet's meat trade. Of course it still does, in a manner of speaking.'

'Still does?' Larn said. 'I don't understand what you mean.'

'He means that this whole damned city is one big meat grinder, new fish,' Davir growled from the bottom of the trench. 'And we are the meat.'

'You should tell the new fish about the promethium, Scholar,' Bulaven said from beside him. 'It is better if he knows what we are fighting for.'

'Ah yes. The promethium,' Scholar said, taking the field glasses back from Larn and placing them in a case on his belt. 'That is what the battle here is about, more or less.' Then, nodding towards Davir, he added: 'Of course, I'm sure if you asked Davir he would tell you the war here is only about survival. Which would be right as well. But you cannot understand the broader issues of strategy here without knowing something about the promethium.'

'Strategy, my broad Vardan arse,' Davir said. 'What does strategy mean to us? You think a man cares about strategy when he feels an ork blade go into his belly? You and Bulaven are fooling yourselves, Scholar. What, you think if it wasn't for the promethium the orks would just go away? If that were the case I'd have found some way of giving it to them myself by now, never mind all this fantasising about killing generals. You make things too complicated, Scholar. The orks want to kill us for one simple reason. They are orks. That is all there is to it. Though by all means tell the new fish about your grand theories. I'm sure they'll come in very handy next time the bullets start flying and he finds himself face to face with a horde of screaming green-skins. Though from what I've seen already, you might be doing him more of a favour if you told him to tie a string around his belt and tie the other end to his las-gun so he doesn't lose it again.'

Grimacing in dismissive annoyance Davir returned his attention to the card game, leaving Scholar to go on with his lecture.

'The promethium, new fish,' Scholar said. 'That's why the orks are here and that's what makes the city important to both us and them. Remember I told you this city started off as a centre for the meat trade? Well, that was thousands of years ago. In more recent times Broucheroc became a centre for the planet's promethium industry. Time was when this city was little more than one giant refinery, where crude promethium would be brought from the drilling fields further south to be refined into fuel. Even though the pipelines that brought that crude here were cut long ago, this city is still rich in promethium. Billions of barrels' worth, stored in massive underground tanks underlying most of the city.'

'But what do the orks want with it?' Larn asked him.

'Fuel,' Scholar said. 'Ten years ago, just as we first made landfall here, it looked like the orks were going to conquer this entire planet. Until they started to run out of fuel for their armour. When that happened they laid siege to Broucheroc, hoping to seize the city's fuel reserves. But we managed to hold out, and without fuel the ork assault elsewhere on the planet simply ground to a halt. Ever since then it has been a stalemate, with us trapped inside the city and the orks outside it trying to get in. A stalemate that shows no sign of ending anytime soon.'

'But what about the Imperial forces in other parts of the planet?' Larn said. 'Or even Imperial forces from offworld? Why haven't they tried to relieve the siege?'

'As for the Imperial forces elsewhere on this planet, it could be they have tried to relieve us, new fish,' Scholar said. 'Certainly, if you asked General HQ they would tell you the city is on the verge of being relieved. However, seeing as they have been saying the same thing for ten years now, no one much believes them anymore. You will find that here in Broucheroc our commanders tell us a lot of things. That we are winning the war. That the orks are leaderless and on the verge of collapse. That the big breakthrough they have been promising us for the last ten years is finally imminent. You will find that after a while hearing the same old things, day after day after day, you simply learn not to listen. For myself, I suspect that our brother Guardsmen in other parts of this Emperor-forsaken world are in no better shape than we are. Not that I can say definitely whether or not this is the case you understand, given that the only part of this

planet I've ever seen is Broucheroc. As theories go however, it seems no worse than any other.'

'But, of course, that doesn't fully answer your question,'
Scholar said, fully lost now in the flow of his own erudi-
tion. 'As to why Imperial forces from off-world don't
intervene; I suspect the war here is simply not important
enough to justify a full-scale landing. From time to time
there are smaller more isolated landings – by a lander say,
or a single dropship – but nothing that could be mistaken
for anything even resembling a real attempt to break the
siege. Sometimes, as in the case of you and your company,
these landings turn out to be simple mistakes. Other
times, it is as though some distant bureaucrat has finally
decided to send us a few more troops or supplies in order
to reassure us we have not been forgotten. For the most
part, these occasional drops are as pointless and ridiculous
as every other aspect of life here in Broucheroc. In the past
we have been sent entire pods full of supplies, only to find
when we fight our way to them the boxes inside the pods
are full of the most useless things imaginable: paperclips,
mosquito netting, laxatives, boot laces, and so on.'

'Remember when they sent us an entire drop-pod full of
prophylactics?' Davir said from nearby. 'I never could
decide whether they wanted us to use them as barrage bal-
loons, or simply thought the orks must have a fear of
rubber.'

'A good example of what I was talking about,' Scholar
said. 'But anyway, I think that pretty much covers everything for now, new fish. Do you have any questions?'

'Never mind his questions,' Zeebers said, suddenly looking up from his cards to gaze at Larn with a sly and
malignant smile. 'You didn't quite cover everything for the
new fish, Scholar. There is still one thing you forgot to tell
him.'

'Forgot?' Scholar said. 'Really? I don't think there was
anything else of importance…'

'Yes there is,' Zeebers said, staring hard at Larn now with cold malice. 'You forgot to tell him why it was Davir said you'd be wasting your time telling the new fish anything. Why all the things you told him already are probably totally useless to him. Why, come tomorrow, there's likely only going to be four men in this trench, not five. Oh yes, I think you forgot to tell him something, Scholar. You forgot to tell him the single most important thing of them all.'

For a moment Zeebers paused, the silence growing tense and ugly as he stared at Larn while the others shifted uneasily in their positions as though suddenly uncomfortable. Then, the corners of his lips rising tightly in a gloating smile of victory, Zeebers smirked at Larn and spoke once more.

'You forgot to tell him about the fifteen hours.'

THEY WERE QUIET at first. Scholar and Bulaven looked down at the ground in apparent embarrassment, while even Davir avoided Larn's eyes as though feeling the same vague sense of discomfort as the others. Only Zeebers looked his way. Staring back at him, Larn found himself party to an unwelcome insight. Zeebers hated him. Though why, or for what reason, he could not even begin to guess.

'What is this fifteen hours?' Larn said at last to break the silence. 'Repzik said something about it just before the last attack. And Corporal Vladek mentioned it as well. He said he would issue me with more equipment if I came back to see him again in fifteen hours' time.'

Long moments passed and no one answered. Instead there was only more silence while Davir, Scholar, and Bulaven looked uneasily at one another as though mentally drawing lots to decide which of them would perform an unwelcome duty. Until at length, still refusing to meet Larn's eyes, Davir finally spoke.

'Tell him, Scholar.'

In response Scholar fidgeted for a moment before, clearing his throat, he turned to face Larn directly.

'It is a matter of statistics, new fish,' Scholar said with a pained expression. 'You must understand that in many ways every marshal and general at headquarters is as much a bureaucrat as the most pedantic scribe in the Administratum. To them war is not just a thing of blood and death; nor entirely a question of tactics and strategy. To them, it is as much as anything a matter of calculation. A calculation based on casualty reports, rates of attrition, the numbers of units in the field, estimates of the enemy's strength, and so on; all the myriad facts and figures that, together, can be used to establish a mathematics of slaughter. Every day, from all over Broucheroc, these figures are recorded, collated and sent to General Headquarters for the bean counters there to work on them. As for this fifteen hours that Zeebers mentioned, it is one of the products of these daily calculations.'

'You are over complicating things again, Scholar,' Davir said. 'It does no good to sugar the pill for the new fish. He asked a direct question; you should answer him accordingly.'

'It is a matter of life expectancy, new fish,' Scholar sighed. 'Fifteen hours is the average length of time a replacement Guardsman survives in Broucheroc after he has been posted to a combat unit at the frontlines.'

'A replacement Guardsman?' Larn said, still unsure whether he fully understood what Scholar had just told him. 'Like me, you mean? Is that what you are telling me? That's how long you expect me to survive here? You think I am going to be dead inside fifteen hours?'

'Less than that, new fish,' Zeebers said, his tone smug and mocking. 'You must have been here at least three hours by now. Leaving you only twelve hours left.

Maybe less. Why do you think Vladek told you to return to him in fifteen hours? He didn't want to risk wasting a lot of good equipment on a dead man.'

'Shut up, Zeebers,' Bulaven rumbled. For a moment Zeebers glared back at him until, seeing the angry expression on the big man's face, he dropped his eyes to look down at the mud of the trench floor in sullen silence. 'Tell him that isn't the way it is, Scholar,' Bulaven began again, his expression softening and his voice almost pleading. 'Explain it to him. Tell him we have every faith he will still be alive tomorrow.'

'What, you think we should lie to him?' Davir said to Bulaven. 'Zeebers here may be an evil little shit with a big mouth, but at least he was telling the truth. You think we should treat the new fish like a child? Tell him that everything will be all right? That his kindly old uncles Davir, Scholar and Bulaven will keep him safe from the mean and nasty orks? Even after ten years of your fat-headed stupidity, you never cease to amaze me, Bulaven.'

'It wouldn't be lying, Davir,' Bulaven said sulkily. 'There is nothing wrong with giving a man some hope.'

'Hope, my arse,' Davir spat. 'I keep telling you, fat-man: hope is a bitch with bloody claws. You'd think after ten years in this damned hellhole you would have learned that lesson by now at least.'

'All the same, Bulaven is not entirely wrong,' Scholar said, turning towards the others to join the discussion. 'The new fish does indeed have some small cause for hope. True. General HQ may have calculated the life expectancy of a replacement to be fifteen hours. But that is only an average figure. Perhaps the new fish will be more fortunate. He could survive longer. He has already beaten the odds once already by surviving that landing.'

'Phah. Sometimes, Scholar, you can be as bad as Bulaven,' Davir said. 'But where he witters on about hope and optimism, you act like you were still in the scholarium. You would do better to remind yourself we are in the real world here. Your talk of odds and averages is all very well, but this is Broucheroc. It doesn't matter that the new fish survived the landing. Any more than it matters whether or not you and Bulaven try to coddle him. He is as good as a corpse already. A dead man walking. Trust me, the orks will see to that. There's nothing they like better than a new fish, still wet behind the ears and ready for the gutting.'

'All I am saying is that we are perhaps being too literal-minded when it comes to talking about this figure fifteen hours,' Scholar said, all three of them so caught up in the heat of their argument now that they ignored Larn as he stood there listening to them. 'It is not an absolute figure. It is only an average. Why, for all we know, the new fish might end up surviving days, weeks, even years.'

'Years?' Davir said. 'You know you really are a wonder to me, Scholar. I've never seen a man talk so eloquently and at such length from his arse before. You think the new fish is going to manage to survive years in this place? Next you will be telling me you expect Sector Command to make Bulaven a general! You obviously haven't seen the new fish in action–'

'Stop it,' Larn said quietly, no longer willing to be talked about as though he were invisible. 'I've heard enough. Stop calling me *new fish*. My name is Larn.'

For a moment, as though surprised by the interruption, the other men in the trench simply blinked and turned to look at him in silence.

'What? You don't like us calling you new fish, then?' Davir said after a time, sarcastically. 'We have offended you perhaps? Your feelings are hurt?'

'No,' said Larn, uncertainly. 'I… You don't understand. I just think you should use my name is all. My real name, I mean. Larn. Not new fish.'

'Really?' Davir said, gazing at him with cold eyes while Zeebers glared at him in hostility and Scholar and Bulaven looked at him in sadness. 'Then, it is you who does not understand the facts of life here, new fish. You think I care what your name is? I have enough baggage in my head already; never mind learning something that will likely be written on a grave marker before the day is out. You want me to remember your name? Tell me it again in fifteen hours' time.

'By then, perhaps it just may be worth knowing.'

CHAPTER NINE

15:55 hours Central Broucheroc Time

A FIGURE MOVING CLOSER THROUGH NO-MAN'S LAND –
STANDING WATCH WITH BULAVEN – MATTERS OF
GRETCHIN AND HUMAN MARKSMANSHIP – A SPLASH OF
COLOUR AMIDST THE WASTELAND – LESSONS ON HOW
BEST TO ACT AS BAIT

HE HAD BEEN moving slowly now for hours.

Crawling on his belly, painted from head to hind claws in grey clay with the long kustom barrel of his blasta wrapped in layers of grey sacking, he crept forward a centimetre at a time through the frozen mud of what the humies called no-man's land. Slow, like a slaver hunting a squig with a grabba stik, he moved an inch and then waited. He moved an inch and then waited. He moved an inch then and waited. Over and over again, always careful in case his prey was watching.

Suddenly, seeing a glint in the distance ahead of him, he stopped. Sure one of the humies' spotters must have seen him, he tensed, expecting at any moment to feel the pain from a lasbeam or hear the sound of a shot, but neither of them came. He remained motionless. Until, as the minutes passed and he became convinced he was none the worse for wear, his journey began again. Moving slowly, inch by inch, across the frozen mud toward his destination.

Finally, perhaps halfway across no-man's land, he reached the lip of a shallow shell crater. For a moment he looked at it. Then, responding to some inner instinct he could have never named, he crawled inside. Out of sight now, he moved more quickly, crawling up the opposite slope of the crater to look through the sights of his blasta in search of a target. At first, nothing. Then he saw a head in a fur-shrouded helmet peeking out of a hole in the ground some way away and he knew the instinct had been right. He had found his kill.

Breathing through his nose, careful not to make any sudden moves that might spook his prey, he aimed at it through his sights, his finger tightening incrementally on the blasta's trigger. As he did, he felt a warm sensation rush through his head as something like a clear and coherent thought occurred to him.

If he made this shot, the boss would be pleased…

'YOU SHOULDN'T TAKE it too much to heart what Davir said before, new fish,' Bulaven said. 'He didn't mean anything by it. It is just his way is all.'

Bulaven was standing on watch on the firing step, looking out into no-man's land with Larn beside him. Meanwhile, in the firing trench below them, the other men were mostly quiet. Wrapped in an extra greatcoat in place of a blanket, his muffler pulled forward to cover most of his face, Davir lay dozing with his back against some spare flamer canisters. Beside him, Scholar sat silently reading from the tattered pages of a battered and obviously well-used book. Only Zeebers was making anything much in the way of noise. Sitting on the trench floor, he could be seen sharpening the blade of his entrenching tool with a whetstone, the low scraping sound of the stone running over the metal added a malicious counterpoint to the occasional hostile glances he periodically made in Larn's direction.

'Yes, that is a good trick, new fish,' Bulaven said, noticing that Larn was looking at Zeebers. 'If you sharpen the blade of your entrenching tool it makes a good weapon if you find yourself in hand-to-hand with an ork. Better than a bayonet, anyway. Of course, you need to be careful you don't sharpen the edges of the spade head too fine. Otherwise, it can split if you actually have to dig the earth with it.'

'Does it happen a lot?' Larn asked him, giving an involuntary shiver as he remembered his earlier encounter with the gretchin. 'Going hand-to-hand with the orks, I mean?'

'Not so much if we can help it,' Bulaven said, tapping the imposing bulk of the heavy flamer by his side. 'For myself, when it comes to killing orks I prefer to use my friend here. Sometimes though, the orks get in close and it can't be helped. Then you just have to kill them with laspistols, knives, spade heads: whatever comes to hand. But you don't need to worry too much about that, new fish. Stay close to me, Scholar and Davir, and you'll be all right.'

'You will forgive me, Bulaven,' Larn said to the big man. 'But it didn't sound too much like that when you were talking before.'

'Ach, I told you: you shouldn't worry about that, new fish,' Bulaven said. 'As I say, Davir didn't mean too much by it. It is simply his manner to sound off from time to time, and you just happened to get in his way. Personally, I think it is because he is shortarse. He likes to talk a lot to make himself seem important. Trust me, you should just put it from your mind as though it never happened.'

'And the fifteen hours?' Larn said quietly. 'What about that?'

In reply Bulaven fell silent for a moment, his broad and kindly features abruptly given over to an almost pensive brooding. Until, at length, he spoke once more.

'Sometimes, it is better not to think too much on such things, new fish,' he sighed. 'Sometimes, it is better just to have faith.'

'Faith?' Larn asked. 'You mean in the Emperor?'

'Yes. No. Perhaps,' Bulaven said, his words growing as slow and thoughtful as his expression. 'I don't know, new fish. I used to believe in so many things back when I first became a Guardsman. I believed in the generals. I believed in the commissars. Most of all, I believed in the Emperor. Now, I certainly don't believe in the first two any more. And as for the Emperor? Sometimes it is hard to see His grace among all this carnage. But a man must have faith in something. And so, yes, I still believe in the Emperor. I believe in Him. And I believe in Sergeant Chelkar. Those are the two articles of my faith, such as they are.'

'But there is something else, new fish,' he continued. 'Something just as important as faith. *Hope.* Davir is wrong about that, you see. A man must have hope, or he might as well not be alive. It is as important as the air we breathe. So, no matter how bad things get, new fish – no matter how bleak they seem – you must remember not to give up hope. Trust me, if you can hold on to your hope, everything will be all right.'

With that, Bulaven fell silent again and Larn found himself remembering his talk with his father in the farmhouse cellar on his last night at home. *Trust to the Emperor*, his father had told him then. And, now,

Bulaven had told him to trust to hope. Though in his heart he knew them both to be good pieces of advice, as he looked out at the desolate and foreboding landscape around him they seemed of little comfort.

A single shot rang out, the sound of it unnaturally loud after the silence. Acting on reflex Larn jumped back from the firing step in search of cover, only to fall backwards into the trench to land on top of Davir, causing the stocky runt to awaken in a flurry of profanities.

'Marshal Kerchan's bloody arse!' Davir cursed as he pushed Larn away. 'Can't a man get any sleep around here without some idiot jumping on top of him with two boots first! What, you have mistaken me for your mother, new fish, and you wanted a cuddle? Get the hell off me!'

'There was a shot, Davir,' Bulaven said, still standing on the firing step, head crouched to peer cautiously over the trench parapet. 'From out in no-man's land. A sniper, I think. That is what the new fish was reacting to.'

'Well, he can react to it all he wants so long as he doesn't keep leaping on me,' Davir said, grabbing his lasgun and stepping up to the firing step beside Bulaven to gaze wolfishly into no-man's land. 'So. A sniper, eh? Scholar, hand me your field glasses and we will see if we can find him.'

Soon, Scholar and Zeebers had joined Davir and Bulaven on the firing step. Then, handing the field glasses to Davir, Scholar turned to look over his shoulder at Larn standing at the bottom of the trench behind him.

'You should come up and watch this, new fish,' Scholar said. 'It is important you learn how to deal with a sniper.'

Taking his place on the step next to Scholar, Larn watched as the other men stared intently into no-man's land, scanning for anything out of place. Until, indicating a shell crater perhaps three hundred metres away from their trench, Davir's wolfish smile became a broad grin of delight.

'There,' he said. 'I see him. Keep your heads down – the little gretch bastard is already looking for his next shot. He's not the brightest of sparks, however. He may have painted himself grey to blend in with the mud, but apparently, nobody told him a sniper's not supposed to fire twice from the same position.'

As though in response another shot rang out, raising a clod of earth as the bullet struck the ground three metres to the left of the trench.

'Ha! He's not much a shot either,' Davir said, handing the field glasses to Bulaven beside him. 'Really, I think we should consider sending a letter of complaint to the orks about the quality of the gretchin they choose for sniper duty. This one is so poor a marksman, killing him seems almost a waste of a lasblast.'

'It is another one of the hazards here, new fish,' Scholar said to Larn. 'Every now and again the orks will equip a particularly level-headed gretchin with a long rifle and send him out into no-man's land to act as a sniper. Of course, gretchin are hardly renowned for their marksmanship, so mostly they are just a nuisance. But we have to take them out, all the same. Which unfortunately means that one of us here will have to act as bait.'

'I vote for the new fish,' Zeebers said, sneering at him. 'He is expendable, after all, and you never known when a gretch might get lucky.'

'Very kind of you to volunteer him,' Davir said, his lasgun at his shoulder as he sighted in on the shell crater. 'Especially since, if memory serves, it is actually your turn to act as sniper bait. Now shut your stinkhole and get out there. And make sure you give the gretch plenty of opportunity to shoot at you. I want a clear view of him so I can be sure of a clean kill.'

Muttering darkly under his breath, Zeebers grabbed his lasgun and put his hands on the top of the trench wall to the side of him. Then, giving Larn a last poisonous glare, he pulled himself up out of the trench and jumped into the open. The moment his feet hit the ground he was off and running; zigzagging with his body half-crouched as he sprinted across open ground to the next nearest firing trench and threw himself inside to safety.

'No,' said Davir, still peering through his sights towards the shell crater. 'He is still in cover. Maybe our friend is smarter than we think. Or perhaps he simply finds Zeebers to be a rather scrawny and uninspiring target. Either way, I haven't got a shot yet.'

'Again, Zeebers!' Scholar yelled, waving toward the next trench.

Discontent clearly visible on every line of his face even from a distance, Zeebers leapt from the trench again and ran zigzag once more toward the next trench in line.

'He's moving,' Bulaven said, gazing through the field glasses towards the crater. 'Looks like he's taken the bait.'

'Quiet.' Davir hissed. 'You are putting me off.' Then, exhaling slowly, he pulled the trigger, producing a single sharp crack as the lasgun fired.

'You got him!' Bulaven said, passing the field glasses to Larn with a smile of exultation. 'Look, new fish. You see that? He got him.'

'Of course I got him,' Davir said. Then, as he clicked the firing control switch on his lasgun to safe, the wolfish smile returned. 'Though it was a remarkably fine shot, even if I do say so myself.'

Gazing through the field glasses Larn looked toward the shell crater, at first unable to distinguish any sign of the gretchin in the grey landscape. Then, he saw it: a

small red stain lying across a grey rock at the lip of the
crater. Abruptly, adjusting the magnification of the field
glasses to take a closer look, Larn realised he had been
mistaken. What he thought was a rock was in fact the
gretchin's head; the red stain being the contents of the
creature's brains as they oozed through the hole in its
ruptured skull and dribbled towards the ground. The
creature was dead; the only sign of its passing a smear
of red against the all-encompassing greyness of the
world around it. A bright splash of colour in the midst
of a wasteland.

'Did you see how Zeebers did it, new fish?' Bulaven
asked him. 'Did you see how he kept crouched and ran
zigzag from one trench to the next, so he wouldn't give
the gretch too much of a target?'

'Yes, I saw it,' Larn said, sensing some unwelcome portent in the concern evident in the big man's manner. It
was almost as though Bulaven was warning him about
something. 'But, why do you ask?'

'Why do you think, new fish?' Davir grunted.
'Because, now Zeebers has been kind enough to show
you how it is done, next time we have a sniper it is your
turn to act as bait.'

CHAPTER TEN

16:33 hours Central Broucheroc Time

A Daily Dose of Hell – Further Musings on the
Frontline – Friendly Fire – Intimations of an
Unwelcome Burial – Another Consultation with
Medical Officer Svenk – Corporal Grishen and
Certain Failures in Communications – Sergeant
Chelkar Finds a Way to Make his Point

'Battery, make ready!' he heard Sergeant Dumat's voice
shouting in his earpiece. 'Gun crews remove camo-covers
and make ready to open the breech!'

As though an army of quiescent insects had been provoked into action, in an instant the artillery park
became a nest of activity. Everywhere, gun crews rushed
to their posts to pull away camouflaged tarpaulins and
make ready for firing. Watching as the camo-covers were
discarded to reveal the huge and gleaming bores of the
dozen Hellbreaker class cannons under his command,
Captain Alvard Valerius Meran allowed himself a

moment of pleasure as he saw the extra firing drills he had ordered for his men had worked. There was no sign of slackness, ill discipline or confusion in the workings of the gun crews. The entire battery operated with all the smooth efficiency of a single, finely tuned, well-oiled machine.

'Load ordnance.' Sergeant Dumat yelled, the strident tones of the command carried to the ears of every man in the battery through the comm-beads inside the ear-protectors they wore to protect them from the sound of their guns. 'High explosive rounds.'

Standing in the shadow of the burnt-out building that served as his de facto headquarters, Captain Meran watched the four-man loading teams attached to each gun crew as they hurried to disappear into the tarpaulin-covered ammunition stacks beside each gun. A moment later they emerged once more, each loading team gently cradling the shining and deadly weight of a metre long high explosive shell between them. Then, carrying them to their guns, the loaders lifted their shells into the open breeches for the other members of the guns crews to ram them home.

'Load propellant.'

Again, delighting at every well-trained movement and flawless action, Meran watched as the loading teams returned to the stacks to fetch the heavy barrel-sized cylindrical sacks of cordite that served as propellant for the cannons. Grunting under the weight, taking even more care with the volatile cordite than they had with the shells, the loading teams lifted the sacks into the guns' breeches, then retreated to their positions beside the ammunition stacks once more.

'Close breeches. Set firing trajectories as follows. Horizontal traverse: five degrees twenty-six minutes. Repeat: zero five degrees two six minutes. Vertical elevation: seventy-eight degrees thirty-one minutes. Repeat: seven eight degrees three one minutes. Windage: zero point five degrees. Repeat: zero point five degrees.'

And so the sergeant's voice went on, repeating the bearings again as the gun crews worked the wheels and gearings of their guns' aiming systems to adjust the Hellbreakers to the proper trajectories. Until, their preparations at last completed, the gun crews stepped back from their guns and awaited the firing instruction.

Yes, Captain Meran thought. *Just like a machine. Really, that was a most excellent display of gunmanship. It is a shame no one from Battery Command was here to see it. If they had been, they would have been sure to have given me a commendation.*

Briefly, he wondered whether he should order an extra ration of recaf for the gun crews by way of a reward. Just as swiftly he abandoned the idea. It might set a dangerous precedent to give the men any additional reward for simply doing their duty. No, it would be pleasure enough that they could all go to their beds tonight knowing they had performed their duties with admirable dispatch. Then, noticing his men looking towards him with expectant faces as they awaited the order to fire, Meran made an elaborate show of taking his pocket chronometer from its chain and opening it to check the time. *16:30 hours exactly*, he thought with a smile, hand going to the comm-stud at the collar of his uniform as he make ready to vox the command to Sergeant Dumat to give the order to let loose the guns.

Time to give the orks their daily dose of hell.

PERHAPS HALF AN HOUR had passed since they had killed the sniper. Half an hour. Yet still, having returned to the trench in the wake of acting as bait, Zeebers sat sullenly in a corner glaring murderously at Davir and the others. Most of all, he glared at Larn; his eyes full to the brim with hatred and loathing. Not for the first time, Larn found himself wondering how it was the man had taken so badly against him for no apparent reason. Though, given Zeebers's current demeanour, he thought better of asking him outright why he hated him.

Elsewhere in the trench, the others had resumed the same positions they had occupied before the sniper's opening shot. Davir had his back against the spare flamer canisters and was wrapped dozing in an extra greatcoat once more. Scholar had returned to his book. Bulaven was still on the firing step, gazing out into no-man's land on watch with Larn beside him. Now, with the passing of the brief excitement caused by the sniper, the big man had fallen as quiet as the others.

So much has changed, Larn thought, finding the brooding silence of the past half-hour had at least given him time to think. *A few hours ago I was with Jenks and the others, getting ready to make our first planetary drop and wondering what to expect. Even in our worst nightmares none of us could have thought of this. Certainly, Jenks wouldn't have expected to die in his chair without even leaving the lander. Any more than Sergeant Ferres would have expected to be killed by a misfiring explosive bolt. The same goes for Hallan, Vorrans and Leden. It is like I remember that old preacher saying one time. You never know what the shape of your death is going to be until it has got you. And, by then, it is already too late to do anything about it.*

Sobered by the thought, shivering against the cold, Larn looked out into no-man's land and tried to make some sense of how it was he had come to be there. Try as he might he could see no sense in it. No sense in the mistake that had brought him to this place. No sense in the deaths of his friends and comrades. No sense to the fact that it seemed his life was now under a fifteen-hour sentence of death. He could see no sense in it. No sense at all.

Turning to glance down at the others from his position on the firing step, Larn noticed he could just about see the faded gold leaf lettering of the title on the cracked leather cover of the timeworn and battered book that Scholar was reading. *Under The Eagle,* the book's title read. *Glorious Accounts of Valour from the Annals of the Imperial Guard.* Larn had heard the book mentioned in basic training. It was a compilation of stirring accounts of the brave actions and past successes of just a few of the many millions of different regiments of the Emperor's armies.

Watching Scholar as he read the book, Larn saw the man's face break into an occasional smile from time to time as though in sarcastic amusement at some passage he had seen there. Again, Larn found himself wondering about Scholar's background. Davir had mentioned something about him no longer being in the scholarium. *Could it be that Scholar had once been a student in some place of higher learning?* He certainly had the disposition for it, and he seemed better informed than any of the other men in the trench. *If he really was a scholar, what was he doing serving in a forward firing position on the frontlines?* It was a mystery. As much of a mystery as everything else about the behaviour and motivations of the men around him.

With a sudden sadness born of isolation, Larn realised he understood nothing about the men who shared the trench with him. Nor for that matter did he understand any of the other men he had met so far in Broucheroc. Corporal Vladek, Medical Officer Svenk, Sergeant Chelkar, Vidmir, Davir, Zeebers, poor dead Repzik – none of them seemed remotely like any of the people he had known before he had come to this planet. By turns they were gruff, sardonic, cynical, world-weary, intimidating, not to say largely contemptuous of all the institutions and traditions Larn had been raised to cherish. Even with Bulaven, the most sympathetic and friendly of the Vardans, Larn could sense a certain reserve as though the big man was wary of getting to know him too well. It was more than that. More than any remoteness of manner or lack of empathy. These men seemed entirely unknowable to him: almost as alien in their own way as the orks. It was as though some strange and entirely new species of Man, far removed from Larn's understanding, had been given life by this place.

A new species, he thought with a shiver that owed nothing whatsoever to the coldness of the air. *A new species, forged in hell and nurtured on the fields of slaughter.*

'You seem caught up in your troubles, new fish,' Bulaven said beside him, the sound of his voice after so much silence making Larn jump. 'As though the weight of this entire world was on your shoulders. It cannot be so bad as that, though. A centi-credit for your thoughts?'

For a moment, wondering if it was possible to give words to all the confused welter of thoughts and emotions whirling inside him, Larn was silent. Then, just as he was about to speak in answer to Bulaven's question, they heard the forboding thunder of artillery fire in the distance behind them.

'Hmm. Sounds like they're firing the HeeBees,' Bulaven said, turning to look toward the sound of firing.

'HeeBees?' Larn asked.

'Hellbreakers,' said Bulaven distractedly, 'A local variant on the Earthshaker, just *bigger*. Now please be quiet, new fish. We need to listen.'

From far away Larn began to hear the high-pitched scream of artillery shells in flight. Moving ever closer, the sound of the shells' passage high in the air above them grew louder by the instant. Until, by the time the noise was directly overhead, the character of the shells' screaming abruptly changed, reaching a terrifyingly shrill and strident crescendo as the shells began their final death-dive shriek.

'Incoming!' Bulaven yelled, grabbing Larn by the collar and pulling him down with him as he suddenly leapt towards the bottom of the trench.

His stomach rebounding hard against an ammunition box as he landed on the trench floor, Larn found he was not alone there. Roused by Bulaven's warning shout, Davir and the others had already thrown themselves prostrate at the trench bottom, hugging the ground with all the fervour of lovers reunited after a long separation. Finding himself face down among a heap of bodies with someone else's boot heel jabbing painfully against his ear, Larn tried to rise, only to find it was impossible to even move so long as Bulaven's not-inconsiderable bulk was lying on top of him. Though any questions Larn might have had as to the reasons behind his comrades' strange behaviour were quickly answered as the screaming of shells in the air above them abruptly ended, replaced by the roar of explosions as the shells began to fall to earth all around their trench.

'The stupid sons of bitches!' Davir yelled, his shouting voice barely loud enough to be heard above the din. 'That's the third time this month.'

His body shaking as the ground quaked from multiple detonations, Larn closed his eyes and buried his face in the mud, his lips mumbling a litany of choked and terrified devotions as he prayed for salvation. As he prayed, his mind raced with desperate and outraged questions. *How can this be*, he thought. *Bulaven said they were our guns. Why is our own side shooting at us?* But there was no answer. Only more explosions and flying soil as the bombardment continued.

Then, abruptly, thankfully, the explosions stopped.

'Move! Move! Move! Out of the trench!' Davir shouted. 'Quickly. Before the bastards finish reloading!'

Scrambling to his feet as the others leaped up and over the rear trench wall, Larn followed them. Clearing the wall, he saw they had already sprinted halfway down the rise towards the line of dugouts. Running desperately to catch up, for a moment Larn was aware of nothing more than the rush of blood in his ears and the pounding of his heart. Then, as though with a slow dawning realisation akin to a nightmare, he heard the deathdive scream of falling shells once more and knew he would never reach the dugouts in time.

Abruptly, an explosion ripped through the air to the side of him, knocking him to the ground and showering him with falling earth. Finding himself on his back and covered in soil, Larn felt a sudden fear at the thought he had been buried alive, before he saw the grey sky overhead and realised he was still above ground. Spluttering out a mouthful of earth as he stumbled to his feet again, he spent long dangerous instants staggering aimlessly about in a daze as more explosions wracked the ground beneath him. Then, relieved, he heard the sound of a familiar voice shouting through the haze of his confusion.

'Here, new fish,' he heard the voice yell. 'This way! Over here!'

It was Bulaven. Standing sheltered within the sandbag walls of one of the dugout emplacements, the big man was gesturing frantically to him. Seeing him, Larn half-ran, half-stumbled towards him, all but collapsing into Bulaven's outstretched arms as he finally reached the safety of the emplacement. Then, hurriedly, Bulaven helped Larn down the steps into the dugout while another grim-faced Vardan slammed the door closed behind them.

'...new fish...' Bulaven said, the words mostly drowned out by the ringing in Larn's ears. '...close one... thought... los.. you...'

'...new fish...' Bulaven said again, what few words
Larn could understand were dim and muffled, as
though the big man's voice was a dying whisper echoing down the length of a long tunnel. '...are... ou... ll...
right...'

'...new fish... ' Bulaven's face was painted with concern as Larn felt a sudden weakness and the world
about him grew dark and distant.

'...new fish...'

And then, everything went black.

HE AWOKE TO darkness and the smell of earth. Opening
his eyes, Larn looked up to see a slim rectangle of cold
grey sky above him surrounded on all sides by dark
walls of soil. As he tried to stand, he found his limbs
would not answer him. He could not move; the fact of
his paralysis accepted with a curious sense of detach-
ment and calm resignation. Abruptly, he saw four bent
and ragged figures appear overheard to peer down at
him as though from a dizzying height. Seeing the lines
and creases on each ancient wizened face, he recognised
them at once. They were the old women he had seen
carting corpses away after the battle. Then, looking
down at him with tired disinterest, the women began to
speak, each one taking up where the other had left off
as though performing some ritual they had enacted a
thousand times already.

'He was a hero,' the first old women said as Larn
slowly began to understand something was terribly
wrong here. 'They all are, all the Guardsmen who die
here.'

'They are martyrs,' one of her sisters said beside her.
'By giving their blood to defend this place they have
made the soil of this city into sacred ground.'

'Broucheroc is a holy and impregnable fortress,' the
third one said. 'The orks will never take it. We will break

their assault here. Then, we will push them back and reclaim this entire planet.'

'So the commissars tell us,' the fourth one added, without conviction.

Turning away, the rustling noise made by their tattered layers of clothing not unlike the flutterings of the black wings of crows, the women disappeared from his sight again. Lying on his back still looking up at the rectangle of grey sky above him, Larn felt his previous sense of calm replaced by a sudden presentiment of terror. *There is something wrong here*, he thought. *They are talking as though I were dead. Are they blind? Can't they see I am still alive.* He made to speak, to call out and tell them to come back and help him up out of this strange pit he found himself lying in but the words would not come. His mouth and tongue were as paralysed as every other part of his body. Then, Larn heard a scratching sound as though somewhere a shovel had been pushed into a mound of earth, and knew all his horrified premonitions of a moment earlier were about to be made reality.

This is not a pit, he thought, his mind frantic with despair. *It is a grave! And they are about to bury me alive!*

'Grieve not for this departed soul,' he heard a stern and even voice say from above as the first shovelful of earth fell towards him. 'Man born of woman was not made to be eternal. And, insofar as he was given life by the Immortal Emperor, so it is by His will that Man should die.'

Feeling the earth strike his face, Larn tried to struggle to his feet. To scream. To shout. To cry out. It was hopeless. He could not move.

'For though the soul may be immortal, the body was made to pass from this world,' the voice smoothly continued. 'And let the flesh of the remains of Man be given over to the processes of decay, for only the Emperor is undying.'

Helpless, Larn found himself blinded as another shovelful of earth landed on his face. Then, as fragments of soil dribbled into his mouth and nostrils, he felt more earth hit his body, the weight of it growing slowly more intolerable as, one remorseless shovelful at a time, the unseen grave diggers went about their work. Soon, his lungs crushed under the weight of the soil on his chest, his mouth and nose choked from the soil inside them, he could no longer breathe. Mute and blind now, his heart growing feeble, in the throes of his last desperate paroxysms of helpless terror the final thing he heard was the words of the calm and pitiless voice droning endlessly on above him.

'Ashes to ashes,' the voice said, uncaring. 'Dust to dust. A life is over. Let the body of this man be given to the earth.'

'THERE. YOU SEE now I was right,' he heard Davir say. 'I told you all he wasn't dead. Naturally I defer to your medical judgement in such matters, Svenk, but I understand it is exceedingly rare to find a dead man who is still breathing.'

Groggily opening his eyes, Larn was briefly confused to find he was lying on his back on the floor of an unfamiliar dugout with the gaunt figure of Medical Officer Svenk kneeling over him. For a moment he wondered what had happened to the open grave and the weight of earth on top of his chest. *It must have been a nightmare*, he thought. Then, becoming aware of a pungent odour making his eyes water, he realised Svenk had broken open a vial of smelling salts and was wafting them under his nose. Weakly pushing the vial away Larn tried to stand, only for Svenk to place a firm hand on his chest to stop him.

'Not just yet, new fish,' he said, raising a hand to hold three fingers up in front of Larn's face. 'How many fingers do you see?'

'Three,' Larn said, noticing Bulaven kneeling on the other side of him and looking down at his face with an expression of concern.

'We thought we had lost you there for a moment, new fish,' Bulaven said. 'When you collapsed I was sure a near miss from one of the shells must have liquefied your insides. The blast does that sometimes, even if the shrapnel does not hit you. I am glad to see you are still all right though.'

'How many now?' Svenk asked, changing the number of raised fingers and holding them in front of Larn once more.

'Two.'

'Good,' Svenk said. 'You can remember your name?'

'Larn. Arvin Larn.'

'And where do you come from, Larn?'

'From? Outside... there was shelling...'

'True. But I mean where is your homeworld, Larn? Where were you born?'

'Jumael,' Larn replied. 'Jumael IV.'

'Excellent,' Svenk said, his face at last cracking into a smile. 'Let me extend my warmest congratulations to you, new fish. You are hereby pronounced fit for duty and free from concussion. Should you find yourself experiencing any sudden dizziness or nausea over the next twelve hours, please take two glasses of water and call me in the morning. Oh, and as for that headache you are no doubt feeling at the moment? Don't worry, it is a good sign. It means you are still alive.'

'The warmth of your bedside manner is most extraordinary, Svenk,' Davir said, suddenly appearing to stand over the medic's shoulder and gaze down at Larn. 'Remarkable, even. Really, you are a credit to your profession.'

'Thank you, Davir,' Svenk replied, putting the loop of his satchel strap over his shoulder once more as he made to stand. 'I always find such unsolicited testimonials deeply moving. Now, if you will excuse me, I had better go and check the other dugouts for casualties. Given the thoroughness of the bombardment our own side are currently subjecting us to, chances are there are others elsewhere who may be in more need of my talents. Though I warn you, new fish,' he added, looking down with mock seriousness at Larn. 'While getting injured twice in one day is scarcely unheard of hereabouts, it does suggest a certain carelessness about your own well-being. Come to me again today, and I may be forced to start charging you for my services.'

With that Svenk turned on his heel and walked briskly away, headed for the doorway at the far end of the dugout. As he watched the medic open the door and start up the stairs towards the surface, Larn became abruptly aware of the muffled sounds of explosions as shells struck the earth overhead. *We are still being bombarded*, he thought, the fog of his mind slowly clearing as he came more back to himself. *And Medical Officer Svenk is about to go out in the middle of it in search of wounded men in need of treatment. Unbelievable. Whatever the strangeness of his manner, he is either insane or the bravest man I have ever seen.*

'You still do not look too well, new fish' Bulaven said, still kneeling beside Larn and frowning at him with concern. 'Your face is very pale.'

'So?' said Davir. 'For all we know that is his normal colour when he has just had the shit knocked out of him. Anyway, you heard what Svenk said, Bulaven: the new fish is perfectly fine. Now, stopping clucking over him like some idiot mother hen and get him to his feet. If the new fish isn't dying he has no right to be taking up valuable space by lying there like that.'

'Come on then, new fish,' Bulaven said, helping him stand up as Larn looked for the first time at the interior of the dugout around them. 'Careful now. If you feel like your knees are about to go, just put your weight on me.'

Inside, the dugout was smaller than the one he had been in before; perhaps a third of the size at most of the barracks dugout where he had first met Sergeant Chelkar and Corporal Vladek. Looking through the crowd of a dozen or so Guardsmen standing near him Larn saw a table in the corner covered in communications equipment. In a chair beside it an unshaven and harried-looking Vardan corporal sat holding a pair of headphones to his ear with one hand, while pressing down the 'send' button of the vox-com before him with the other.

'Yes, I understand that, captain,' the corporal said, talking into the vox-com. 'But regardless of what your situation maps may say, I assure you we are still in possession of sector 1-13.'

'That is Corporal Grishen,' said Bulaven once he had seen Larn watching the man. 'Our comms officer. Right now he is talking to the commander of the artillery battery that is shelling us.'

'What? You mean they *know* they are shooting at us?' Larn asked in disbelief.

'I wouldn't sound so surprised, new fish,' said Davir. 'This is Broucheroc, after all. Here, such snafus are not uncommon. You have heard the expression by now, I take it? Snafu? I tell you: there could be no better term for describing this whole damn war.'

'It is usually a question of parts, I understand,' Scholar said as he came over to join them. 'The cause of these incidents when our own artillery suddenly starts shooting at us, I mean. Old parts wear out; the new ones are incorrectly calibrated, or else they have been recycled and refurbished so many times as to be all but useless. Whatever the cause though, I'm sure once the battery commander has become aware of our situation the shelling will stop.'

'*Phah*. More groundless optimism,' Davir spat. 'Really, Scholar, you are getting as bad as this fat oaf Bulaven here. Grishen has been at the comm-link working his way up that battery's chain of command for the last twenty minutes. So far, the most he has managed to accomplish is for his backside to go numb from sitting in that chair. No, I wouldn't expect this bombardment to end any time soon. For that to happen the moron shooting at us would have to admit he has made a mistake. And why should he do that, after all? If he kills us, some arsehole at General Headquarters will probably pin a medal on him.'

'Yes, captain, I know you have your orders,' said Corporal Grishen nearby, still talking into the vox-com before pausing to listen to a reply through his headphones. Then, with every man in the dugout now silent as they stood listening to the stop-start rhythms of Grishen's side of the conversation, the corporal began once more.

'Yes, I realise that, captain,' Grishen said. 'And you are right: the Guardsman's first duty is obedience. But, even granting that you have your orders and it is your duty to obey them, if those orders are mistaken...'

A pause.

'No, of course, you are right, sir. The divinely ordained command structure of the Imperial Guard precludes any possibility of your orders being mistaken. If I may rephrase myself, however? What I really meant to say, of course, was that perhaps the problem here lies not in the orders themselves, but in the practical aspects of their execution...'

Another pause.

'Oh no, sir. I wasn't for a moment questioning your competence...'

And another.

'Yes, sir, as you say: your battery runs like a well-oiled machine. But you must concede that, seeing as we are unquestionably under bombardment, a mistake must have occurred somewhere…'

Another pause.

'Yes, of course, sir. You concede nothing. Yes, I understand. No, sir, you are correct. General Headquarters is not known for promoting fools to the rank of captain…'

And so it went on, while from above Larn heard the distant roar of explosions as the bombardment continued. Until, at last, he heard a door open behind him and turned to see Sergeant Chelkar step grim-faced into the dugout. Then, as the group of assembled Vardans huddled in the dugout silently parted to give way before their sergeant, Larn saw Chelkar stride purposefully over to Grishen at the comms system.

'Yes, sir,' Corporal Grishen said, raising his eyes as he saw Chelkar approach him. 'Naturally, you are right. If there is any mistake here it was ours in being present in a sector scheduled for bombardment. But, if you will excuse me for a moment, my company commander has just entered the room. Perhaps it would be better if you and he discussed this matter directly.'

'What is going on, Grishen?' Chelkar said, laying the shotgun he had been carrying down across the table before him. 'Why in hell are those idiots still shelling us?'

'I am on the line to the captain commanding the battery in question now, sergeant,' Grishen said, diplomatically releasing the 'send' button on the vox-com so his listener at the other end could no longer hear them. 'I have tried to explain things to him, but he refuses to accept anything I say. He claims that according to his situation map this entire sector fell to the orks three days ago – meaning he would be quite within his rights to bombard it even if he didn't already have signed orders from Battery Command telling him to do so. And as for ending the bombardment? He says in keeping with his orders the shelling will cease in precisely one hour and twenty-seven minutes' time. Not a moment sooner. He is most definite on that point, sergeant. Frankly, some might even say a little intransigent.'

'I see,' said Chelkar. 'Hand me the vox-com, Grishen. I want to talk to this son of a bitch myself.'

'This is Sergeant Eugin Chelkar,' he said, taking the headphones and pressing the button to activate the vox-com. 'Acting regimental commander of the 902nd Vardan Rifles. Who am I speaking to?'

For a moment, like Grishen before him, Chelkar went quiet as he listened to the voice on the other end of the line through his headphones. Then, his tone becoming grave and forceful, he spoke once more.

'Captain Meran, the 16th Landran Artillery?' Chelkar said. 'I see. Well, I have a message for you, captain. No, I am well aware you outrank me, but you will listen to what I have to say all the same. I am giving you two minutes, captain. Two minutes. And, if this bombardment hasn't ended by then, I am going to come over to whatever hole you are hiding in and kick you up the arse so hard that you will taste leather every time you swallow. Not that you will have to worry about that for long, you understand. The arse kicking will only be for my own amusement. After that, I fully intend to put a shotgun blast through your skull. Have I made myself clear?'

Again, there was another pause while Chelkar listened to the captain's reply on his headphones.

'No, it is you who does not understand the situation, captain,' Chelkar said after a moment. 'I don't give a damn about your rank or your orders. Nor do I care if you report me to the Commissariat. In fact, please feel free to do so: if nothing else, they can serve as pallbearers at your funeral. What you fail to understand is that, even if you have me arrested, there is an entire regiment of men standing around me who are quite prepared to make good on my threat. And, if you think the Commissariat will be willing to arrest an entire frontline combat unit to save you, I think you overestimate your own value to the war effort of this city. Oh, and by the way, captain, the chronometer is counting down. You now have only one minute and twenty seconds to make a decision. Chelkar out.'

Giving the vox-com and headphones back to Grishen, Chelkar stood waiting beside the table. Listening intently, like every other man in the dugout to the sound of shelling going on above their heads.

'I don't understand,' Larn whispered. 'Surely the sergeant has just written his own death warrant by talking to an officer that way?'

'Maybe,' Bulaven whispered back. 'You don't know Chelkar though, new fish. In seventeen years I have never seen him be afraid of anything. If there is something that needs to be done, he is the man to do it. Whatever the cost. All the same, I wonder if even he has gone too far this time. If the captain should vox a complaint to the Commissariat…'

'Ach, you are both like children frightened of your own shadows,' Davir muttered beside them. 'You especially should know better, Bulaven. When has Chelkar ever failed us? The sergeant knows what he is doing. These artillery monkeys always think frontline troops are crazy to begin with. This arsehole captain won't dare call the Commissariat. Trust me, he is probably already soiling himself in fear and is giving the order to cease fire even as we speak.'

Above, as though in confirmation of Davir's opinions, the guns abruptly fell silent. At first no one spoke, all of them listening to hear whether the shelling would begin again. Until, as the seconds passed into a full minute with no further sound of explosions, it became clear the bombardment was ended.

'There, you see, Grishen?' Chelkar half-smiled. 'It is simply a matter of knowing how best to talk to these people to get your point across.' Then, taking up his shotgun once more and turning away from the corporal, Chelkar noticed every man in the dugout was looking at him with faces caught in expressions of awe and gratitude.

'It was nothing so much,' Chelkar said to them. 'Still, it was probably better that I let our friend the captain think he was going to have an entire regiment after his blood if he didn't stop the shelling. If he'd known the 902nd Vardan was only made up of a single company perhaps he would have felt man enough to take us all on. It is not unusual for these rear echelon heroes to have a bloated sense of their own abilities.'

At that the men smiled, some even laughed in nervous relief. Seeing the mood of reverence had been successfully dispelled, the sergeant's manner became more business-like.

'All right,' he said. 'Now, enough of this hiding underground. Back to your posts. We don't want to leave the firing trenches undefended and make the orks think it is a worthwhile time launching another attack. Go on. Get moving, all of you.'

As the men in the dugout began to hurry out towards their trenches again, Larn's last sight of Chelkar came as he saw the sergeant turn to towards Corporal Grishen once more with further instructions.

'Grishen, I want you to contact General Headquarters,' he heard the sergeant say. 'Inform them Sector 1-13 is most certainly not in ork hands and make it clear we would consider it a great personal favour if they would adjust their situation maps accordingly. Oh, and you had better try voxing Battery Command as well to ask them if in future they could please refrain from ordering people to shoot at us. It probably won't work, of course. But I suppose we should at least pretend we believe the men in charge of this war have some idea of what it is they are doing.'

INTERLUDE

As Above, So Below
or Grand Marshal Kerchan and the Genius of Command

By any standard of measurement, the war was going badly.

Brooding as he sat through yet another interminable briefing His Excellency Grand Marshal Tirnas Kerchan, Hero of the Varentis Campaign and Supreme Commander (All Forces) of the Most Glorious Armies of the Emperor in Broucheroc, considered the facts he had learned so far that day and found there was nothing there to please him. For the best part of two hours now, from his place at the head of the long table inside General HQ's Central Briefing Room One, he had listened as a succession of his commanders read aloud their latest situation reports to the assembled General Staff. Through it all, through all their pasty-faced dissemblings and pathetically transparent attempts to lay the blame for their failures on others, the message at the heart of each man's report was exactly the same.

They were losing the war.

'Grand Marshal?' he heard his adjutant, Colonel Vlin, whisper from his chair by the side of him, breaking his train of thought.

Disturbed from his despairing reverie, the Grand Marshal abruptly realised he had lost track of the briefings. Looking up he saw the eyes of every man at the table were turned to gaze his way, nervously awaiting his reaction to the substance of the last report. For a moment, unable to remember the name of the man standing before him who had presented it, he found himself stymied.

'Yes, good. Very good,' Kerchan harrumphed, then floundered. 'Most cogent and concise. An excellent analysis, General… ah…'

'Dushan,' Vlin said *sotto voce*, raising a sheath of papers in front of his mouth to hide the words as he spoke them.

'Yes, General Dushan,' the Grand Marshal said, inclining his head toward the officer in question and giving him a curt nod by way of encouragement. 'Your grasp of the situation is to be commended.'

Clearly relieved, his face all but beaming at the praise, the ferret-faced Dushan puffed out his chest with pride and bent forward in a low bow in grateful acknowledgement before taking his seat once more.

Look at him, the Grand Marshal thought sourly. *The man is an idiot. Still he is hardly unique in that regard. I am surrounded by idiots. This whole damned city would seem to be staffed from first to last with idiots, cowards and incompetents.*

Briefly, the Grand Marshal idly wondered whether it might not be better to make an example of Dushan. To denounce him, here and now, and order him taken away to stand court martial on charges of incompetence. *That might put the fear of the Emperor into the rest of them for a while*, he thought. *Force them to buck their ideas up for fear they'd be facing more of the same themselves.* As attractive as the idea was, he found himself forced to dismiss it. He had just praised the man, after all. To go back on that praise so quickly might make him seem indecisive. No, like it or not, for the rest of the day at least the idiot Dushan was beyond arrest; almost as inviolable to the Grand Marshal's powers as the body of an Imperial saint. It was a matter of maintaining the proper respect for the chain of command. Once the Grand Marshal had given voice to an opinion on a man there could be no turning back.

And besides, thought Kerchan, *I was the one who gave Dushan his position in the first place. To punish him for his inadequacies now might be perceived as an admission I was wrong to promote him. No matter what, a Grand Marshal can never admit to having made a mistake. He must be seen to be infallible. To give credence to any thought otherwise would be to fatally undermine the rightful awe every Guardsman naturally feels for the wisdom of their superiors. Well, the awe that most of them feel anyway. It is the nature of war that, occasionally and inevitably, there will always be dissenters.*

With a distant stab of quiet anger, the Grand Marshal found himself remembering the officer whose place Dushan had taken on the General Staff. *What was the man's name,* he thought. *Minar? Minaris? Minovan?* He was about to turn to Colonel Vlin to ask him the name of Dushan's predecessor, when abruptly it came to him. *Mirovan! That was the man's name.* The remembered name brought with it a clearer picture in his mind of the individual to whom it belonged and Grand Marshal Kerchan found his bleak and unhappy mood growing even darker.

Of all the men on his staff, Mirovan had always seemed the best and brightest. An exemplary field officer with an admirable record of citations for bravery behind him, Mirovan had made general in a creditably short space of time. If the man had any flaw at all, it was in the one single characteristic Kerchan could never abide in a subordinate.

Insolence.

Mirovan had been so insolent in fact that two weeks ago he had even had the temerity to question one of the Grand Marshal's military decisions during a staff meeting. Enraged, Kerchan had demoted the man on the spot, busting him down to the rank of common trooper and ordering him to be immediately posted to a front-line combat unit. Next, in a hasty decision the Grand Marshal now bitterly regretted, he had promoted the man's less than able second-in-command, the then-colonel Dushan, and ordered him to serve on the General Staff in Mirovan's place. Though he had felt quite sure humbling Mirovan had been the right thing to do at the time, the Grand Marshal now experienced a troubling sense of ill-defined unease. *In many ways Mirovan was an admirable man*, he thought sadly. *Certainly, he was a damn sight more competent than most of the toadies and feckless lackeys who bedevil me sitting around this table day after day. I wonder what happened to him?*

'He was a good man in his way,' the Grand Marshal said. 'It would be a pity if such a man were dead.'

All around the table, the others were staring at him. Kerchan realised he must have inadvertently spoken his musings aloud, interrupting the flow of conversation around him as the members of the General Staff discussed the significance or not of Dushan's report. On every side of him, as though not entirely sure how they should react, generals stared towards him with expressions ranging from uncertainty to quiet trepidation. Even the ever-faithful Vlin seemed to be looking at him strangely. Kerchan, however, felt no embarrassment. If nothing else, a lifetime spent commanding soldiers had taught him a simple truth. A man with the absolute authority of life-or-death over others should never feel any need to have to apologise for his own behaviour.

'I was remembering Mirovan,' he said, turning to look toward General Dushan. 'After his demotion he was given over to your command, Dushan. What happened to him?'

'I… I am not sure, your excellency,' Dushan said, almost squirming before the Grand Marshal's gaze. 'I left the matter of assigning him to a new posting to one of my aides. As to where precisely he was sent, I should have to check the battalion rosters…'

Faltering, failing miserably to hide his discomfort, Dushan's voice gradually trailed away to guilty silence. *He probably had the man posted to the worst unit and the most dangerous duties he could find*, Kerchan thought. *Somewhere right in the thick of the action no doubt, where Mirovan would have been lucky to survive a week. After all, with their former general still alive there would always be the danger of dissent and mutiny among the men who had served under him. So, Mirovan is likely dead then. Not that I can fault Dushan's decision-making in that regard, of course. Dissent is a cancer. If I had been in his position, I would have done the same myself.*

Then, looking at the eyes of the men seated around him, the Grand Marshal realised his mention of Mirovan's name had apparently had an entirely unforeseen consequence. Every man there seemed in the grip of the same queasy discomfort as Dushan, as though the recollection of Mirovan's sudden fall from grace had spooked them. Watching them, the Grand Marshal began to understand he had quite inadvertently achieved his original purpose. *Mentioning Mirovan did the trick*, he thought. *That seems to have put the fear of the Emperor in them, all right.* Not for the first time, Kerchan was left dazzled by the extent of his own genius when it came to motivating the men under his command. *I didn't even realise I was doing it*, he thought. *And yet still, by some happy accident, I seem to have created exactly the effect I wanted. No, not an accident.. Unconsciously or not, the fact I achieved my aim means I must have intended to do so all along. There are no accidents when one is a Grand Marshal.* Then, making the effort to summon his most carefully unreadable sinister half-smile, the Grand Marshal spoke to Dushan once more.

'No matter, Dushan,' he said, noting with satisfaction that the man seemed little reassured by his manner. 'It was simply an idle thought, nothing more. Now, on to other matters. Colonel Vlin? Who is scheduled to give the next briefing?'

'Magos Garan, your excellency,' his adjutant said. 'He wishes to advise us on the monthly production figures from the city's munitions manufactoriums.'

His brief mood of good humour abruptly evaporating, the Grand Marshal watched with a sinking heart as the hooded figure of the archmagos of the Adeptus Mechanicus in Broucheroc rose slowly to his feet. As much machine as man, covered in whirring devices that had kept their owner alive for far past the normal span of life, what could be seen of the magos's aged and withered body from beneath his cloak no longer looked entirely human. Most disquieting of all were the mechadendrites: four thin tentacle-like mechanical arms that would periodically emerge from the folds of the magos's cloak to make minute adjustments to the other machines that covered his flesh.

Though as disturbing as he had always found the creature's appearance, the real root of the Grand Marshal's dislike of Magos Garan lay more in practical considerations than in anything so flighty as matters of aesthetics. Unlike the rest of the men seated around the briefing table, Magos Garan did not serve at the Grand

Marshal's whim. As the most senior member of the Adeptus Mechanicus in the city Garan was not here as a subordinate. Without the machine-adepts to keep the city's manufactoriums working, the Grand Marshal would have no munitions for his troops. No new lasguns. No missile launchers. No replacement power packs. No grenades, mortar rounds, artillery shells, or any of the hundreds of other things the Guardsmen of the city needed daily to help them keep the orks at bay. As such, the Grand Marshal found himself forced to deal with Magos Garan as though he was the representative of some foreign power. A man to be negotiated and entreated with, but never commanded. An equal, not an inferior. Not being by inclination a man much given to the subtle intricacies of diplomacy, Kerchan had long found dealing with the haughty Magos to be a difficult burden to bear.

'In the last thirty days the productivity of the city's manufactoriums has fallen by a figure of four point three four per cent,' the Magos said in a dry monotone voice, apparently so long past remembering what it was to be human he made no attempt to leaven the bad news as he delivered it. 'The reasons for this fall in productivity are as follows. One, the loss of five manufactoriums in Sector 1-49 when the sector in question was partially overrun by the orks. Two, the destruction of another manufactorium in Sector 1-37 by an ork raiding party who had gained entrance past the city's defensive perimeter by unknown means. Three, damage to a further fifteen manufactoriums in Sectors 1-22 through 1-25 caused by the orks' long-range artillery. Four, further damage to three of the same manufactoriums caused by gretchin suicide bombers. Five, the slowness of repair to these facilities caused by a chronic lack of qualified personnel. Six, the outbreak of an unknown viral pathogen among the lay manufactorium workers of Sector 1-19, causing the loss of 180,757 working man-hours through either sickness or death. Seven, the loss of 162,983 working man-hours caused through civil unrest occasioned by food shortages among the lay manufactorium workers of Sector 1-32, said unrest having since been suppressed at the result of a further 34,234 working man-hours lost through either injury or death…'

His face emotionless, the magos continued, droning out an apparently endless catalogue of doom. As he listened, Grand Marshal Kerchan once more found himself falling into despair. According to his strategic calculations, the battle for Broucheroc should have been won weeks, if not months, ago. More than that, by now they should have broken out of this Emperor-forsaken city and be pushing the enemy back on every front. Yet, impossibly, after ten years of warfare the orks still showed no sign of defeat or collapse. While day after day, hour after hour, Grand Marshal found himself confronted by defeatism at every turn: his every waking moment spent in the company of dozens of mewling incompetents, all of them with their pleas of extenuation and tales of woe.

The Adeptus Mechanicus complained about not having enough workers or raw materials for the manufactoriums. The Medical Corps complained of not having enough surgeons or medicines for the apothecariums. The militia authorities he had placed in command of the civilian infrastructure complained of not having the resources to provide enough food or clean water for the city's population. Worst of all, his own generals complained of not having enough men, or arms, or artillery support, or any other damned thing. Complaint, after complaint, after damn complaint. All the while, the Grand Marshal knew all these complaints for what they truly were. Excuses. It was hardly any wonder that sometimes he felt such outrage he was tempted to pick out one of his generals at random and put a lasblast through his head just as an example to the others.

A lasblast, he thought, hand straying unconsciously to the finely filigreed surface of the ceremonial laspistol at his side. *Right here and now. That really would put the fear of the Emperor into them!*

'Fifteen, the loss of 38,964 working man-hours through reason of power shortages in Sectors 1-42 through 1-47,' the magos droned relentlessly on, his mechadendrites still attending to the machines of his body as though with a life of their own. 'Sixteen, the loss of a manufactorium to explosion in Sector 1-26, said explosion believed to have been caused by a malfunction in an incorrectly fitted power conduit. Seventeen...'

And on and on and on. Seeking relief from the depressing tedium of the Magos's report, hearing the sound of a door opening behind him the Grand Marshal turned his head enough to the side to watch from the corner of his eye as one of Vlin's aides stepped into the briefing room from the anteroom outside. Holding a data-slate the aide advanced to the table to hand it to Colonel Vlin, before saluting and smartly turning on his heel to march away. Pressing the display stud to bring up the report stored on the data-slate, Vlin studied it for a full minute. Then, his face visibly growing pale, he raised his eyes to look uneasily toward the Grand Marshal.

'What is it, Vlin?' Kerchan asked as, from further down the table, the magos's briefing continued inexorably.

'I have just received the latest estimates from the Office of Strategic Analysis, your excellency,' Vlin said, a wavering tone of uncertainty in his voice. 'But there must be some mistake–'

'Let me see it,' the Grand Marshal said, holding his hand out for Vlin to give him the data-slate.

For a moment, as though unsure whether he should surrender it, Vlin hesitated. Then, the habits of obedience engrained by fifteen years in the Grand Marshal's service proving too strong to resist, he reluctantly complied. Curious as to what could have so unnerved his adjutant, Kerchan took the data-slate and skimmed through the report to see for himself. At first glance it seemed no more than Vlin had said: another dry analysis of facts and figures from the number crunchers in the OSA. At least until the Grand Marshal happened to look at the report's conclusions.

'Damnation!' he roared.

Incensed, before he even knew what he was doing the Grand Marshal had thrown the data-slate away in a rage, flinging it across the room to smash against the wall in a crash of breaking plexiglass as its display screen shattered. Stunned by his outburst, mouths gaping open in idiot expressions of surprise, the men around the table sat frozen in shock. Even Magos Garan was not immune, his mechadendrites becoming suddenly motionless, he paused in his report and stood gazing at Kerchan as though unsure how best to react. All of them silently staring at the Grand Marshal with wary expressions whose combined meanings were almost palpably clear.

They think I have turned into a madman, Kerchan thought, the storm of his anger having subsided immediately he had vented his rage against the helpless data-slate. *The old man is losing it. That is what they are all telling themselves.*

'Leave me,' he said quietly, his face a mask, his mind feeling suddenly tired and no longer willing to see the looks in their eyes. 'Leave me,' he directed. 'All of you. Get out of here now.'

Cowed, heads bent so as not to meet his gaze, the members of the General Staff stood, bowed at him, and filed from the room in uneasy silence. All except Vlin. Treading cautiously over to the fallen data-slate while the others went to the door, the adjutant picked it up and made to take it with him.

'Leave it, Vlin,' the Grand Marshal said. 'Put it on the table, and then get out with the rest of them.'

Soon, he was alone. The mammoth expanse of the briefing room seemed desolate and empty about him now it was deserted, Grand Marshal Kerchan began to wonder if he perhaps should have held himself better in check. Generals were by their nature inveterate gossips. Within the hour news of his outburst would be known throughout General Headquarters; by tomorrow it would likely be known across the city. In these trying times even a Grand Marshal must be careful. Whatever the rules and regulations of the Imperial Guard might say to the contrary, as the commanding officer of a besieged city his position was precarious. Idle gossip about the data-slate incident could easily lead to discussions about the state of his mental health; discussions that in turn might undermine his authority, creating fertile soil in which the twin ugly flowers of dissent and mutiny could grow. He was not afraid. Experience had taught him there was always one sure way for a Grand Marshal to maintain order.

It is time for another purge, he thought. *Tonight, I will tell Vlin to contact the Commissariat and have them send over a list of anyone above the rank of major they suspect of disloyalty. A few show trials and shootings should nip any problems in the bud in that regard. And while we're at it, I will tell Vlin to add Dushan to the list. Yes, another purge. That is exactly what is needing here.*

Calm and satisfied now, he turned his attention back to the object that had originally provoked his displeasure. Lifting the data-slate from its position on the table where Vlin had left it, the Grand Marshal looked again at the words and graphs of the report still visible on the shattered surface of its display screen. The findings of the report were bleak. Based on current estimates of ork birth-rates and the rate of attrition of men and materiel inside the city, it concluded Broucheroc could only survive another six months at most.

Six months, the Grand Marshal thought grimly. *I shall have to remember to tell Vlin to add the name of whatever traitor compiled this report to the list as well. Imagine claiming this city has only six months left to live, when any fool knows the siege is on the verge of crumbling and victory is within our grasp.*

Mentally making another note to himself to have the report suppressed, Kerchan tossed the data-slate away and sat in silence for several minutes. Feeling weighed down by the heavy burden of responsibility on his shoulders, his brooding mood of earlier returned. *I am assailed on all sides by troubles*, he thought. *Bad enough after a long and glorious career for a man to find himself shunted to a sideshow war on a planet of no importance. Worse, to then be condemned to a long siege with no prospect of relief from other sources. But it does not matter. The genius that won me my battles in the past has not deserted me. I am still a great leader, and my plan is sound. Soon, I will break this siege and reclaim this planet for the Emperor. And, when I do, the fools among the Lord Generals Militant responsible for sidelining me to this awful place will find themselves embarrassed to see me celebrated and revered for all my victories. I am the Grand Marshal Tirnas Kerchan. I am still in control of my own destiny. I will win this war. And, soon enough, I will be able to add the name 'Hero of Broucheroc' to all my different titles. I will not allow matters here to go any other way.*

Then, noticing a single page sitting alone among the flotsam spread of maps and documents lying across the table, the Grand Marshal saw something there that excited his interest. It was the latest edition of *The Veritas*, the city's twice-daily newsletter and, as so often in the past when he felt weighed down by all his troubles, the Grand Marshal turned to the newsletter in the hope of comfort.

Orks Defeated in Sector 1-13, the headline read. *Jumael 14th Victorious!*

Yes, he thought, reading the story written below it. *It doesn't matter what the others say, here is the proof that I was right all along. The proof of impending victory and the proof my battle plans are sound. We are winning victories. We are defeating the orks. We are winning this war.*

It says so right here in the news.

CHAPTER ELEVEN

17:54 Central Broucheroc Time

Boy and the Taking of Broucheroc's Children –
Trench Repairs Parts 1, 2 & 3 – Questions as to the
Whys and Wherefores of Survival – A Reappraisal of
the Tale of his Fathers

His name was Boy. Granted, his Ma had given him
another name but she had been dead for more than
three something years now and he had been so young
he could no longer remember what it was she had
called him. Instead, he had taken the name the auxies
used for him when they tried to catch him to take him
to the machine-men and their big making-places. *'Come
here, boy'* they would say. *'We don't want to hurt you, boy'*,
their voices breathless from running, their stupid faces
red and panting, trying to chase him as he danced away
from them across the rubble. Some of them, the clever
ones he guessed, would even try to trick him. *'We have
food, boy,'* they'd say. *'Come down here and we will share*

some with you.' But they could never fool him. He was Boy, and he lived wild and swift and free in the ruins of this city. Try as they might, the auxies and the machine-men would never get him.

Now, the cloak he had made from rat skins and scavenged sacking-cloth wrapped tight about him to keep out the cold, Boy crouched hidden in a hollow in the rubble waiting to see if one of the children of Cap'n Rat would take his bait. The pickings had been good this week, with Cap'n Rat sending at least one of his children along each day for Boy to kill and eat. In return Boy had done right by the Cap'n just liked he'd promised him: forsaking all other gods and praying to Cap'n Rat over each of his kills. As far as agreements went Boy reckoned it had been a pretty good one. Only problem was, despite the fact he had been waiting in the same place for hours now, so far today the Cap'n didn't seem in any great hurry to live up to his end of the bargain.

Then, at last, Boy saw signs of progress. Tempted from his burrow by the promise of easy pickings, a rat emerged from a nearby hole in the rubble and moved quickly across the rocks towards the bait. Until, coming to the small piece of greasy flesh Boy had set out as a lure, the rat paused with whiskers twitching warily as though some inner instinct had alerted it to danger.

Too late to be twitching with your whiskers now, Brother Rat, Boy thought, a feral smile playing across his cracked lips as he aimed his slingshot and loosed the taut string to let fly with a two-inch metal nail. *Shouldn't oughta have been so greedy, coming out in the open in the suntime like that.*

Flying fast and true the nail took the rat square in the back of the neck, stabbing through its spine and into the skull. On his feet and moving before the nail had even hit its target, Boy jumped from cover to race scampering across the rubble to retrieve his prize. Grabbing the dead rat by the tail, he turned and ran back to find refuge again in his hiding place. Then, pulling the nail free and daubing two smears of the rat's blood across his cheeks, he knelt to send a silent prayer of thanksgiving to his unseen benefactor.

Praise'm, Cap'n Rat, he thought as he looked down at the body of his catch and considered its worth. *Praise'm for making so many of your children. Praise'm for making them big and fat. And praise'm for sending them to me so I don't starve.*

It was a good rat, fine and sleek, with the kind of big meaty haunches he knew would make for tasty eatings. Nor did the value of the rat to Boy end there. He could make clothing from its pelt, sewing thread from its sinews, needles and traphooks from its bones, teeth, and claws. No part of the rat's body would go wasted. By virtue of the survival skills he had learned first by watching his mother and then on his own after her death, Boy could find a use for anything.

Abruptly, he found himself thinking of how things used to be when his Ma was still alive. He remembered the cellar where they used to live, her kind and care-worn face, the soft lullabies she would sing to drift him off to sleep. He remembered sitting on her knee as she told him the reasons they must stay in hiding. *'They say we must give up our children,'* she had told them. *'The generals. They say children are a distraction in wartime; that the people of Broucheroc must all serve in the auxiliaries while their children are cared for in the orphanariums. But I don't believe them. I think they want to give the children over to the Adeptus Mechanicus – the machine-men – so they can train them to be workers in the manufactoriums, the big dangerous making-places. But I won't let them do it, my baby boy. I won't let them take you. No matter what happens, you can always know your Ma will keep you safe.'*

His heart growing heavy, Boy remembered other things
as well. He remembered the sound of thunder rolling
across the ground above their heads one night while they
crouched huddled in the cellar. He remembered the cave-
in and his mother's body lying crushed among the rubble.
He remembered her eyes staring at him, cold and dead
from a face covered in a thick layer of dust. He remembered crying for hours, scared and lonely, not
understanding how it was she could have left him. Then,
his own eyes stinging wetly at the corners, Boy found he
didn't want to have anything more to do with remembering for a while.

Sucking a breath of air and rubbing the back of his hand
across his face to clear his eyes, Boy decided it was time to
head back to his warren and get to eating Brother Rat. Too
smart to just head there directly in case anyone was looking, he took the long way, cutting a twisting path through
the maze of shattered buildings and mounds of rubble all
around him. Then, as he crossed near the summit of one
of the mounds, he noticed something that gave him pause.
A smell, almost. Something gathering on the wind…

For a moment, feeling a sudden chill at the base of his
spine, Boy stood looking out toward the east. Before him
the city seemed quiet, its deserted streets appearing every
bit as dead and lifeless as the ruined burnt-out buildings
that surrounded them on every turn. Boy was not fooled.
After three something years living alone among the rubble
now he had developed a sixth sense when it came to the
city and its ways. A sense that, right here and now, told him
he had best be wary.

*Oughta be getting myself back underground and staying there
a while,* he thought as he finally turned to make for home.
*There's trouble brewing: the wind says it clear and loud. A bad
day is coming, and like as not a lots of peoples is gonna die…*

* * *

'WHAT WAS LIFE like where you were born?' Larn asked Bulaven, lifting another shovelful of earth onto the blade of his entrenching tool as the big man stood beside him. 'On your homeworld, I mean?'

'On Vardan?' Bulaven said, pausing in his work long enough to wipe the sweat from his chapped brow before it could freeze. 'It was good enough I suppose, new fish. Certainly, there are a lot of worse planets a man could be from.'

They were standing in the trench with shovels in their hands, Davir and Scholar beside them while Zeebers stood on the firing step on watch, trying to repair the damage done to the trench in the course of the shelling. Returning to their trench in the aftermath of the bombardment, the fireteam had arrived to find the explosion of a nearby shell had caused part of the trench's rear wall to collapse, half-burying the trench interior in clods of frozen earth. Now, after half an hour of backbreaking labour the trench floor was mostly cleared, the excess earth having been piled out of the way into another corner of the trench.

'Personally, I would say you are doing our homeworld a grave disservice, Bulaven,' Davir said, sitting on the end of his shovel and watching them as they moved the last of the fallen earth. 'Frankly, my own recollections suggest Vardan was every bit as much a stinking hell-hole as Broucheroc. Granted, we didn't have all these orks to contend with there. I'm sure I don't remember having to do so much digging back home though.'

'I don't seem to have noticed you doing too much digging here either,' Bulaven said. 'Most of the time in fact you have been standing there and leaving all the work to others.'

'Phah. It is a simply a matter of maintaining a proper division of labour,' Davir said. 'Each man performs the task to which he is best suited. Which, in this case,

means that you, Scholar, and the new fish do the don-
keywork while I oversee your labours in a supervisory
capacity. Besides, someone must watch to make sure the
new fish can tell one end of a spade from the other.'

'Not to mention your vital role in keeping us all
warm,' Larn said, so annoyed now at the ugly dwarf's
constant insults that he found himself responding in
kind without even thinking. 'Emperor knows, if it
wasn't for all your hot air spewing about this trench we
might have frozen to death long ago.'

For a moment, shocked at his response, the others
looked at him in silence. Then, abruptly, Scholar and
Bulaven broke into surprised laughter. Even Davir's face
briefly cracked into a grudging smile. Only Zeebers
seemed unmoved, scowling down at Larn from the firing step with the same hostile expressions he always
wore.

'Hah! Hot air!' Bulaven said, laughing. 'That's a good
one. The new fish may not have been here very long,
Davir, but you have to admit he got your number fast
enough!'

'Yar, yar, yar. Keep on laughing, pigbrain,' Davir said,
his gruff demeanour abruptly restored as he turned to
look at Larn in tight-lipped derision. 'So, it seems our
little puppy has claws. Very good, new fish. Well done.
You made a joke. Ha, ha, you are very funny. But don't
let your head get too big now. The orks like nothing better than to see a new fish with a big head. It gives them
more of a target to aim at.'

THE REPAIRS CONTINUED. Having finally cleared the
trench of earth, they laid down their shovels. Then, as
Larn watched them, Bulaven and Scholar picked up an
oblong sheet of metal lying across the trench floor and
pressed it against the ragged hole in the trench wall,
holding upright it as Davir took a wooden prop and

used his shovel to hammer the prop in place to keep the sheet in position.

'There,' Davir said, checking the hole was fully covered and putting his weight against the prop to make sure it was tight. 'That should hold it long enough for us to finish the repairs.'

'What now?' Larn asked. 'We have cleared the floor. How do we repair the hole itself?'

'How?' said Davir. 'Well, first thing, you pick up your shovel again, new fish. You see that pile of earth over there?' he said, pointing towards the clods of frozen earth they had already moved over to the corner of the trench. 'The pile you just moved? Well now, you take your shovel and move it back over here. Then, you use it to fill in the original hole. I know, I know, you needn't say it. With all this endless excitement, who can believe that anyone ever told you that life in the Guard might be boring?'

'I DON'T UNDERSTAND how this is supposed to work,' Larn said later, his hands blistered through his gloves and his back aching from using the shovel as they refilled the hole in the trench wall with soil. 'Even after we have filled the hole in, won't the wall just collapsed again the moment we take the prop away?'

'We don't take the prop away, new fish,' Bulaven said, shovelling beside him. 'Not at first, anyway. First, we fill in the hole. Next, we wet the soil. Then, we tamp it all down and leave it to freeze for a while. Then, after a couple of hours, we finally remove the prop and the wall will be as good as new. Trust me, new fish, it always works. You wouldn't believe how many times we've had to repair this trench since we first dug it.'

'Wet it?' Larn asked. 'Don't we need a bucket then to fetch more water? We haven't got much left in our canteens.'

'Bucket? Canteens?' Bulaven said, pausing in his labours to look at Larn with raised eyebrows. 'We are repairing a trench wall, new fish. We don't use *drinking* water for that.'

'But then, what do we use?' Larn asked, beginning to feel foolish as he realised the others were smirking at him.

'What do we use, he says,' Davir said, rolling his eyes towards the heavens. 'My broad Vardan backside. I swear, new fish, just when I was starting to think you might not be a total idiot you say something stupid and ruin my good opinion of you. If it helps you to answer your question, here are a couple of hints. One, it is always better to use warm water when repairing trench walls in frozen conditions. Two, every human being carries a ready supply of the stuff in question about their person.'

'Warm?' said Larn, a new understanding slowly dawning on him. 'You mean we…'

'Ah, finally, he understands,' Davir said. 'Yes, that's right, new fish. And guess what? It's your turn first. Now, get up there and start pissing. I only hope to hell you haven't got a nervous bladder. Emperor knows, I have better things to do with my time than standing around here waiting for you to piss.'

'WHAT ABOUT YOUR own world then, new fish?' Bulaven asked afterwards, as they sat in the trench waiting for the newly repaired wall to freeze. 'You asked me about Vardan before. What was your own homeworld like?'

Trying to think of an answer, for a moment Larn was quiet. He thought about his parents' farm, the endless golden wheatfields swaying in the breeze. He thought of his family, all of them sitting at their places around the table in the kitchen as they made ready for their evening meal. He thought of that last beautiful sunset, the sky reddening as the fiery orb of the descending sun fell slowly towards the horizon. He thought of the world he had left behind, and of all the things he would never see again.

It all seems so long ago and far away now, he thought. *As though all those things were a million kilometres away from me. The sad thing is they are even farther away than that. Not just a million, but millions of millions of kilometres; however far it was we came in that troopship.*

'I don't know,' he said at last, unable to find the words to say what he really felt. 'It was different anyway. A lot different from this place.'

'Hnn. I think our new fish is starting to feel homesick,' Davir said. 'Not that I blame him, you understand, any place would seem rosy when compared to this damn stinkhole. You find me in a strangely magnanimous mood however, new fish, so let me give you a piece of advice. Whatever wistful longings you may harbour for the world of your birth, forget them. This is Broucheroc. There is no room for sentiment here. Here, a man must keep himself hard and tight if we wants to live to see tomorrow.'

'Is that it then?' Larn asked. 'I remember Scholar told me you were all that had survived from over six thousand men. Is that how you did it? By keeping yourselves hard and tight?'

'Ah, now there you have touched upon an interesting question, new fish' Scholar said. 'How was it we survived when so many of our fellows didn't? You can be sure it is a regular topic of conversation hereabouts. Each man has his own opinions. Some say that to have managed to live so long in Broucheroc at all, we must have been born survivors to begin with. Others say it must have been a combination of fate and good judgement, or perhaps only a matter of poor dumb luck. As I say, everyone has their own opinions. Their own theories. For myself, I am not sure I put much store in any of them. We survived where others died. That is all I can tell you.'

'I always thought the Emperor must have had a hand in it,' Bulaven said, his expression quiet and thoughtful. 'That perhaps He was saving us for some greater purpose. At least, that is what I used to believe. After so many years in Broucheroc, a man begins to wonder.'

'The Emperor?' Davir said, throwing his hands up in a gesture of frustration. 'Really, this time you have excelled yourself, Bulaven. Of all the lumpen-headed stupidities I have heard pouring from your mouth over the last seventeen years since we were inducted into the Guard, that is without a doubt the most idiotic. The Emperor! Phah! You think the Emperor has nothing better to do than watch over your fat backside and make sure it comes to no harm? Wake up, you big pile of horse manure. The Emperor doesn't even know we exist. And, if he does know, he doesn't care.'

'No!' Larn shouted, the sudden loudness of his voice in the trench startling them. 'You are wrong. You don't know what you're talking about!' Then, seeing the others looking at him in bewilderment, Larn began to speak again. More quietly now, the words spilling heartfelt from his mouth.

'I am sorry,' he said. 'I didn't mean to yell. But I heard what you were saying and… You are wrong, Davir. The Emperor does care. He watches over all of us. I know he does. And I can prove it. If the Emperor wasn't good and kind and just, he never would have saved my great-grandfather's life.'

And then, as about him the others sat quietly in the trench and listened, Larn told them the same tale his father had told him in the farmhouse cellar on his last night at home.

* * *

HE TOLD THEM about his great-grandfather. About how his name was Augustus and he had been born on a world called Arcadus V. He told them about his being called into the Guard, and how sad he had felt at leaving his homeworld. He told them about the thirty years of service and his great-grandfather's failing health. He told them about the lottery and the man who had given up his ticket. He told them it was a miracle. A quiet miracle, perhaps. But, a miracle all the same. Then, when he had told them all these things word for word the same as his father had told him, Larn fell quiet and waited to hear their reaction.

'And that is it?' Davir said, the first to speak after what felt to Larn like an age of silence. 'That is the proof you talked about? This tale your father told you?'

'It is an interesting story, new fish,' Scholar said, his expression ill at ease.

'Hah! Story is right,' Zeebers said, looking sarcastically down at Larn from up on the firing step. 'A fairy story, like parents tell their children to make them sleep. You believe that crap, new fish, maybe you should go tell your story to the orks and see if a miracle saves you then.'

'Shut up, Zeebers!' Bulaven snapped. 'You're supposed to be on watch, not flapping your lips about. And it is not as though anyone asked for your opinion. Leave the new fish alone.' Then, seeing he had cowed Zeebers to silence, Bulaven turned towards Larn again. 'Scholar was right, new fish. It was a very interesting story, and you told it well.'

'Is that all you are going to say?' Larn asked, surprised. 'You all sound like you think something is wrong. As though you don't believe what I just told you.'

'We don't believe it, new fish,' Davir was blunt. 'Granted, Scholar and Bulaven are trying to be soothing about it. But they don't believe it either. None of us do.

Frankly, if the story you just told us is what passes your benchmark for a miracle, you are even more of an innocent than you look.'

'I would have expected you to say that Davir,' Larn said. 'You don't believe in anything. But what about the rest of you? Scholar? Bulaven? Surely you can see that what happened to my great-grandfather was a miracle? That it is proof that the Emperor watches out for us?'

'It is not a matter of believing you,' Scholar said, lifting his shoulders in a helpless shrug. 'It is just that even if we accept the details of your story are true, new fish, those same details are open to a variety of interpretations.'

'Interpretations?' Larn said. 'What are you talking about?

'He is saying you are being naive, new fish,' Davir said. 'Oh, he's doing it in that scholarly way of his, of course – just tip-toeing around the subject rather than coming right out and saying what is on his mind directly. But he thinks you are naive. We all do.'

'You have to understand our experience of life makes us see these things differently,' Scholar said.

'But how is there any different way to see it?' Larn said. 'You heard the story. What about the man giving my great-grandfather his ticket? Surely you can see that must have been the hand of the Emperor at work?'

'Far be it for me to shatter your illusions, new fish,' Davir said. 'But I doubt the hand of the Emperor had anything to do with it. No, likely the only hands involved in it at all would have belonged to your great-grandfather.'

'I… What do you mean?'

'He killed him, new fish,' Davir said. 'The man with the ticket. Your great-grandfather killed him and took his ticket from him. That's your miracle.'

'No,' Larn said, looking quietly from face to face in disbelief. 'You are wrong.'

'Course I can see how it could have happened,' Davir said. 'There's your great-grandfather. He's sick. Ailing. He knows winning the lottery is his only chance of making it out of the Guard alive. Then, when someone else gets the winning ticket, he realises only that one man's life stands between him and freedom. And he was a soldier. He'd killed before. *What is one more life in the grand scale of things*, he tells himself. It's a dog-eat-dog universe, new fish, and it sounds like your great-grand-father was a dirtier dog than most.'

'No,' Larn said. 'You're not listening to me. I'm telling you, you're wrong about this. You are sick, Davir. How could you even think something like that?'

'It is the name, new fish,' Scholar said sadly. 'Or the lack of one, I mean.'

'Yes, the name,' Davir said. 'That's what clinches it.'

'What are you... I don't understand...'

'They're talking about the name of the man who gave your great-grandfather the ticket, new fish,' Bulaven said with a sigh. 'It wasn't part of the story. And you must be able to see that makes all the difference? I am sorry to tell you this, but that is what proves your great-grandfather killed him.'

'The name?' Larn was floundering now, his stomach churning, his head dizzying as though the world about him had suddenly begun to turn strangely on its axis.

'Think about it, new fish,' Davir said. 'This man is sup-posed to have saved your great-grandfather's life. Your great-grandfather must have known his name. He was a comrade of his, remember? A man who had fought side-by-side with him through thirty years in the Guard? And yet, years later, when your great-grandfather tells the tale to his son he somehow neglects to even mention the name of the man who saved his life? It doesn't add up, new fish. Especially considering you told us your great-grandfather was a pious man. A man like that, if somebody does them a good turn they remember them in their prayers to the Emperor for the rest of their life.'

'It does have the ring of a guilty conscience about it, new fish,' Scholar said. 'Though, if it is any consolation to you, it also suggests your great-grandfather was not given easily to murder. If he'd been a more cold-blooded man, presumably he'd have just told his son the man's name and thought no more about it.'

'Not really, Scholar,' Davir said. 'Even though years had passed by then, he could've still been worried about his crime being found out. Maybe he thought it was better to let bad dogs lie, and never mention the name ever. Either way, it doesn't really make any difference. Your great-grandfather killed the man, new fish, and stole his ticket. That's all there is to it. So much for miracles.'

'No. You've got it wrong,' Larn said. 'There must be another explanation. One you haven't thought of. Surely you can see that my great-grandfather wouldn't have done anything like that?' But as Larn looked at them it was clear to him that was exactly what they did believe. Davir, Scholar, Bulaven, Zeebers. All of them. Looking at the faces of each man in the trench, Larn could see their minds were made up. There had been no miracle. No example of the Emperor's grace. To them, it was a simple matter. His great-grandfather had killed a man, then lied about it afterwards.

'No,' Larn said at last, hating how weak his voice sounded and way it wavered. 'No. You are wrong. You are wrong and I don't believe you.'

CHAPTER TWELVE

18:58 hours Central Broucheroc Time

SECTOR COMMAND AND THE PORTENTS OF A COMING
STORM – LARN SULKS – DAVIR AT LAST FINDS A REASON TO
BE CHEERFUL – MEAL TIME IN BARRACKS DUGOUT ONE –
THE CULINARY ARTS AS ACCORDING TO TROOPER SKENCH
– A DISCUSSION AS TO THE ADVANTAGES OF ARTILLERY IN
THE HUNTING OF BIG LIZARDS

'HERE ARE THE raw contact reports for the last half-hour,
sir,' Sergeant Valtys said, holding out a sheaf of papers as
thick as his thumb in his outstretched hand. 'You said
you wanted to see them immediately, before they were
collated.'

Sitting at his desk in his small office at Sector Command Beta (Eastern Divisions, Sectors 1-10 to 1-20),
Colonel Kallad Drezlen turned to take the papers from
Valtys and begin to read them. *There must be two hundred
reports here at least,* he thought. *Each one recording a sep-
arate incident of contact with the enemy. Two hundred, when*

usually at this time of day we would expect to get no more than eighty or so in an hour. It looks like the orks are getting restless hereabouts and that is never a good sign. Something must be coming.

'How bad is it, Jaak?' he asked, raising his eyes from the reports to look at the sergeant.

'Bad enough, sir,' Valtys replied, still standing ramrod-straight beside the colonel's desk as though he thought he was on a parade ground muster. 'Five of our sectors report coming under heavy shellfire from the orks. Another two report incidents of massed assaults. Then, we have received something like a hundred different reports from across all sectors of contacts ranging from raiding parties to an increase in the number of gretch snipers and scouts in no-man's land. Looks like there's a real shitstorm brewing, colonel, if you pardon my language.'

'Hhh. You are pardoned, Jaak,' Drezlen said, looking up at the non-com's grizzled face with a quiet amusement born of long familiarity with his ways. 'What about Sector Commands Alpha and Gamma? Are they having the same problem with flying faeces?'

'No and I have to admit that's what put the wind up me, sir. Our neighbouring Sector Commands say they're having a quiet time of it. Too quiet, if you ask me.'

'As though the orks were planning something, you mean?' Drezlen said, his face serious now as he gave voice to the thought hanging communally in the air between them. 'Concentrating their forces here, as though they are about to launch a major offensive?'

'Yes, sir. Course, I know that's not supposed to happen. I know General HQ say the orks aren't smart enough to coordinate something like that. But I've got a metal pin in me, holding my left knee together from the time an ork shot blew a fist-sized hole in it. Ever since I got it, that pin has always started itching whenever the

orks were up to something. And right now it's itching
worse than a red-arsed monkey that's been sitting in a
mound of firebugs.'

'I know what you mean, Jaak,' Drezlen said. 'My gut's
the same way. All the same, I wouldn't want to go to
General Pronan asking him to order an alert based on
the combined evidence of your pin and my digestion.
I'll need something a bit weightier than that. Get me the
collated statistics and summaries for these contact
reports ASAP. Then, I'll go see the general and see if we
can get him to take some action.'

'Begging your pardon, sir, but the general's not on
site. He still hasn't returned from the Staff Briefing at
General HQ.'

'Spectacular,' Drezlen said, sighing in irritation. 'The
one time we really need the old man he's off enjoying
flatcakes and recaf with Grand Marshal Kerchan. All
right, then. Looks like I'll have to be the one to put my
head in the cudbear's mouth. Get comms to vox General HQ. Tell them Colonel Drezlen wants to put
Sectors 1-10 through to 1-20 on Alert Condition Red.'

'YOU SHOULD TRY not to take it so much to heart, new
fish,' Bulaven had said, going over to join Larn as he sat
alone in a corner of the trench. 'So, your great-grandfather
killed a man and stole his ticket. What of it? It hardly
matters now, does it? It was a long time ago, after all,
and anyone it might have been important to is long
dead by now.'

'It is not as though we meant anything by it, new fish,'
Bulaven had said then, once it had become clear Larn
was not going to answer him. 'We were just talking is all.
You have to find some way of passing the time in the
trenches. So, sometimes we tell stories and afterwards
everyone gives their opinion. You have to understand it
is nothing personal.'

'Granted, maybe we should not have been so forth-right,' Bulaven had said next, while Larn stared fixedly ahead and refused to look at him. 'Your story was important to you, I can see that now. We should have been kinder perhaps.'

'Perhaps you are right, new fish,' Bulaven had said at last. 'Perhaps it was a miracle and we are all full of manure. I am not a preacher. I don't know about such things. But really, new fish, it is making your own life hard on yourself if you just keep sitting there in silence.'

'Ach, leave him, Bulaven,' Davir had said. 'All your feeble-fabbling around the new fish is giving me a headache. If he wants to sulk, let him. Emperor knows, it'll be a damn sight more quiet around here without all his stupid questions.'

TIME PASSED. SITTING alone in his corner of the trench while Zeebers stood on watch and the others played cards, Larn found the heat of his anger had slowly cooled. With it, he became gradually aware of other things, sensations that until then had been masked from him by the intensity of the emotions boiling within him ever since the Vardans had defamed his great-grandfather's memory and ridiculed his story of the miracle.

Emperor's tears, but it is cold, Larn thought, suddenly realising he had been sitting in the same spot so long his backside had gone to sleep. Just as he was about to stand and stretch, to move about in the trench in the hope of getting his circulation working, some lingering residue of his anger stopped him.

If I get up and move now the others will think I have for-given them, he thought, hating how childish the thought made him feel and yet at the same time helpless to resist it. *It would be like giving in,* he thought. *Like I was admit-ting I believed all the nonsense they talked before about my great-grandfather stealing the ticket.* Then, his anger re-igniting at the thought the others might think him weak, he resolved to sit where he was in silence a while longer.

Of course it doesn't really matter what they think, he thought after some further time had passed. *It doesn't matter if they think I have given in. It doesn't matter whether they think my great-grandfather stole the ticket or murdered anyone. All that matters is that I know those things aren't true. So long as I know that, they can believe whatever they like.* Still, he was not content. Something deep inside him refused to let him move.

They have all been in this place too long, he thought at last. *That's what it is. That is why they see dark motives in everything and can't accept the fact of miracles. Really, it is not even a matter of forgiving them. I should feel sorry for them. Not angry.*

Then, just as he had all but finally summoned the will to swallow his pride and move, Larn heard the sound of a shrill whistle that seemed to come from the direction of the dugouts.

'Ach, at last,' Davir said, as around him the other men began to stand and collect their weapons. 'It's about time. I have been getting so hungry sitting here I was beginning to think about eating Scholar's boots.'

'Really?' said Scholar mildly, checking to see if he still had his book with him. 'And there was perhaps some special reasons you were considering eating my boots rather than your own, Davir?'

'What, you think I should eat my own boots and risk getting frostbite?' Davir said. 'No thank you, Scholar. Besides, you have such big feet there would be plenty of boot to go around. Happily though, we seem to have averted that particular catastrophe. Time to get to the barracks and see what culinary pleasures are awaiting us.'

'Come on then, new fish,' Bulaven said, standing over Larn. 'If you are last to the mess line there won't be much left for you.'

'You mean it is meal time?' Larn asked.

'A meal, yes,' Bulaven said. 'And a two-hour rest-period as well. They rotate us off the line in groups of ten fireteams at a time. One whistle means it is Barracks Dugout One's turn. Our turn. Now, come on, new fish. The food will be getting cold.'

'Yes, come on, new fish,' Davir said. 'Believe me, you think your day has been bad enough so far? Well, you haven't tasted Trooper Skench's cooking yet.'

AFTER SO LONG in the cold of the trench, the interior of Barracks Dugout One seemed warm and inviting to him now. So inviting, in fact, that Larn found he barely even noticed the stifling stench of smoke and stale sweat that permeated the air of the dugout. Inside, a line of Guardsmen had already formed up by the time they arrived. Waiting, with mess tins in their hands, as a lanky rat-faced Vardan trooper with only one arm dolefully served out portions of gruel from a battered and gigantic pot from on top of the stove.

'Ah, the inestimable Skench,' Davir purred as he reached the head of the line. 'Tell me, good friend Skench – what delightful delicacy are you attempting to poison us with today?'

'Hhh. It's gruel, Davir,' Skench said sourly. 'Why? What does it look like?'

'Between you and me, I wasn't entirely sure,' Davir said as he watched Skench ladle a steaming dollop into his mess tin. 'Gruel, you say? And you have followed your normal recipe, I take it? Sawdust, spittle, and whatever dubious organic refuse you could lay your hands on?'

'Pretty much,' said Skench, humourlessly. 'Though you can be sure I made certain you got an extra helping of spit in yours.'

'Why thank you, Skench,' Davir said, favouring the one-armed cook with his most irritating smile. 'Really, you are spoiling me. I must remember to write to Grand Marshal Kerchan and recommend you for a commendation. If you got a nice medal it would give you something extra to put in the soup.'

'Hhh. Always the funny man, Davir,' Skench muttered, watching Davir walk away. Then, turning back to see Larn standing next in line, he squinted at him in wary hostility.

'I haven't seen you before,' Skench said. 'You a new fish?'

'Yes,' said Larn.

'Uh-huh. You got something funny to say about my cooking, new fish?'

'Umm... no.'

'Good,' Skench said, dropping a ladleful of greasy brown gruel into Larn's tin, then nodding towards a pile of ration bars lying on a nearby table. 'Make sure you keep it that way. As well as the gruel you get to take a ration bar. *One* bar, mind, new fish. I've counted them, so don't try taking two. Oh, and if tonight you should have the runs, don't do what the rest of them do and come round here blaming me. There ain't nothing wrong with my cooking. We clear on that?'

'Uhh... yes. We're clear.'

'Good. Then get moving, new fish. You're holding up the line. And remember what I told you. There ain't nothing wrong with my cooking.'

'This is disgusting,' Larn said. 'Really disgusting, I mean. I thought the food they gave us in basic training on Jumael was bad enough. But this is ten times worse.'

'Well, I did warn you, new fish,' Davir said, as he shovelled another spoonful of gruel into his own mouth. 'Such is Skench's extraordinary mastery of the culinary arts, he can make bad food taste even worse.'

Having collected his ration bar, Larn now sat with Davir, Bulaven and Scholar among the bunks inside the barracks. Meanwhile, still occasionally glowering at Larn as though to assure him his feelings of hostility had not waned, Zeebers sat alone and apart from them against one of the dugout walls. Though, while he still wondered at the source of Zeebers's strange antagonism towards him, Larn found he was more directly concerned at that moment with the small white shape he saw wriggling among the slop in his mess tin.

'There is some kind of maggot in my food,' he said.

'A Tullan's worm-grub,' Scholar said. 'They are quite plentiful hereabouts, new fish. And an excellent source of protein.'

'They add to the flavour as well,' Bulaven said. 'But make sure you chew up your food properly. If the grub is still alive when you swallow it they can lay eggs in your stomach.'

'Eggs?'

'Don't worry about it, new fish,' Bulaven replied. 'It's not as bad as it sounds. Gives you the runs for a couple of days, that is all. Course, if Skench cooked them properly, the grubs would be dead by the time they got to us.'

'Sweet Emperor, I can't believe you act like it is normal to eat things like this,' Larn said.

'Normal?' Davir said, mouth open to reveal a mashed lump of half-chewed gruel. 'In case you hadn't notice you're in the Imperial Guard, new fish. And in the Guard you eat what you can get. Anyway, you think this is bad you should've seen the whipsaw grubs we had to eat on Bandar Majoris.'

'Actually, I seem to remember they were quite flavour-some, Davir,' Scholar said. 'Tasted a bit like ginny fowl.'

'I'm not talking about how they tasted, Scholar,' Davir said. 'I'm talking about the fact they were as big as your leg with a metre-long tongue covered in razor-sharp barbs. Not to mention they were strong enough to tear a man's arm off. And if you want know *how* we know that, new fish, just go ask Skench.'

'Don't listen to him. He is just fooling with you, new fish,' Bulaven said. 'It was an ork axe that did for Skench's arm right here in Broucheroc, not a whipsaw grub on Bandar Majoris. Though we did lose a lot of men to those grubs.'

'Do you remember Commissar Grisz?' Scholar said. 'Went behind a bush one morning to see to his daily bowel movement only to find he was squatting over a whole nest of the damned things. You could have heard his scream halfway across the planet.'

'Phah. Good riddance to bad rubbish,' Davir said. 'Grisz always was a pain in the arse. No pun intended.'

'You ask me,' Bulaven said, 'the thing I remember most from Bandar is Davir hunting the terranosaurs.'

'Ah yes,' Scholar said. 'You mean the wager.'

'Ach, you're not still going on about that, Bulaven,' Davir scowled. 'Emperor wept. Once a man wins a bet against you, you never forgive him.'

'You should have seen it, new fish,' Bulaven said, smiling. 'We'd been on Bandar a week maybe, at most. It is a jungle planet and there were these deathworlders. Ach, you tell it, Scholar – you always do a better job of it than me.'

'All right, then,' Scholar said, leaning intently forward. 'Imagine the scene, new fish. It is midday; the jungle is hot and humid. We have come back into camp after being out on patrol when we smell the most delicious and mouth-watering aroma. Following our noses we find a group of Catachans are roasting a metre-and-a-half long two-legged lizard on an open spit. Naturally, we enquire whether we can join in their feast. But, being Catachans, they refuse. "Go catch your own terranosaur," they say. Now, you thought that would have been the end of it. But Davir refuses to let matters rest. Soon, he begins bragging to us that he is more than capable of capturing a terranosaur just as the Catachans had. And, before you could say *small man, big mouth* we have agreed to enter into a wager with him on the matter.'

'He bet us he could hunt down a terranosaur, new fish,' Bulaven jumped in excitedly. 'He bet us a hundred credits he could hunt one, kill it, and bring it home for dinner.'

'So,' Scholar continued, 'armed with a lasgun, our intrepid, if diminutive, hunter goes alone into the jungle in search of his prey. Only to re-emerge two hours later, running back into camp in a panic as though he had a daemon on his trail!'

'Ach, you and Bulaven can laugh all you like,' Davir said, holding a hand high above his head like a fisherman describing the size of his catch. 'But nobody told me the one the Catchans killed was only a baby, and that the adults were ten metres tall when full-grown. Or, for that matter, that they hunted in packs. I tell you: I only got out of that damn stinking jungle by the skin of my teeth. And, besides, you have to admit I did what I said I'd do in the end. I did kill a terranosaur and I did bring it home for dinner. About three of them, in fact.'

'Only because you bribed someone in comms to let you call in an artillery strike against them!' Bulaven said, outraged. 'Then, after the batteries had been pounding that patch of jungle for an hour straight, you got a search party together and brought back the remains of all the terranosaurs that had been killed by the shellfire. That doesn't count, Davir.'

'Of course, it counts. What, you think I should have dug a pit trap like some idiot deathworlder and waited for one of the big dumb beasts to wander by and fall into it? I keep telling you, Bulaven: you should have been more specific about the conditions of the bet. You didn't say anything about not being able to use artillery.'

The argument continued: Davir and Bulaven squabbling comically about the details of the decade-old bet while Scholar attempted to act as arbiter. As he listened to them, Larn became aware of how different the three men's manner had become since the whistle had blown and they had come to the dugout. Here, they did not seem as gruff and intimidating. They seemed more relaxed. More at ease with themselves and their surroundings.

Looking around, Larn saw it was the same everywhere. All about him he could see Vardans talking, joking and laughing amongst themselves, their faces animated, their gestures more free and expansive. It was almost as though here in the dugout, for the moment at least, there were no orks. No constant threat of death. No Broucheroc. Here, the Vardans seemed almost like the people Larn had known back home. As though, momentarily released of the shadow of war and horror, they had reverted to their true selves.

As he watched them, Larn began to understand for the first time that each of the Vardans had once been like him. Each of them had been a green recruit. Each of them had once been a new fish and he realised there was hope for him in that thought. If each of these men had somehow learned how to survive the brutalities and privations of this place, then so could he. He would learn. And he would survive.

And then, comforted by that warm and happy thought, before he even knew it, Larn was asleep.

CHAPTER THIRTEEN

20:01 hours Central Broucheroc Time

A Mosaic Coloured in Blues, Greens, and Reds – A
Dream of Home – A Bombardment Again – Zeebers's
Behaviour is Perhaps Explained – Sergeant Chelkar
Rallies the Troops – The Myth of The Big Push

'You ordered us to Alert Condition Red!' the general
roared, his voice so loud that the Guardsmen and
militia auxiliaries seated at their work stations
around them in the Situation Room gave a collective
jump. 'Have you taken leave of your senses?'

'If you would allow me to explain, sir,' Colonel Drezlen said, his expression tight as he stood facing the
older man, fighting visibly to keep his own temper in
check.

'Explain?' General Pronan thundered. 'What is
there to explain? You have grossly exceeded your
authority, colonel. I could have you court-martialled
for this.'

'I had no choice, sir,' Drezlen said. 'We were faced
with an emerging situation, and you were elsewhere–'

'Don't try and lay the blame for this debacle at my
door, Drezlen.' The general's cheeks grew florid with
rage. 'You will only end up making matters worse for
yourself, you hear me? I know very well I was away
from Sector Command. I was at General Headquarters, where fortunately I was made aware of your alert
order in time to quash it before all hell could let
loose.'

'You... *quashed* it?' Drezlen said, appalled. 'You
countermanded the alert?'

'Of course I did. Have you any idea of the fuss an
alert order can cause? Troops are seconded from other
sectors all across the city; extra supplies are sent up;
reserve units are brought forward to the front. Sweet
Emperor, man! Don't you know a sector has to be on
the verge of being overrun before an order to go to
Alert Condition Red is warranted? Never mind the fact
that, by issuing an alert on your own authority, you
violated the chain of command!'

'You countermanded the alert,' Drezlen said quietly,
his face ashen. 'I can't believe it...'

'Yes. And by doing it I likely saved you from a firing
squad,' the volume of the general's voice had fallen,
his manner growing more composed as his anger
abated. 'But you can thank me for that later, Drezlen.
First, I want you to start giving me some answers.'

'Answers?' Drezlen was curt. 'Very well, general. Let
me give you all the answers you could want.' He
turned towards a nearby Guardsman seated beside a
control panel covered in dials and switches. 'Corporal
Venner? Activate the pict-display and bring up the current situation map for our sectors. Let us see if we can
show the general exactly why I believed we had
reached Alert Condition Red status.'

At the flick of a switch the large rectangular pict-display set into one of the Situation Room's walls suddenly hummed into life, a small white dot appearing in the middle of the black screen before expanding to cover its entire surface. Then, as Corporal Venner worked another series of switches, the situation map for Sectors 1-10 through 1-20 appeared on screen. A mosaic coloured in blues, greens, and reds: blue for the areas under Imperial control; green for the parts held by the orks; red for the territories whose ownership was currently being contested.

'I don't understand,' the general said, looking up at the pict-display in confusion. 'I don't remember seeing all this red on the board when I left for General Headquarters this morning.'

'Matters have developed considerably since then, general,' Drezlen said. 'As of fifteen minutes ago no less than *ten* of the eleven sectors under your command are currently being attacked by the orks. In each case, the pattern is the same: massed assaults preceded by lengthy bombardment by enemy artillery, as well as coordinated attacks on vital facilities by gretchin suicide bombers and ork troops. Currently, it is unclear how many of these assaults are the real thing and how many are intended only as diversions to put pressure on our resources.'

'Diversions? Lengthy bombardments? Coordinated attacks?' the general's expression was incredulous. 'Have you lost your mind, man? You're talking as though the enemy were working to some kind of coherent plan of action. For the Emperor's sake, these are orks we are talking about! They don't have the brains or organisational ability to put anything like that in motion.'

'Be that as it may, sir, it appears that is *precisely* what they are doing. So far, we are holding on by our fingernails. But if you want to see just how *bad* things here could get, take a look at Sector 1-13.'

'1-13?' the general said. 'What are you talking about Drezlen? The situation map says Sector 1-13 is blue.'

'Yes, sir. And what is more, it is the only sector that has yet to be attacked. And I ask you, leaving aside for a moment the fact that our enemies are orks, what does that suggest to you?'

'You don't mean?' the general blustered. 'But that is impossible, colonel…'

'Ordinarily I would agree, sir. But there seems to be a pattern here. And, given that pattern, we have to ask why would the orks launch a major offensive against every sector to the side of it and leave Sector 1-13 unmolested? Unless what we are seeing on the situation map are only the opening moves of a larger assault intended to tie up our forces and allow the orks a clear run at their *real* target. Imagine it, general: if the orks were to launch a full-scale assault on Sector 1-13 now, there would be precious little we could do to stop them achieving a sector-wide breakthrough.'

'But if that happened, our forces in other sectors would have to retreat or risk being cut off. It could turn into a rout. No. It is just not possible, Drezlen. They are orks. Savages. They are not clever enough to have…'

For a moment, turning to gaze intently at the pict-display before him the general fell quiet. Watching the old man's troubled face as he silently wrestled with all he had heard, Colonel Drezlen felt a sudden sympathy for him. General Pronan was an old school solider, thoroughly indoctrinated by his forty years in the Guard in the belief that all aliens were little better than animals. The idea he might have been outmanoeuvred by them, and by orks for that matter, would be hard for him to swallow but it was a matter of evidence. Slowly, Drezlen saw a grim look of resolve come over the general's face. He had made his decision.

'All right, then' the general said at last. 'Let us assume for the sake of argument your theory is correct. Can we reinforce Sector 1-13?'

'No, sir. As I say, all our forces are tied up fighting off the orks in other sectors.'

'What about our forces already inside Sector 1-13? Who do we have stationed there?'

'Company Alpha, the 902nd Vardan Rifles, commanded by Sergeant Eugin Chelkar.'

'A single company?' the general's voice was a dry whisper. 'Commanded by a sergeant? That's all we have? But, Holy Throne, if you are right and the attack comes–'

'Yes, sir,' Colonel Drezlen said. 'If that happens, then two hundred and something Guardsmen are all that stands between us and this entire map going green.'

HE DREAMED OF home. He dreamed of spring: the earth of the fields wet and rich as the seeds were planted. He dreamed of summer: the sky blue and endless overhead as rows of golden wheat grew ripe below it. He dreamed of autumn: the same sky now thick with lazy smoke from the burning of the stubble after the harvesting was done. He dreamed of winter: the fields dizzyingly empty, the ground hard with frost. He dreamed, his dreams a jumbled montage of people, places, memories, recollections.

He dreamed of home.

He dreamed of the days of his youth. Of the change of the seasons. Of happiness, peace and contentment.

And then, he awoke to hell once more.

STARTING AWAKE AT the sound of an explosion overheard, for an instant Larn had no idea where he was. Gazing blearily about him in confusion, he recognised the dugout and realised he must have fallen asleep on one of the bunks while the others were talking. Then, he heard another explosion much louder than the first and looked up to see a thin trickle of soil fall downwards through the gap between two of the wooden planks that made up the dugout's inner ceiling.

'That was a close one,' he heard Bulaven's voice say calmly. 'I wouldn't like to be above ground in the middle of this one.'

Becoming fully awake, Larn realised he had inadvertently fallen asleep on top of his mess tin. Wiping away a chunk of congealed gruel that had stuck to his uniform, he turned to see the Vardans were still gathered nearby. Bulaven sat in one bunk rubbing dubbing into his boots; Scholar sat in another reading his book; while, incredibly, despite the now continuous roar of explosions overhead, Davir lay in another bunk sound asleep.

'Ah, you are awake, new fish,' Bulaven said, gesturing up with his thumb toward the ceiling at the sound of more explosions overhead. 'I can't say I am surprised. They are making enough noise up there to wake the dead.'

'They are shelling us again?' Larn asked. 'Our own side, I mean?'

'Hmm? Oh no, new fish,' Bulaven said. 'It is the orks this time. If you listen closely you can hear the difference, ork shells have a duller sound to them when they explode. Still, you needn't worry. These dugouts are built to last. We should be quite safe so long as we are in here.'

'Unless, of course, a shell scores a direct hit on the dugout's ventilation chimney,' Scholar raised his eyes from his book. 'Even if the shell doesn't break through it, the chimney is still likely to funnel the explosion down here.'

'True,' Bulaven said. 'Ach, but that hardly ever happens, new fish. You needn't worry about that. Anyway, this bombardment won't last long. The orks have no staying power when it comes to these things, you see. Chances are whichever ork is in charge of their big guns has become overexcited for some reason and has decided to let off a few rounds in celebration. Trust me, new fish, in ten minutes' time or so it will all be over.'

'How LONG HAS it been now,' Larn asked, listening to the muffled thud and whump of shells striking the ground above the dugout.

'About an hour, I'd say,' Bulaven shrugged, now busy cleaning the trigger mechanism of his heavy flamer. 'Maybe three-quarters. Looks like the orks must be very excited. Still, I wouldn't worry too much about it. Don't let it ruin your barracks time, new fish. They are bound to get tired of shelling us sooner or later.'

Finding himself far from reassured, Larn looked upward to see another trickle of soil falling from the gaps between the wooden planks of the ceiling. Remembering a dream of tattered crones standing around his grave as shovelfuls of earth hit his face, Larn felt an involuntary shiver run through him. *Those explosions sound close*, he thought. *What if one of the shells hits the dugout entrance and we are trapped down here? Would anyone on the surface be able to dig us out? Would they even try? Sweet Emperor, it might be better if what Scholar talked about happened instead and a shell hit the ventilation chimney. At least then it would be quick. You would be dead before you knew it. Not buried alive in this tomb of a dugout, waiting for your air to run out or to slowly die of thirst and starvation.*

Abruptly, realising his nerves were beginning to shred at the constant sound of explosions and the thought of what those explosions might cause, Larn begin to scan the interior of the dugout in search of something – any-thing – to take his mind from what was going on above

them. Around him, the dugout had become crowded
with men who had taken refuge from the shelling.
Among them he saw Sergeant Chelkar, Medical Officer
Svenk, and some of the men from Repzik's fireteam.
While the din of explosions continued overhead, here
life inside the dugout seemed to be proceeding just as it
had before the shelling started. He saw Vardans eating,
talking, laughing, drinking recaf; some of them even trying to sleep like Davir. Then, Larn noticed Zeebers was
still sitting alone against one of the dugout walls, idly
tossing a knife around in his hand to catch first the
blade, then the hilt.

Watching Zeebers playing with his knife, Larn felt a
sudden urge to have the answer to a question that had
been gnawing at him ever since he had first met the
man.

'Bulaven?' he asked. 'Before, remember when you told
me that I shouldn't worry too much at the things Davir
said? That it was just his way?'

'Of course I remember, new fish,' Bulaven said. 'Why
do you bring it up?'

'Well, I was wondering about Zeebers...' Abruptly
Larn paused, uncertain how best to broach the subject.

'Zeebers, new fish? What about him?'

'I think he has noticed that Zeebers has been showing
a certain hostility towards him, Bulaven,' Scholar said,
raising his eyes from his book once more to look at
Larn. 'I am right, yes, new fish? That is what you were
about to ask?'

'Ah, I see,' said Bulaven. 'Well, there is no great secret
there, new fish. Zeebers just gets nervous whenever
there are any more than four men in our fireteam.'

'Nervous?' asked Larn. 'Why?'

'It is a matter of superstition with him,' Scholar said.
'Apparently, on Zeebers's homeworld the number four
is considered lucky. Then, when he first came to

Broucheroc and joined us there were only three men left in our fireteam – Bulaven, Davi, and myself. Hence, Zeebers was the fourth man, lucky number four to his mind, and he has convinced himself that is how he survived his first fifteen hours – not to mention how he has survived ever since. So, you see, whenever they send us a new replacement and there are five men in the fireteam he tends to believe his luck has become endangered somehow. You remember before I said every man here has his own theory as to how he survived where so many others have died? Zeebers's beliefs are but another example of the same thing.'

'You see, new fish, no great mystery,' Bulaven said, before abruptly turning his head to look over at another part of the dugout. 'Hmm, looks like something is brewing.'

Following the direction of Bulaven's gaze, Larn saw Sergeant Chelkar standing deep in conversation with Corporal Vladek by the quartermaster's table in the corner of the barracks. Then, while Sergeant Chelkar walked away to talk to someone else, Vladek turned to open a wooden crate beside him and, one-by-one, began to carefully pull out a number of heavy demolitions charges and stack them on the table before him. As he did, Larn noticed that Bulaven's face had grown suddenly uneasy as though the big man had seen something in Vladek's actions to worry him.

'What is it, Bulaven?' he asked. 'What have you seen?'

'A bad sign, new fish,' Bulaven said. 'Between me and you, a very bad sign indeed.'

'WE ARE AT Alert Condition Red,' Chelkar said, his face grave as he addressed the Guardsmen standing before him while overhead the sound of explosions continued. 'Sector Command says we can expect an assault. A big one, probably timed to begin the moment this bombardment ends. Looks like the orks are going to hit us hard this time. Leastways, harder than any of the other attacks we've had to deal with today.'

A few minutes had passed and in the wake of his conversation with the quartermaster, Sergeant Chelkar had ordered the men in Barracks Dugout One to arm themselves and assemble around the iron stove for an impromptu briefing. Scholar, Bulaven, Davir, Zeebers, the other fireteams, even Vladek and the one-armed cook Skench, stood in their battle gear listening intently to Chelkar's words, their expressions every bit as grave and serious as their sergeant's. Looking about him, Larn saw that the easy and relaxed manner with which these men had enjoyed their time in the barracks was gone now. They were soldiers once more. Guardsmen. They were ready for war.

'I won't lie to you,' Chelkar said. 'Things look grim. Every other sector in the area is under heavy assault and all reserve units are tied up elsewhere. Which means no there is no potential for reinforcements – at least not for several hours. Worse, Battery Command is already tasked to the limit, so we can't expect artillery support either. We still have our own mortars, of course, and our fire support teams but, other than that, we are on our own.

'Now for the good news. Sector Command has made it clear that if we lose here there is the danger of a major ork breakthrough into the city. Accordingly, they have ordered that we are to hold this sector at all costs. *Stand or die*, they say. No matter how many orks come at us or how hard they hit us, we are to hold on until we are reinforced, the ork assault fails, or the Emperor descends to fight alongside us – whichever one of those comes first. We hold the line. I don't care if hell itself comes calling. We hold the line no matter what. Not that we have much choice here anyway, you understand.

You all know what happens if we retreat. The commissars don't even bother with a court martial any more: it's just a bullet in the back of the head and a place on the corpse-pyres. This is Broucheroc: between the orks and our own commanders, there's just nowhere else left for us to go.

'As for our plan of defence, I have ordered Vladek to distribute four extra frag grenades to each man and one demolition charge per fireteam. Once the assault begins we will hold the forward firing trenches for as long as possible, only retreating to the dugout emplacements when the situation there becomes untenable. Then, once we're at the dugout emplacements we will make a stand. That's as far as we go. After that, it's hold the line or die.

'Are there any questions?'

No one spoke. Silently, the Guardsmen stood gazing back at their sergeant with resolve and determination etched into every line of their faces. For better or worse, they were ready.

'All right, then,' said Chelkar. 'We have been in this situation often enough before to make saying anything else irrelevant. You all know what is ahead of us. I will say only this. Good luck to every one of you. And, fates willing, let us all see each other again when the battle is over.'

'MAYBE IT IS The Big Push,' Larn heard one of the Vardans say as he hung the extra grenades Vladek had given him on his belt and went over to join the other members of Fireteam Three. 'Emperor knows, it was bound to happen sometime.'

'It can't be,' said another man nearby. 'General Headquarters would have told us.'

'Phah. You are fooling yourself,' a third man said. 'The damn generals refuse to even admit The Big Push exists.

When it finally does come they'll be caught as much by surprise as the rest of us.'

The Big Push. By then Larn had heard the phrase used several times already, whispered amongst themselves by grim-faced Guardsmen as they stood in the dugout making final adjustments to their weapons and equipment as the bombardment continued above them. Each time he heard it, Larn found something in the tone of the way they said the phrase that made him uneasy. It was a tone, he realised, of nervousness and quiet anxiety. *The tone of fear*, he thought with a sudden shudder.

'Bulaven?' he asked the big man beside him. 'What is The Big Push?'

For a moment the Vardan was silent, his usually affable manner replaced by the bleak and brooding expression of a parent who realises he can no longer protect his child from the dark realities of the world.

'It is a bad thing, new fish,' Bulaven said. 'A story you could call it, I suppose. Or a myth. You know when the preachers talk in church of the Last Judgement when the Emperor will finally step forward from His throne once more and judge humanity for its sins? The Big Push is like that.'

'It is something in the manner of a folktale,' Scholar said, standing next to him. 'The Big Push is the mythic apocalypse that every Guardsman in this city dreads. A Day of Judgement, as Bulaven puts it, when the orks will at last mount their long-expected final assault and the city of Broucheroc will fall. It is a nightmare, new fish. The one thing that the defenders of this city fear more than anything else. And, as such, I am not surprised you heard it mentioned. For the orks to launch so many assaults across different sectors at once and coordinate them with artillery bombardment is highly unusual. So unusual in fact that it is easy to see in it the portent of something larger.'

'The Big Push is bullshit, new fish,' Davir said. 'A story that the mothers of this city scare their children to sleep with, nothing more. Put it from your mind.'

At that, they became silent and, looking at the faces of his companions, Larn saw the same thing there as had been hidden in the whispers of the men he had heard discussing The Big Push to begin with.

He saw fear.

And he was not reassured.

CHAPTER FOURTEEN

21:15 hours Central Broucheroc Time

BOOKKEEPING AND THE TRAGEDY OF WAR – MATTERS OF
TACTICS WHILE WAITING FOR AN ETERNITY TO PASS –
PREPARATIONS AND PRELUDES IN THE TRENCHES – HOLDING
THE LINE – SHOT IN THE HEAD AND SAVED BY DAVIR – LAST
STAND BY THE DUGOUTS – THE SOUND OF SALVATION

FOR CAPTAIN ARNOL Yaab it had been a long and tiring day. A day spent like every other day of the last ten years in a cramped windowless office in the lower levels of the General Headquarters building in the centre of Broucheroc, ceaselessly compiling the twice-daily Imperial Guard casualty statistics from the reports and logs of the various Sectors Command throughout the city.

Sector 1-11, he wrote in a neat and ordered hand in the pages of the ledger before him. *12th Coloradin Rifle Corps. Commanding Officer: Colonel Wyland Alman. Previous Strength: 638 men. Total Casualties in Last Twelve*

Hour Period: 35 men. Current Adjusted Strength: 603 men. Percentage Loss: 5.49%.

Sector 1-12, he continued, carefully allowing the ink time to dry so as not to risk smudging the previous entry. *35th Zuvenian Light Foot. Commanding Officer: Captain Yiroslan Dacimol (Deceased). Previous Strength: 499 men. Total Casualties in Last Twelve Hour Period: 43 men. Adjusted Strength: 456 men. Percentage Loss: 8.62%.*

Sector 1-13. 902nd Vardan Rifles. Commanding Officer: Sergeant Eugin Chelkar (Temporary Appointment). Previous Strength: 244 men. Total Casualties in Last Twelve Hour Period: 247 men. Current Adjusted Strength: −3. Percentage Loss: 101.23%.

Abruptly, gazing down at the entry he had just written, Yaab became aware that there seemed to be some problem with his figures. *101.23%? That cannot be right,* he thought. *How can a unit have lost more than one hundred per cent of its original strength and be reduced to a current adjusted strength of minus three? It is an impossibility. How can you have minus three men?*

Pursing his lips in annoyance, Captain Yaab rechecked the figures in the Sector Command Beta casualty log. There, in black and white, the same statistic was confirmed. Out of a total strength of 244 men, the 902nd Vardan had somehow conspired to lose no less than 247 of their number in the last twelve hours. Then, just as deep in his pen-pusher's soul he began to fear he had made an error that would see him reprimanded – or worse – posted to the frontlines, Yaab noticed a sheet of paper clipped to the back of the log and realised he had perhaps found the source of the mistake.

It was a supplementary report, recording that a lander had crash-landed in Sector 1-13 at around midday and deposited an additional 235 Guardsmen into the sector. *Ah, now that would account for the discrepancy,* Yaab thought, making a quick series of mental calculations. *An extra 235 men would put the total strength of the sector at 479. Then, the loss of 247 men would leave us with a current adjusted strength of 232, constituting a percentage loss of 51.57%. All in all, a much more acceptable figure.*

Happy again, Captain Yaab adjusted his ledger in line with the new calculations only to find himself aggravated once more as he noticed the unsightly mess the alterations had made to the clean, well-ordered columns of his figures. Sighing as he returned to compiling his statistics, Yaab tried to take comfort from the thought that it could not be helped. It was the tragedy of his life that certain amount of unsightliness was to be expected.

War, after all, could be a messy business.

'SWITCH YOUR COMM-BEAD to our command net on frequency five,' Bulaven told Larn through the roar of shellfire shaking the ground above them. 'You will know we are about to go when the shelling stops. Then, when we get the order, we run back to our firing trench. No crouching or trying to stay in cover this time, new fish. You just sprint there as fast as you can. We have to be back in the trench and ready to shoot before the orks reach the kill zone at the three hundred metre mark.'

They were standing with the rest of the Vardans next to the steps leading from the dugout up to the surface. As his fingers fiddled to change the frequency of the comm-bead in his ear, Larn's mind turned to a lesson he had learned in his last battle. *This is the worst time*, he thought. *While you are waiting for the attack to start, before the battle even begins. Once the fighting is underway you are still afraid. But it is having time to think about what is coming that makes the fear worse. And the orks would seem to know it. They are giving us plenty of time to dwell on our fears. Right now, it feels like waiting for an eternity to pass.*

'All right, new fish,' Bulaven said. 'Now, I have told you everything you need to know about what we are going to do after that. I want you to tell it back to me now so I can be sure you have understood it.'

Can he see that I am afraid, Larn thought. *Is that it? Is he trying to keep me busy and take my mind off the fact we could all be dead in a matter of minutes? And if Bulaven can see it what about the rest of them? Are they all standing here watching me wondering if I am going to turn and run? Do they think I am a coward?*

'Our tactics, new fish?' Bulaven prodded. 'What are they?'

'Once we reach the firing trench we will hold it as long as we can,' Larn said, silently praying to the Emperor his voice did not sound as frightened and nervous as he suspected. 'Then, if it looks like we are going to be overrun, Scholar will set the demolition charge to buy us enough time to fall back. You will be carrying the flamer, I will be carrying a spare fuel canister for you, Davir and Zeebers will give us covering fire with their lasguns.'

'And if any of us are dead by then?' Bulaven asked. 'Or too badly wounded to move on their own? What then, new fish?'

'Then the three most important things are the demolition charge, the flamer, and the spare fuel canister, in that order. Other than that we will help the wounded if we can. If not, we will leave them behind.'

'Remember that one, new fish. It is important. Now, where will we fall back to?'

'To the sandbag emplacement above this dugout,' Larn said, repeating everything Bulaven had drilled into him while they waited for the shelling to stop. 'After that, it is like Sergeant Chelkar was saying. We do not fall back any farther. Once we are at the emplacements, we stand or die.'

'Very good, new fish,' Davir said sarcastically from the side of them. 'It sounds like you have got it.'

ABRUPTLY, THE SHELLFIRE stopped. The brief silence that followed it felt strange and eerie after so long a bombardment.

'Go! Go! Go!' Sergeant Chelkar yelled, as beside him Vladek threw open the door to the dugout and the assembled Vardans ran pell-mell up the steps toward the surface. 'Get to your trenches!'

Before he even knew it Larn was above ground, emerging blinking into the cold grey light of the sun outside to turn and sprint towards the firing trench with Bulaven and the others beside him as the rest of the Vardans spread out to run for their own positions. Then, with barely a few metres gone, he heard Corporal Grishen's voice in his ear through his comm-bead.

'Auspex reports activity in the enemy lines,' Grishen said, frantic through a squall of static. 'The orks are moving.'

Larn could already see them. On the other side of no-man's land, a horde of orks had risen up and were now charging screaming towards them. For a moment Larn heard a still small voice in his head questioning what he was doing, running towards the orks when every fibre of his being told him he should be running away from them as fast as his legs could take him but he ignored it. Ignored it and raced instead towards the trench to take his place with the other members of the fireteam as they made ready to repel the assault.

'Five hundred metres,' Scholar said, already squinting at the oncoming orks through a targeter by the time Larn threw himself into the trench and took his place on the firing step beside Bulaven.

'Remember, new fish,' Bulaven said. 'When you hear the order to fall back, you grab a spare fuel canister and stay close to me.'

'Yes, new fish,' Davir said from across him. 'And while you're at it, don't go losing your lasgun again. I will let you into a secret: your helmet is for protecting your head, not for the hitting of gretchin. Now, get ready, puppy. Time to show the orks your claws.'

'Four hundred metres,' Scholar said.

Remembering this time to click off the safety catch, Larn hurriedly ran through his pre-battle ritual, silently reciting the Litany of the Lasgun in his mind before adding a quick prayer to the Emperor for good measure. Beside him he saw Davir, Scholar and Zeebers sighting in on the orks, while to the side of them Bulaven checked the pump pressure on his flamer. Then, from behind him, he heard the sound of mortars being fired and knew the battle was about to begin in earnest.

'Three hundred metres,' Scholar yelled. 'On my mark… fire!'

LASBEAMS. MORTARS. AUTO-CANNON rounds. Frag missiles. From all across the line the Vardans opened up with everything they had. All the while, as Davir, Scholar and Zeebers fired their lasguns from the side of him Larn fired with them, remembering to aim high for the orks as Repzik had once told him. And through it all, the orks kept coming.

There are more of them this time, Larn thought. *Ten times more at least than when I was in the trench with Repzik. Sweet Emperor! And we barely managed to hold out then!*

'One hundred and twenty metres,' Scholar said, the orks having seemed to cover the intervening distance between them with impossible swiftness. 'Change magazines and switch to rapid fire.'

The orks came closer. Some of them were already gruesomely wounded by the Vardans' remorseless hail of fire, all of them were red-eyed and eager in an apparently endless barbaric tide.

'Fifty metres,' Scholar's voice counted down calmly. 'Forty metres. Thirty.'

'Any time now would be good, fatman,' Davir said to Bulaven. 'Are you actually going to use that damn flamer, or just wait until the orks get close enough for you to try and fart them to death instead?'

In response, Bulaven lifted the nozzle of the flamer, extending himself to his full height to point the barrel over the trench parapet and unleash an expanding cone of yellow-black fire towards the closest enemy group. Screaming, the orks disappeared in a burning agonised haze while Bulaven sprayed bright fire at their comrades around them. Soon, all Larn could see directly ahead of him was a rising curtain of flame while the air grew thick with smoke and the sickly odour of burning *Xenos* flesh.

'Shoot to the sides, new fish!' Davir yelled. 'Bulaven can deal with the orks ahead of us – it's our job to stop the others flanking round them!'

Following Davir's lead, Larn began to shoot at the orks charging towards them from the right of the curtain of fire created by the flamer while Scholar and Zeebers shot at those on the left. For an instant, seeing the carnage inflicted on the orks, Larn thought he could see the beginnings of the greenskins' charge starting to falter. *We are winning*, he thought, exultant. *We have beaten them. There is no way for the orks to get past the flamer.*

And then, abruptly, the tongue of fire jetting from the flamer spluttered and died.

'Canister's empty,' Bulaven said, hands already at the fuel line. 'Reloading.'

'Grenades.' Davir yelled, his own hands at the grenades on his belt.

While Bulaven transferred the fuel line from one canister to another, the others threw two grenades each towards the orks. By the time the last of the grenades had exploded, the line was attached and Bulaven's flamer was once more spewing fire. More orks died but it seemed to make no difference. As though they had been given fresh impetus by the brief cessation in the flamer's attentions, the horde of orks crashed relentlessly nearer, some enveloped from head-to-toe in flame and yet still they kept coming. Thirty metres became twenty-five. Twenty-five became twenty. Twenty…

'Fall back!' Davir yelled. 'The bastards are right on top of us. Scholar, arm the demolition charge. The rest of you fall back.'

THE RETREAT BEGAN.

Scrambling over the rear trench wall with his lasgun slung across his shoulder and dragging the heavy weight of a spare flamer canister behind him, Larn began to run for the dugout emplacement while Scholar threw the demolition charge at the advancing orks.

'Faster, new fish,' Scholar ran past Larn, his long legs eating up the distance. 'It's only a four second delay!'

Suddenly, Larn heard a tremendous explosion behind him as clods of earth flew past his head. For a moment, caught at the furthest edge of the blast, he stumbled and almost fell forward, only to be saved as the weight of the canister served as an accidental counterweight behind him. Then, as he tried to heft the canister on to his shoulder and pick up pace, he felt a painful blow at the back of his head, the jarring force of it sending him spinning towards the ground.

Landing in the frozen mud, Larn felt a warm wetness spreading across his scalp. Putting his hand to his head, when he brought it away again he saw red blood staining his fingers. He saw his helmet lying upside down on the ground before him – a large dent left in its side by whatever unknown missile had knocked it from his head. Incongruously, as he rose shakily to his feet, he wondered what would have happened to him if he had fastened his helmet strap instead of leaving it loose. Then, the guttural bellow of an alien war cry behind him put the thought abruptly from his mind.

Whirling to look, Larn saw an ork charging towards him with an enormous pistol in one hand and a broad-bladed cleaver in the other. The creature was huge; its body inhumanly and disproportionately muscled. Larn saw a jutting jaw, yellowed, sickle-shaped tusks, a line of three severed human heads hanging like grotesque spectators from a trophy harness above the monster's shoulders. He heard a bullet scream past him as the pistol fired. As though of its own volition his lasgun responded, the first lasblast flying wide over the ork's shoulder to hit one of the trophies.

Steadying himself, Larn fired again, hitting his enemy in the chest. Unfazed, the ork did not miss a step. Larn shot at it again, firing off a rapid series of blasts that hit the creature in the neck, the shoulder, the chest again, then the face. Until finally, just as Larn began to fear coming within reach of its jagged blade, the ork gave a last enraged bellow, collapsed, and died. Though whatever brief sense of elation Larn felt at his victory quickly evaporated as he saw more greenskins come charging towards him in the dead ork's wake.

'Get a move on, new fish!' he heard a voice yell behind him as a hand grabbed his shoulder. 'Damnation! Are you trying to take on the whole damn ork mob on your own?'

It was Davir. Firing his lasgun one-handed towards the approaching orks, Davir began to tug Larn in the direction of the dugouts. Realising he had dropped the flamer canister when he had fallen, his head still groggy from the blow, for a moment Larn tried to resist as his eyes scanned around in search of the canister.

'It is too late for that, new fish,' Davir shouted, pulling hard now at his shoulder. 'Leave it. I need that canister right where it is.'

Giving in, Larn turned to flee with Davir at his side, catching a last sight of the fallen canister lost among the legs of the screaming phalanx of oncoming orks. Then, turning briefly back as they ran towards the emplacements, Davir fired a snap shot toward it – the lasbeam ruptured the canister's body and it exploded in a plume of orange flame, incinerating the orks around it and buying him and Larn time enough to reach their destination.

'You see there, new fish?' Davir said as the outstretched hands of eager Guardsmen helped them to safety. 'I *told* you I wanted the canister right where it was. Oh, and I saw you feeling at your head earlier? You needn't worry in that regard: it is still attached. Though for all that you seem to use it, you might as well have left it with the orks.'

'You came back for me…' Larn said incredulously. 'Even after what Bulaven said about leaving the wounded, you came back and saved me…'

'I wouldn't get too starry-eyed about it, new fish' Davir said. 'What I *really* wanted to save was the flamer canister – events just got ahead of me, is all. Now, shut up and start shooting. You have killed one ork. Only another twenty or so thousand to go.'

THEY WERE OUT of grenades. They had used the last of the flamer fuel. The auto-cannons, missile launchers and lascannons had fallen silent. Even the las-packs were running short. And still, no matter how many screaming greenskins died, the ork assault refused to falter.

Standing on the firing step along one wall of the emplacement, the barrel of his lasgun so hot in his hand now it burnt his fingers, Larn fired a lasbeam into the face of an ork as it tried to climb over the bodies of the dead towards him. Then another, and another. Firing without thought or pause, barely even needing to aim so thick was the press of alien bodies charging towards him in wave after screaming wave. They were surrounded now, cut off from the other emplacements by vast throngs of orks; each emplacement a besieged and lonely outcrop amid an endless churning sea of savage green flesh.

From the corners of his eye Larn caught glimpses of the others around him. He saw Bulaven, a lasgun in his hands taken from another fallen Guardsman. He saw Davir. Scholar. Zeebers. He saw Chelkar, his expression cool and detached, working the slide of his shotgun to send round after round into the enemy. He saw Vladek. Medical Officer Svenk. The cook, Trooper Skench, a laspistol blazing in his one remaining hand as he stood beside the others. He saw their faces: Scholar drawn yet steadfast, Bulaven dutiful, Zeebers nervous, Davir spitting obscene and angry oaths at the advancing orks. He saw steely determination and a refusal to go easily to death. As he saw it, Larn felt a fleeting shame that he had doubted these men when he had first met them. Whatever their manner they were all what a Guardsman should be. Brave. Resolute. Unbending in the face of the enemy. These were the men on which the Imperium had been built. The men who had fought its every battle. Won its every victory. Today, they were hopelessly outnumbered.

Today, it was their final stand.

'I'm out!' Davir yelled, pulling the last expended power pack from his lasgun and flinging it towards the orks as his other hand went for the laspistol on his hip.

All about him, it was the same for the others. Around him, Larn saw the Vardans draw pistols or fix bayonets, while he wondered how many shots he had left in his own power pack. Five? Ten? Fifteen? Then, just as he rejected the idea of saving the last shot for himself, the question was answered as he pulled the trigger and heard a final despairing whine from his lasgun as it died.

This is it, he thought, his hands moving with nightmare slowness to attach his bayonet to the lasgun as an ork raised a bloodstained cleaver and charged towards him. *Merciful Emperor, please! It is so unfair. I can't die here. You have to save me.*

Abruptly, as though halted in its tracks by his silent prayer, the ork stopped and raised a bestial face to look up towards the sky. For an instant, Larn was left dumbstruck. Then, he heard a sound and suddenly knew what had given the ork pause. As from the sky above them, there came a cacophony of shrill and strident screams which at that moment sounded to Larn every bit as sweet as the voices of a choir of angels.

Shellfire, he thought, recognising the sound. *Hellbreakers. They are giving us artillery support at last! We are saved!*

'Into the dugout, new fish.' he heard Bulaven's voice beside him. 'Quickly. We have to get to cover!'

Racing to the entrance of the dugout with the Vardans, Larn stumbled down the steps to safety just as the ground began to shake with explosions. Breathing heavily and bolting the door behind them to prevent the orks from following, they stood there for long minutes of silence. Listening, as shells shrieked and roared and boomed above them.

'It makes a refreshing change don't you think, new fish?' Davir said, after a while as the bombardment continued. 'For our own side to be shooting at the orks rather than us, I mean. Now, assuming Battery Command keep this up long enough, I would say that is the last we will see of this particular ork assault.'

He was right. Hearing the shelling finally end after several minutes, the Vardans cautiously emerged from the dugout with Larn beside them to be greeted by the sight of a battlefield now left deserted save for the mounds of the sundered bodies of the dead. The orks had fled. The battle was over. Looking out at the scene of carnage and devastation before him, Larn felt a sudden dizzying sense of joyful exhilaration.

Against all expectation, he was still alive.

CHAPTER FIFTEEN

22:35 hours Central Broucheroc Time

The Corpse-Pyres – Matters of Disposal and the Varied
Uses of an Entrenching Tool – To See a Perfect Sun

By necessity, he had long ago become inured to the
stench of burning flesh.

Sweating at the heat, Militia Auxiliary Herand Troil
used the hook of the long pole in his hands to push
another ork body into the enormous burning mound
of corpses before him, then stepped away for a
moment to catch his breath. Finding it difficult to
breathe through the charcoal-filled filtration tube of his
gas mask, he pulled it back from his face, opening his
mouth wide to gulp at the smoky air around him. Inadvertently swallowing a drifting fragment of ash he
coughed, retching at the taste as he tried to summon
enough spittle to clean his throat, before hawking up a
greasy wad of brown phlegm and spitting it towards the
fire.

I am getting old, he thought. *I've only been working my shift three hours now, and already I'm exhausted. Ten years ago I seem to remember having more staying power than that.*

Ten years, he thought again. *Has it really been that long? Can it really have been so long since I came to work on the corpse-pyres?*

Weighed down by a sudden sadness, Troil looked around him at the place where he had spent virtually every waking moment of his life since being press-ganged into service with the militia at the age of sixty. He was standing on a hillside, the ground beneath his feet barren after so many fires, surrounded on all sides by tall mounds of burning ork corpses. Through the smoke and ash he could see other auxiliaries in masks tending to the pyres with long hooks, their figures little more than silhouettes through the burning haze. Looking at it, he was struck once more by grief. Grief not for the orks, but for himself. Grief for the life he had lost. Grief for his family and his loved ones long dead. Grief for his days spent working on the corpse-pyres. Most of all though, he felt grief for the city of Broucheroc and the horror the war had made of it.

It was a beautiful place once, this city, he thought. *Not beautiful as most people think of these things perhaps. But it was alive and vital with an energy, an industry, a character all its own. All that is gone now though. Gone and lost for good, taken away by the war. Now it might as well be a city of the dead.*

Sighing, finding his eyes starting to water at the smoke, Troil pulled his mask down back in place and began to walk towards the corpse-pyres to resume his labours. As he did, he spared a last glance down the hillside towards the endless lines of other auxiliaries dragging ork bodies up the slope towards him. He did not linger on the sight though because he expected it.

The flow of bodies for the pyres never stopped. This was Broucheroc.

Here, there were always more corpses.

'YOU NEED TO put your spade here, new fish,' Bulaven said, standing over the body of a dead ork and pressing the blade of his entrenching tool against its throat. 'Next, you draw the spade head back and forth a bit to cut through the skin. Then, you put your weight on it. Here, let me show you how it is done.'

Standing beside him, Larn watched as Bulaven stamped down to push the sharpened spade head partway through the thick muscles of the ork's neck. Then, occasionally wriggling the spade around to slice through the worst of the tendons and break the spinal vertebrae, the big man stamped down on the spade several more times until the creature's head had been completely severed.

'There. You see? Granted, ork skin can be tougher than reptile hide – especially on the big ones. But if you keep your spade head nice and sharp, and remember to let your body weight do the work, their heads come off pretty easy. All right, new fish. Now you try one.'

In the aftermath of battle came the clean-up. Around them, while other Guardsmen tended to the wounded or repaired the shell-damaged emplacements and militia auxiliaries carried in new ammunition and supplies to replace those expended in the fighting, Larn and Bulaven had been detailed to the task of beheading fallen orks. Dubiously, Larn picked an ork at random from the dozens of bodies lying nearby and placed the sharp end of his entrenching tool across its neck. Following Bulaven's earlier example he drew the blade back and forth, feeling the resistance as it cut through the skin and into flesh. Then, raising his foot he stamped down on the spade head, pushing the blade perhaps a quarter of the way into the ork's neck. Read-justing his position to put more force into it he stamped again, harder this time, then again, until at the fourth blow the ork's head finally came free to roll away across the frozen ground.

'That's good, new fish,' Bulaven said. 'Try to make sure you are standing right over the spade though when you stamp on it. That way you will put more of your weight behind it. It makes the work easier and takes less effort. We have a lot more corpses to do before our job is done.'

'But why do we need to do it?' Larn said to him. 'They are dead already, aren't they?'

'Maybe,' Bulaven said. 'But is always better to make sure with an ork, just to be on the safe side. They are tough bastards. You can shoot one in the head and think he's dead, only for him to suddenly get up and start walking about a few hours later. Believe me, I've seen it happen.' Then, noticing Larn casting worried glances at the bodies lying all around them, he smiled. 'Ach, you needn't worry about these ones, new fish. If any of them were capable of moving, they'd be trying to kill us by now already. We'll have their heads off long before any of them that are still alive have had time to heal. Then, the militia auxiliaries will take the bodies away for burning to get rid of the spores.'

'Spores?' Larn asked.

'Oh yes, new fish. Orks grow from spores. Like mold. Leastways, that's what Scholar says. I can't say I've ever seen it myself, mind. But I'm prepared to take his word for it. You should ask him about it later. He'll tell you all about it. You know Scholar, he loves telling people about things.'

Apparently satisfied that Larn now knew what he was doing, Bulaven turned away quietly whistling a cheerful tune to himself as he began to deprive more dead orks of their heads. In his wake, Larn set to the same task of decapitation. It was gruesome and tiring work, and Larn quickly found his boots and the spade head were stained black with viscous alien blood. Soon, he was sweating under his helmet; the salt of his sweat irritating the head wound he had sustained during the battle.

In the aftermath, telling him he was lucky and it was only a scalp laceration, Medical Officer Svenk had bandaged it for him while Corporal Vladek had supplied him with a new helmet – something for which Davir had been particularly scathing. *What is it with you and helmets, new fish,* Davir had said. *First, you use one to beat a gretch's brains in. Then, you go and get yourself shot in the head. What will you use the next one for? A soup bowl perhaps, or a planting pot for some flowers?* But, much to his own surprise, Larn found he was longer irritated by Davir's constant complaints and insults. He owed him a debt now. No matter how much the runtish trooper might protest to him that it had all been a mistake, even an accident, Davir had saved his life.

Then, pausing in his work to wipe the sweat from his forehead, Larn noticed a gathering redness in the sky. Turning to face the ork lines in the east, he saw the sun was setting. He saw it, and he was amazed.

It was beautiful. Extraordinary. More breathtaking and vivid even than the sunset he had seen on his last night at home. The sun that had so often seemed cold and distant above him had at last grown to become a warm red orb; the sky once grey around it had transformed and given way to a dazzling symphony in flaming shades of scarlet. Watching it, Larn found himself enraptured by awe. Moved to the very depths of his soul, he stood there transfixed. Hypnotised. *Who knew there could ever be such a sun,* he thought in wonder. *Who knew there could be such beauty here?* And no sooner had that thought occurred than it seemed to him it had all been worth it. All the things he had been through. The fear. The hardship. The danger. The isolation. All the carnage he had seen and all the horrors he had witnessed. All of them now seemed worthwhile. As though by right of his passage through hell he had paid the price that had allowed him this brief perfect moment of quiet and reflection.

'Are you all right, new fish?' he heard Bulaven say beside him. 'Is your head wound bothering you? You have been standing there a long time now, just looking at the sky.'

Turning, Larn saw Bulaven facing him and felt moved to tell him about the sunset. There were no words for his epiphany; no way to communicate what he was feeling to another. Unable to express his emotions, for a moment he was silent. Then, seeing Bulaven staring at him in concern and curiosity, Larn felt he should say something – anything – lest the big man should start to think he had lost his mind.

'I was just struck by how strange this place is,' he said, forced to retreat to more commonplace matters. 'To have a sun that sets so late in winter.'

'Winter?' Bulaven asked in good-natured confusion, looking around at the frozen corpse-covered battlefield around them. 'But it is summer hereabouts, new fish. Good thing, too. In winter, life in Broucheroc can really start to get nasty.'

CHAPTER SIXTEEN

23:01 hours Central Broucheroc Time

A Visitor from General Headquarters – The
Reconnaissance Mission – Expressions of Disquiet
Among the Ranks – Into No-Man's land –
Alone in the Darkness

'You have done well, sergeant,' Lieutenant Karis said. 'By holding out against that last assault you have delivered a crippling blow to the activities of the orks in this sector. And you may be assured your efforts in that regard have been recognised and will be rewarded. It is not official as yet, of course, but between you and me I understand you are to be decorated while your unit is to receive a citation.'

In reply, Chelkar was silent. Five minutes ago he had been supervising the repairs to the company's defences when Grishen had voxed him with the news an officer had arrived and was waiting to see him in the command dugout. Hurrying tiredly to meet him, Chelkar had found himself confronted with a fresh-faced junior

237

lieutenant, all spit-shine boots and folded creases, a
swagger stick poking out at a jaunty angle from beneath
his arm. Though Chelkar had at first wondered if Sector
Command had finally got around to sending them a
new CO, it quickly became apparent the lieutenant had
come here on behalf of General Headquarters. A
situation that, to Chelkar's experience, was unlikely to
bode anything but ill.

'Did you hear me, sergeant?' the lieutenant said. 'They
are going to give you a medal.'

'I will have to remember to put it with the other ones,
lieutenant,' Chelkar said, feeling so exhausted and
bone-weary he no longer cared if his tone was properly
diplomatic. 'But I am sure you didn't come all this way
and dragged me away from my duties just to tell me
that.'

Stung by his bluntness, the lieutenant's face briefly
tightened into a look of displeasure. Then, abruptly, his
mood softening and becoming patently false, he
adopted a more conciliatory manner.

'You are right, of course, sergeant. And may I say what
a pleasure it is to hear some plain speaking for a change.
That is why I was so happy to get this chance to come to
the front. Not that I find my duties at General Headquarters in any way irksome, you understand, but at
GHQ one can so often forget the realities of frontline
life in the Guard. We are soldiers, you and I. We don't
do what we do for honours and medals. We do it self-
lessly in the name of duty and for the greater glory of
the Imperium.'

I don't know what is more sickening, Chelkar thought
bleakly. *The fact that someone has obviously told him an
officer should try to strike up a rapport with the lower ranks,
or the fact that he is so inept and insincere in trying to do it.
Why is it whenever you hear one of these rear echelon heroes
talk about selflessness you always know they are desperate to*

win a medal? This one's a glory hound, all right, you can see it in his eyes. He probably heard about some suicide mission at GHQ and volunteered right away.

'Yes, lieutenant,' Chelkar said, hoping that at last the pipsqueak pedant before him might get to the point. 'And, talking of duty, I am assuming there is some matter with which you need my company's assistance?'

'Not the *whole* company, sergeant,' the lieutenant replied blithely. 'I just need some men to accompany me into no-man's land on a mission towards the ork lines. A five-man fireteam to be precise. Of course, I leave it entirely up to you which fireteam to pick. Though I have always considered three to be a lucky number.'

'WE WILL BE going into no-man's land tonight,' the lieutenant said, while Larn heard a sharp intake of breath from the other members of the fireteam beside him. 'General Headquarters wishes to know whether the orks' hold on their territory has been at all weakened by their recent losses. Accordingly, we are ordered to advance by stealth to within sight of their lines and scout out their defences and dispositions under cover of darkness. Then, we will return to our own lines before the orks are any the wiser. A simple and straightforward enough mission, I am sure you will all agree.'

Going about their duties as the clean-up proceeded outside, Larn and the others had been summoned to the command dugout to hear a briefing from a stiff-necked young lieutenant called Karis. Now, standing before the sector map pinned to the wall behind him, the lieutenant pointed at something on the map with his swagger stick as the briefing continued.

'Let me make it clear this is strictly a reconnaissance mission,' he said. 'And, as such, it relies entirely on stealth. We are not to engage the enemy unless forced to do it by the direst circumstance. With that in mind we will maintain total light and noise discipline at all times and follow a route through no-man's land designed to aid us in our attempts to stay unseen. If we are spotted by scouts or lookouts, we will attempt to dispose of them in as quick and quiet a manner as possible – only withdrawing from no-man's land if it is clear our mission has become untenable. Now, I think that about covers everything. Are there any questions?'

No one answered and looking at the faces of the men about him – Davir, Bulaven, Scholar, Zeebers – Larn saw a subtle disquiet among them. As though they were every bit as uneasy at the prospect of a mission into no-man's land as they had been earlier when it seemed The Big Push might be upon them. Watching them, Larn was gripped by a sudden revelation that he realised would have seemed quite commonplace to the others. In Broucheroc the danger never ended; there were always new battles to fight. New ways for a man to get himself killed.

'Good,' Lieutenant Karis said when it became clear there were to be no questions. 'You now have twenty minutes to check your equipment and make your preparations. Zero hour is at 00.00 hours. We go into no-man's land at midnight.'

'A SIMPLE MATTER, he says,' Davir grumbled afterwards. 'I tell you, someone should take that stupid bastard's swagger stick and shove it right up his arse.'

They were in the barracks dugout. In the wake of the briefing with the lieutenant, they had returned there to be issued with black dubbing and lasgun lubricant by Vladek. Now, their faces and all their equipment painted black, their knives and pistols oiled to glide silently from their sheaths, they made their final preparations while time counted down to midnight. As they did, Larn was suddenly struck by the thought he had been in Broucheroc almost exactly twelve hours. *Another three hours to go*, he thought, *and I will have made my fifteen.*

'You ask me, it is the new fish's fault,' Zeebers spat with sudden venom. 'He is unlucky. A jinx.'

'Shut up, Zeebers,' Davir spat back. 'Bad enough I have to go stumbling around no-man's land in the dead of night, without having to hear you mewl and puke about luck and numbers like some halfwit gambler on a losing streak. Shut up, or after I'm finished shoving the swagger stick up the lieutenant's arse I'll stick my lasgun up yours.'

'How do you explain it then?' Zeebers said, defiant. 'We've had nothing but a bad day ever since the new fish got here. He's a jinx. You saw what happened to the men he came here with in the lander.'

'Shut up, Zeebers,' Bulaven rumbled. Then, while Zeebers fell silent and scowled at him, he turned to Larn. 'Don't worry about what Zeebers said, new fish. You're not a jinx. I only wish today *had* been a bad day. Fact is, every day in Broucheroc is pretty much as bad as this, one way or another. After a while you just get used to it.'

'But going out into no-man's land at night is bad?' Larn asked, hoping the big Vardan could not hear the nervousness in his voice. 'Worse than usual, I mean?'

'Yes, new fish, it is worse,' Bulaven said. 'Especially after a battle. You remember I told you how sometimes a wounded ork will seem dead, only to get up and start walking about a few hours later? Well, right now, no-man's land is full of the bodies of orks we shot during the battle. By now some of them could be healed already, just about ready to wake up and start killing again while we'll be right in the middle of them. Then, to make matters worse, we've got to worry about running into gangs of gretchin looking for spare parts as well.'

'Spare parts?'

'Orks are remarkably tough creatures, new fish,' Scholar said by the side of him. 'If one of them loses an arm or leg their surgeons will just staple the limb from another dead ork to them to take its place. After a battle such surgeries are in great demand – so they tend to send gangs of gretchin out into no-man's land to cut undamaged limbs from the corpses. Of course, the real threat lies not so much in the gretch themselves, but in the danger of getting into a firefight in the middle of no-man's land while the entire ork army is on top of us.'

'The short version, new fish, is that this whole damned business has the makings of a first class snafu from start to finish,' Davir said. 'So, this is what I say I we do. We will follow Lieutenant Arsehole's orders so long as there's no shooting. But the moment the shit starts to fly we get each other out of no-man's land as fast as we can and to hell with his orders. Now enough talking and let's get outside. We need to spend at least ten minutes in the dark to get our night vision working. Considering what's ahead of us, I'd say we're probably going to need every advantage we can get.'

'REMEMBER THE SIGNAL, new fish,' Bulaven whispered quietly as they crouched in the darkness of one of the forward firing trenches with the lieutenant and the others waiting for the order for the mission to begin. 'We keep to comms silence. But if you make contact with the greenskins you squeeze the comm stud at your collar to create a squelch over the comm-link. You squeeze it three times. Three squelches. You understand? That way we'll know it's you. Now, tell me it again so I'll know you've got it.'

'We go quiet,' Larn whispered back, reciting the things Bulaven had already told him twice. 'Staying low and keeping together until we get halfway into no-man's land. Then, while Davir and the lieutenant go forward to scout out the ork lines, the rest of us spread out into a wide diamond formation with you at the base, Zeebers on the left flank, me on the right, and Scholar on point. If any of us see or hear orks we squelch on the comm-line: one squelch for you, two for Zeebers, three for me, and four for Scholar – so that way the others will know where the orks are.'

'Noise discipline, troopers,' Lieutenant Karis whispered testily. Then, cupping his hand over the chronometer on his wrist as he pressed an illumination stud to briefly light its face, he gave the order. 'Zero hour. Time to move out.'

With Davir in the lead, they climbed over the lip of the trench and crawled out into no-man's land. Then, at a hand signal from Davir showing the way before them was clear, they stood into a half-crouch and began to move slowly and quietly forward. Ahead, the night seemed impossibly dark, the stars dim and distant. Seeing no sign of a moon in the sky to guide them, Larn found himself wondering if the planet even had a moon or whether it was just hidden from his view. Whatever the case, keeping close to the others he followed them further and further into the forbidding wasteland between the human and ork lines. His every step wary, his senses sharp, his heart beating a tattoo of restless anxiety in his chest.

Around them no-man's land was silent, made even more threatening in the darkness now its flat and desolate surface was covered over with the shadowy foreboding shapes of so many bodies. There were corpses everywhere, strewn haphazardly across the landscape and fallen together so deeply in places the going was made treacherous with splayed limbs and uncaring torsos. Feeling the outstretched fingers of

unseen hand touch his ankle, Larn looked down in
sudden terror expecting the monstrous form of a
wounded and reawakening ork to rise up before him.
Only to see he had inadvertently brushed against a
severed hand lying in the mud. Another dead hand
like so many more around it.

They advanced further, slowly spreading out further
apart from each other until they reached the centre of
no-man's land. Then, as Davir and the lieutenant disappeared from view to go scout the lines, Larn
abruptly realised he could no longer see the others.
For a moment he fought the urge to call to them on
his comm stud. Then, he reminded himself they had
been ordered to maintain vox silence: even if he did
use the comm, no one would answer. Nor could he
go in search of them. Robbed of all sense of direction
by the darkness and the unfamiliarity of the landscape around him, it would take him a miracle to
find anyone. Worse, hopelessly lost, he could easily
stray into the ork lines. Terrified, Larn held his position and did the only thing he could.

Alone in the darkness, he waited.

Time passed and as he stood waiting, afraid that
every shadow might belong to some subtle and stalk-
ing enemy, Larn realised it was the first time he had
been on his own in weeks. More than that, here in
no-man's land, surrounded by corpses and barely
within a stone's throw of thousands of sleeping orks,
he felt more alone than he had before in his entire
life. So alone now, in fact, he might as well have been
the last man left in the entire galaxy.

Then, deep through the gathering haze in his mind
of fear and loneliness, Larn heard a sudden sound
that set cold fingers at his spine and turned his blood
to ice. A single squelch on the comm-bead in his ear.
Bulaven's signal. The signal that meant the big man

had made contact with the enemy and from Larn's point of view it meant something worse.

It meant the enemy was behind him.

CHAPTER SEVENTEEN

00:37 hours Central Broucheroc Time

GIVING AID AND COMFORT TO THE WOUNDED – AS HELL
BREAKS LOOSE LARN IS FORCED TO A DECISION – A FINAL
MADNESS IN ZEEBERS'S SMILE – UNKNOWN, A BULLET
FINDS ITS MARK

ONE OF THE *orks was moving...*

Standing alone in the darkness of no-man's land, not
quite sure if it was only his imagination or if he had
really seen a slight movement in the legs of one of the
corpses lying on the ground before him, Zeebers
decided it would be better to make certain the creature
was dead. Sliding his combat knife from its sheath as he
dropped to his knees beside the body, he quickly pulled
the ork's unresisting jaws open and silently stabbed the
blade up through the weak point in the roof of the
mouth and into the brain. Then, pulling the knife free,
he glanced briefly at the other corpses around him and
wondered if he should do the same with them as well.

I will do another three of them, he thought, wiping the blade on his trouser leg as he crept towards a second body. *That way I will have done four altogether. And I could do with some extra luck, what with that bastard new fish being such a jinx.*

'Help me,' he heard a failing voice whisper in Gothic as he knelt beside a second ork.

Startled, Zeebers turned to see an arm rise falter-ingly from beneath a nearby pile of bodies. Going over to it, he saw a human face peering out from among a nest of greenskin limbs. One of the Guards-man from the lander he realised, mortally wounded and left for dead in no-man's land but still clinging desperately to life.

'Please... help me,' the Guardsman said again, the weak voice was loud against the silence and forced Zeebers to clamp a firm hand over his mouth to keep him quiet.

Weakly, the Guardsman began to struggle, his free arm flailing and flapping around him. Feeling the man grab pleadingly at the edge of his greatcoat, Zee-bers felt a sudden flush of disgust and anger to find yet another new fish was endangering his life.

It cannot be helped, he thought as he pushed down once more with his knife. *He is too far gone to live much longer anyway. And he will bring the orks down on both of us if I don't make him quiet.*

Seeing the arm fall and the Guardsman's spasms grow still, Zeebers pulled his knife free and turned to get back to the orks. The Guardsman did not count, he decided. He was not part of the pattern. Leaving Zeebers with another three orks to deal with if he was going to improve his luck.

Then, abruptly, he heard the signal. A single squelch over his comm-bead. The fathead Bulaven must have run into some trouble.

For a moment Zeebers considered leaving him to it. He did not like Bulaven, or any of the Vardans for that matter. It would be easy enough to slip back towards the line and claim he had lost track of the others in the darkness. Just as quickly he was forced to abandon the idea; if Bulaven or any of the others survived and thought he had left them to die they would frag him without even thinking. No, for better or worse, he had better go and try to save the fat man's hide.

Putting his knife back in its sheath, Zeebers turned to hurry in Bulaven's direction. Then, as he picked his way past a particularly large pile of ork corpses he saw shadowy movement at the corner of his vision and realised he had blundered upon a gang of gretchin harvesting limbs. Swinging his lasgun towards them while the gretchin were still dumb with confusion, Zeebers fired, hitting the nearest gretch in the chest. Swiftly, he fired again, unleashing another half-dozen lasbeams, hitting two more gretch and causing the rest to flee. As Zeebers made to hurry once more on his way he heard something scraping wet and eager behind him followed by the whine of whirring motors. Turning, he saw a threatening shadow loom up in the darkness and knew the day he had feared for months was finally upon him.

Tonight, his luck had finally run out…

'FALL BACK! REPEAT: fall back!' Davir's voice shouted forcefully in his comm-bead as Larn heard the sound of shots and all hell began to break loose around him. 'Everyone back to the trenches!'

Lost and still on his own, Larn turned to move quickly towards what was his best guess at the position of the human lines. Suddenly, he saw a staccato burst of white tracer lines in the distance to the right of him as somewhere in the darkness a lasgun fired.

'Help me.' he heard Zeebers yell in fear and agony over the comm-line. 'Sweet Emperor, it's got me! Someone help me.'

Unsure what to do, for the briefest instant Larn stood rooted to the spot. Then, as Zeebers's voice in his ear became a jumble of incoherent screams, he made a decision. Turning in the direction the lasfire had come from he ran towards it, jumping and stumbling over the ork corpses littering his path as he raced to help the pleading trooper. Seeing two shapes coming together in the darkness ahead of him, Larn ran closer, only to find a scene of horror. He saw Zeebers, arms flailing in useless spasms, belly ripped open and guts hanging out, held like a limp puppet in the hand of an enormous ork while with its other hand the creature used a whirring circular blade to further eviscerate Zeebers's screaming flesh. Then, tossing Zeebers's rag doll body aside, the ork turned to look at Larn and began to advance towards him.

It was huge, wearing a bloodstained apron across its body and a thick-lensed monocular over one of its eyes. Seeing the cruel curiosity written in the creature's monstrous inhuman features, Larn knew at once it must be one of the ork surgeons Scholar had mentioned. Instinctively raising his lasgun to ward off its advance, he fired, the first blast flying wide to hit one of the corpses lying on the ground behind it. Adjusting his aim, Larn fired again, hitting the monster in the stomach. Then again. The chest. Again. The shoulder. Again. The face; the lasbeam briefly flaring brighter as it burned through the lens of the monocular. Tearing the melted mounting of the device away uncaring from the scorched socket of its now-blind eye, the ork kept coming no matter how many times Larn hit it. It seemed unstoppable; as inured to the pain of its own flesh as it was to the agonies of others. All the time, the whining blade in its hand grew closer and closer, as eager as its master to test its edge against the outlines of Larn's body.

Then, incredibly, salvation came from an unlikely source. As if from nowhere, Larn saw Zeebers appear in the darkness behind the ork and jump screaming onto the creature's back to wrap his arms about its throat. Horribly wounded, the spool of his intestines unravelled in the mud behind him, as the ork tried to pull him off, Zeebers briefly smiled towards Larn in pain-fuelled madness, before raising a hand above his head and letting out a bloody-mouthed and psychotic roar of triumph. Seeing the gleam of a half-dozen rings around Zeebers's fingers, Larn realised the madman must have pulled the pins from every grenade on his belt.

Knocked on his back as Zeebers and the ork disappeared in the roar and flash of the resulting explosion, Larn staggered to his feet once more and became aware the volume of firing about him had risen dramatically. All around him no-man's land was alive with bullets as, fully roused now from sleep, the orks fired blindly from their lines in search of targets. A last glance confirming there was no more he could do for Zeebers, Larn turned to run for the human lines in the hope of safety. Only to trip, not realising at first he had been shot, before he could go even a dozen steps.

THE SUN WAS rising in the west, the first red fingers of dawn revealing the brooding and foreboding shape of Broucheroc on the horizon. And still lying wounded in no-man's land in the same place where he had fallen, Larn looked up at the brightening sky above him and knew he should fear the sun. With the gathering of the light soon the orks would be able to see him from their lines. But where once he would have felt anxiety, even perhaps terror at that prospect, now all those things had left him. Instead, he lay on his back watching the sun slowly rise and he felt peace. He watched it and he knew contentment.

I have made it past fifteen hours, he thought, at last given answer by the coming of the dawn to the question that had plagued him throughout the night. *More than that even, now the sun is rising. And with it I have proved the others wrong. I have beaten the odds. I have survived this place. I have passed the test. The orks cannot kill*

*me now. The laws that rule this monstrous city will not let
them.*

Certain now that his fate had been decided in his
favour and it was only a matter of time before someone
came to rescue him, Larn settled calmly down to wait.
All the fear had passed through him now. All the loneliness. The desperation. The despair. They were gone,
replaced instead by a growing sense of detached seren-
ity.

Over the last fifteen hours he had faced the worst this
city could throw at him. It was over now and with it he
was forever free. Free from doubt. Free from worry. Free
from his fears. He did not even feel the cold any more.
He felt safe and warm. He felt whole. He had survived
his fifteen hours. He had lasted. He had proved himself.
This place could no longer hurt him and with that last
happy thought, Larn smiled and closed his eyes. Closed
his eyes to drift away to dreamless sleep, the last shreds
of his consciousness flying away from him like dead
leaves on the wind as the relentless babble of his mind
gradually gave way to silence. Drawing a last contented
breath, his beating heart slowed and stilled.

Then, finally, there was only darkness.

About the Author

Mitchel Scanlon is a hot new talent residing in the sheep-infested valleys of Derbyshire. His first break was with the Black Library's *Warhammer Monthly* comic and the character *Hellbrandt Grimm*. He has since penned the adventures of the assassin *Liliana Falcone* and the ruthless vampire *Helmar von Carstein* for *Warhammer Monthly* and several short stories for *Inferno!* as well as superhero tales for the UK market.

Fifteen Hours is his first novel.

MORE STORMING ACTION FROM THE BLACK LIBRARY

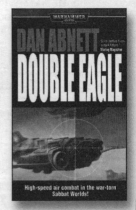